KU-510-745

SPECIAL MESSAGE TO READERS

THE ULVERSCROFT FOUNDATION
(registered UK charity number 264873)
was established in 1972 to provide funds for
research, diagnosis and treatment of eye diseases.
Examples of major projects funded by
the Ulverscroft Foundation are:-

- The Children's Eye Unit at Moorfields Eye Hospital, London
- The Ulverscroft Children's Eye Unit at Great Ormond Street Hospital for Sick Children
- Funding research into eye diseases and treatment at the Department of Ophthalmology, University of Leicester
- The Ulverscroft Vision Research Group, Institute of Child Health
- Twin operating theatres at the Western Ophthalmic Hospital, London
- The Chair of Ophthalmology at the Royal Australian College of Ophthalmologists

You can help further the work of the Foundation
by making a donation or leaving a legacy.
Every contribution is gratefully received. If you
would like to help support the Foundation or
require further information, please contact:

THE ULVERSCROFT FOUNDATION
The Green, Bradgate Road, Anstey
Leicester LE7 7FU, England
Tel: (0116) 236 4325

website: www.foundation.ulverscroft.com

Kate Clanchy was born and grew up in Scotland, and now lives in Oxford. Her poetry collections have earned her many literary awards and an unusually wide audience. She was the 2009 winner of the BBC Short Story Award, and has also written extensively for Radio 4.

MEETING THE ENGLISH

Struan Robertson — orphan, genius, and just seventeen — leaves his dour native town of Cuik, and arrives in London in the freakish fine summer of 1989. His job is to care for Phillip, dumbfounded and paralysed by a massive stroke; because, though two teenage children, two wives, and a literary agent all rattle round Phillip's large house, they are each too busy with their peculiar obsessions to do it themselves. As the city bakes, Struan finds himself tangled in a midsummer's dream of mistaken identity, giddying property prices, wild swimming, and overwhelming passions. For everyone, it is to be a life-changing summer.

KATE CLANCHY

◆

MEETING
THE ENGLISH

Complete and Unabridged

CHARNWOOD
Leicester

First published in Great Britain in 2013 by Picador
an imprint of
Pan Macmillan
London

First Charnwood Edition
published 2015
by arrangement with
Pan Macmillan
a division of
Macmillan Publishers Limited
London

A catalogue record for this book is available
from the British Library.

ISBN 978–1–4448–2308–0

Published by
F. A. Thorpe (Publishing)
Anstey, Leicestershire

Set by Words & Graphics Ltd.
Anstey, Leicestershire
Printed and bound in Great Britain by
T. J. International Ltd., Padstow, Cornwall

This book is printed on acid-free paper

For Matthew

It is easier for them; they are English.

Alasdair Gray,
The Fall of Kelvin Walker

Bathgate no more
Linwood no more
Methil no more
Lochaber no more.

The Proclaimers,
Letter from America

1

It was March, 1989, and the weather was unseasonably warm; but no one worried about that, then.

Phillip Prys, playwright, novelist, was brushing his teeth in the en-suite bathroom of his large house in Hampstead. The incisors had yellowed over the years with nicotine — much like his study ceiling — and there was a brown crack in the left canine, but Phillip was pleased with the molars. Sound to a man. Every morning, he counted them in and rubbed them over with his noisy hard-bristle toothbrush; jaw wide as a crocodile's as he shone up the back ones.

In the mirror his head, brown and speckled as a breakfast egg, dipped, spat, rinsed. On the windowsill, the padded Roberts radio belly-ached on about Salman Rushdie and failed to mention the letter to *The Times* Phillip had put his name to, just two days ago. Not that the letter was his idea: Giles had sprung it on him: and you could hardly say you were pro-fatwa, could you, these PC days? Not even to your agent in the privacy of Simpson's.

Absurd. He'd married one now, hadn't he? A foreigner. An Iranian, no less. The ravishing, the twenty-six-year-old, the petite, the scented Shirin, slowly dressing at this very moment in the adjoining room. Some racist he was. No, what Phillip felt — and he'd said this to Giles, openly, after a few drinks, mind — was, when it came right down to it, Rushdie had stolen a bit of a march on the rest of them with the whole business. Because, look, Giles, Rushdie might be brown, but he was a posh boy at bottom, wasn't he? Went to Eton, didn't he? Oxford? And with fairy tales like *Midnight's Arses* and *One Hundred Years of Buggery* hogging the book market, people were forgetting about the class system here in Britain, weren't they? Pulling the splinter out of the brown chappie's eye and forgetting the bloody pit-prop in bloody Wales, isn't it? Phillip always became more Welsh when he drank.

Giles had said nothing. In fact, he'd had the cheek to start folding his napkin. So Phillip had asked him directly — of course Giles was a queer, that wasn't the point — he must have noticed that the real stories, stories of the men of the valleys, rugby-playing men and their sons, those stories were going out and this posh namby-pamby gossamer was coming in instead, written by women half of it. Angela bloody Carter. And Giles had said, gesturing at Phillip's latest royalties statement, open between them on the table, but Angela sells, old chap, so does Rushdie. They *sell*. And then he'd told Phillip he was going to retire.

Retire. Giles! Giles gone grey all of a sudden, all his soft sideburns, grizzled. Shocking. As if they'd thrown a bucket of talc on him between the acts, while Phillip was in the circle bar, lining up the pink gins. Giles, in the name of Heaven! You could weep for him, so you could, like poor bloody Arthur Scargill and his men and all the other victims of Thatcher, no such thing as society and other bollocks. In the other room, Shirin yawned: small visceral noise from a strong pale throat.

Phillip wiped the last foam from his lips. He breathed in. Today was, after all, a beautiful day. The new leaves on the chestnut tree were un-furling, and Shirin was sitting on his bed, putting on her lipstick with an exact, exquisite hand. Listen! The tootle of birds, the tiny fire-cracker of Shirin's dress being electrically tugged over Shirin's tights. Phillip laid down the flannel and picked up the TCP.

Thirty years he'd lived in the house in Yewtree Row. Twenty his MG had twinkled at him from its snug parking place across the street. Giles at the end of the phone for what — thirty-five? Longer than Shirin had been alive, clever little orchid in the greenhouse of Tehran. But the MG would stay and Giles could be replaced. One of the smart young men in the office would be hon-oured, honoured. Of course he would. Phillip would ring him up and say: 'Bird tootling in a tree, what's the bugger called, for chapter 2?' and get the answer, just as he always had. The thought was worth a song. Phillip liked to carol through his TCP — 'Bread of Heaven', in Welsh, with his head thrown back — a special knack of his.

★　★　★

His jaw was at its very widest when the spasm hit. The TCP gurgled down his throat, and its

3

precise burn, etching the tonsils, was Phillip's last clear memory. He fell to the ground and jerked as if he were being shaken by an invisible policeman. He made a series of bad plumbing noises, rusty groans and burps. Spittle leaked from a corner of his mouth. His legs thrashed, then his head, and this all went on for a very long time, as if Phillip were being uncharacteristically brave, as if he were refusing to give up an answer.

All the while, and evenly as a flag in a steady breeze, the radio talked about the fatwa and moved on to the weather, and then to news just coming in about an oil spill, a very large one.

★   ★   ★

Of course, it was all a terrible shock for Shirin. They kept telling her so in Intensive Care, after she had revived Phillip, carried him downstairs in a fireman's lift, and delivered him to Casualty at speed in the MG which she was not, in fact, licensed to drive. Phillip was stable now, and Shirin should have a cup of tea, one with sugar, said the handsome young consultant. She should place her narrow hips on a plastic chair and smooth back her heavy shining bob of hair, and he would draw up his matching chair and explain everything in his best, grown-up, low voice.

You see, probably, the blood clot had been around for ages, bobbing around in Phillip's bloodstream. Phillip was sixty-two? A vulnerable age. Did Phillip smoke? Untipped? And drink? Pink gin was a strong choice. The young consultant looked like a jogger. His eyes were preternaturally bright, blue as glass. He explained that Phillip's arteries might, because of the smoking, be furred and narrower than average. It must all be hard for Shirin to understand, especially just now, but —

'He is suffering a revolution?' asked Shirin, in her tremendously posh voice with its just perceptible Iranian 'r', fixing the consultant the while with her famously lucent amber eyes.

'Well,' said the consultant, 'you could say that. Are you familiar with the circulatory system, Mrs Prys?'

'Yes,' said Shirin, looking at the ceiling, 'terrifically.' And so the consultant started on about Phillip's clot, how it would have started as something barely tangible —

'All revolutions start like that,' said Shirin, 'do they not? Just a few people? A few, did you call them, platelets? We need a strong tyrant, perhaps, to put them down?' There was a pause.

'Was Mr Prys recommended,' asked the consultant, 'aspirin? At any point?'

'Possibly. He would never take such a thing,' said Shirin. The consultant shook his head.

'It's not always easy to make that generation see that drink is not a friend,' he said.

'His ally,' said Shirin, brightly, 'his comrade. From the days of the Long March!'

'You know,' said the consultant, 'you should consider putting your feet up for a minute.'

'I think,' said Shirin, 'that after all, this is not a revolution, so much as a coup? We have a roadblock, do we not? This clot it is blocking the circulation? And now . . . '

'I think I'm losing your thread,' said the glassy-eyed consultant, who had grown up in Harrogate. And so he went off to fill in forms, and Shirin, who was a painter, sat looking at Phillip's liver-spotted hands with the tubes stuck in them, laid out by his sides, like a pietà. She knew about all this.

After the roadblocks comes the random firing. Rapidly, the streets fill with the injured and the lost, with backfiring ambulances, with gunfire and the reports of gunfire; in moments, the storm troopers arrive and the fires start. Then, the black government vehicles, the ones you'd hoped were rumours, cruise the streets in their sleek silence. Now, the city puts up its shutters, and gets behind them. Now, the new order, the months and years of damage. Last time, she had got away.

She picked up one of Phillip's hands, carefully. It was only slightly cooler than normal, but it felt hard, like the cast of a hand.

'Darling,' said Shirin, 'you'll be in for months.' And, as if in reply, Phillip's catheter bag filled with pee.

★   ★   ★

1989: at that time, hardly anyone carried phones, and the phones that were carried were ridiculous, and their bearers objects of fun. There were still messages, then: phone boxes, faxes, answer-machines, pagers, telegrams, Filofaxes, bike couriers, notes. There were pigeonholes in all sorts of places and out-of-the way organizations, and billets-doux and death threats were put in them.

Of course, things often went wrong. You could hang a movie or a novel on a missed message, then; Phillip in his weary later years had done so several times. Conversely, *getting through* to people was a full-time job for legions of loaf-haired ladies — women who should have been sent to university instead of typing school; who, if they had, would have been running the company instead of the sweaty oafs in pinstripe behind them. Shirin was particularly good at *getting through*, though she operated on an entirely autodidactic, freelance basis. If she hadn't been, as she pointed out to Phillip the first time she opened her little green Filofax containing the home numbers of the American ambassador, Douglas Hogg, Salman Rushdie and Charles Saatchi, she would be dead by now, or barefoot and nameless in a prison in Tehran.

Getting through wasn't just about contacts, you see, it was also about focus, delegation, and intuition. For instance, reaching Phillip's children from his second marriage would have taken Shirin several hours from the call box at the Royal Free Hospital, so, despite the names that Myfanwy, Phillip's second wife, had called her at their previous meeting, Shirin phoned her directly, and, when she found her not at home, succeeded, in a single brilliant swoop, in having her paged in Waitrose on the Finchley Road.

In fact, this was the kind of thing Waitrose

7

liked to manage particularly well. Whisked to the Manager's teak-lined office, Myfanwy was kindly sat down in the Manager's own leather chair with lean-back feature. She used this to the full as she listened to Shirin saying *en suite* and *crisis*. And when she replaced the receiver and murmured, 'My husband. Stroke,' and closed her eyes, the Manager did not hurry her, but slipped discreetly forward with a glass of water.

Myfanwy was in a *reverie*. She was seeing a *tableau*. She would have said both these words with a pronounced French accent which would have enormously irritated her daughter, Juliet. She'd learned it at RADA, in the late fifties. There, she'd also learned to celebrate, even indulge, her visual imagination. 'Picture it!' said the curious Polish movement teacher, Myfanwy's second or was it third lover, in his heavy accent. 'Picture it, Myfanwy, and let your body act the picture!'

On her vast bosom, Myfanwy's be-ringed hand executed a dying fall for the long-lost Zbigniew. Myfanwy's mind was picturing Phillip dead in his study (though Shirin had said *stable*, and *en suite*, several times): dead, yes, quite dead. Yellow, slumped on his vast desk like Marat in his bath, his horn-rimmed specs in his outstretched hand, harmless at last.

And then, into the *reverie*, entering stage left, gently removing the specs, and folding their legs, came her very good friend and colleague, the young estate agent from Hamptons. He was talking about Yewtree Row; he was saying, 'More than a million, Mrs Prys, with renovations.' And with that, the agent opened his hands to show

8

the details of a pair of railway cottages in Cricklewood, property of Myfanwy Prys, that were unaccountably failing to sell, and folded into the brochures, the interest statements from the bank. The agent threw them in the air, like doves, all the bothersome papers, and they flew —

'Madam?' said the Waitrose Manager, for Myfanwy had involuntarily described an arc in the air with both hands. Myfanwy kept her eyes shut, raised one hand flat in a Popish gesture.

Now in her vision she saw, under Phillip's bent yellow fingers, her deed of the divorce, and beside it, the agreement she had providentially pushed through with her lawyer: *that in the event of the death of Phillip Prys before the majority of both his children, the estate should pass in trust to Myfanwy Shirley Davies Prys.* Majority was twenty-five. Jake was twenty. Juliet was just sixteen. Myfanwy opened her eyes and smiled dazzlingly at the Manager.

'Not fatal, I trust?' he said.

'Stable,' said Myfanwy, 'but critical.' She blew her nose. 'So no change there,' she added, shocking the poor man to the core.

Myfanwy's eye fell on the Manager's phone. State of the art, push-button, black, and not her bill. Myfanwy adored Directory Enquiries. 'May I make a few calls?' she said.

★ ★ ★

And so it was that shortly, in a girls' private school in Baker Street, an excited sixth-former

9

went in search of the form mistress of that hopeless skiver, Juliet Prys: and, in a college in Oxford, a porter in a bowler beckoned a random undergraduate across the quad. The form mistress consulted a timetable, and set off for the gym: the porter simply handed over a note, confident that such a conspicuous young man as Jake Prys, one equipped with the quiff of the year, the open shirt of the month, and, the porter strongly suspected, the *lipstick* of the day would be easily located.

Juliet was found in the gym changing room with her best friend, Celia. Celia was crouched on the slatted bench wearing two coats and clutching a book. Celia was anorexic: her hand on the book was yellow and light as a leaf. Juliet was used to this. Juliet hardly cared. Juliet was standing in her knickers: Aertex on and school skirt off; a small, round, pink girl with a dark pony fringe, aggrieved, up-tilted eyebrows, a loose glossy lower lip and an out-thrust tummy like a toddler.

'Kirwan,' said Celia. 'Heading for you.'

'I'm in my pants,' said Juliet, pouting.

'It's OK,' hissed Celia, 'she's looking really sympathetic. Whatever it is, I'm coming with you, yeah? I'll die if I have to pick up a hockey stick.' Celia might, actually: you could see the double bones of her forearm, clear as a biology diagram. Juliet turned to her teacher, and held out the silly pie-frill skirt.

'Miss Kirwan,' she said, priggishly, 'I'm changing.' Unnecessary. A nearly dead father *on its own*, it soon transpired, was top dollar for

10

skivers. Not only good enough to miss PE but also double French, and Celia was warmly urged to take Juliet all the way home. And within minutes the girls stood smoking in Baker Street, just outside the Tube. Though:

'I should go to French, actually,' said Celia. 'I need to revise.'

'Celia,' said Juliet, inhaling importantly, 'you're a monomaniac. My dad's had a stroke.'

'I need all As,' said Celia, 'I need to go to Oxford. You know that. And besides, you haven't even cried yet.'

'I know,' said Juliet, grinding her fag out beneath her pixie boot, 'mad, isn't it?' She wandered into the station, trying to remember what her father looked like. She had his yellowy eyes in mind, and his reddish shining head, and his wide cross mouth, and his knees in tweed beneath his keyhole desk, but she couldn't picture his middle. 'He must have a middle,' she said, aloud. 'What sort of jumpers does he wear?'

'You're in shock,' said Celia, maternally. 'Sugar. Shall I buy you some sweets?' Every day, in this their sixteenth year, Celia had bought a family pack of Minstrels and fed them to Juliet: it was behaviour neither seemed able to stop. And now, she did it again.

'Do you know what I thought when Mrs Kirwan said it?' said Juliet, on the platform, munching. 'About my dad? I mean, what I thought at that exact minute?'

'No,' said Celia, sourly.

'Well,' said Juliet, 'first I thought, can I still go to Italy?' (For Juliet was supposed to be going to

11

Tuscany — then, a reasonably recherché destination — that summer with Celia and her family, and she was concerned that Celia was losing enthusiasm for the project. Or was getting too thin.) Celia raised a contemptuous eyebrow.

'Then,' said Juliet, 'I wondered if it would make me thin. You know, grief.'

Celia's dark pupils flickered in the stretched mask of her face, and her hand came up to cover her mouth, and then she howled with laughter, and Juliet saw in the harsh light of the platform that Celia was the wrong colour, now, the waxy yellow of preserved flesh, and the possibility of death, both for her father and her friend, occupied her mind for its necessarily brief space, like the train for Swiss Cottage rattling just then into the station, so very aluminium, so utilitarian and so large.

★ ★ ★

In Oxford, the note from the porter travelled out of the quad to the King's Arms, and thence to a room in Merton where a pretty, smudged girl was still in a rumpled bed, and thence again to the Playhouse where Jake was sitting on the edge of the stage, a script on his knee, his quiff in his hand. The messenger, a chemistry student in Jake's year who had never previously spoken to him, waited respectfully by his side as he read it. Jake refolded the paper, and handed it back. He looked at the chemist for a moment, then pushed back his quiff and sighed. 'Just gotta channel it,' said Jake, looking at his handsome, ringed hands.

'Death, life, it's all the same, isn't it?' Then, seeing the young man was still there: 'Hey, man. Thanks.' And the chemistry student went out to study the buses in George Street and be thankful he had never been drawn to the Arts.

Later, though, Jake did ring Myfanwy's flat, and got Celia. Myfanwy was up at Phillip's house, tidying it or something. Fighting with Shirin, probably. Juliet was chain-smoking on the sofa, making 'v' signs at the phone.

Jake said: 'Look, how is he?'

And Celia, modest and calm, said, 'Critical but stable.'

Jake said: 'See, I'm on stage tonight. You know. A new piece. I know Dad would want it this way.'

'Oh yes,' said Celia.

Jake said, 'But I'll ring, you see. I'll need someone to be in, to tell me how it's going, even if it's late.'

'Well,' said Celia, 'that could be me. I'm staying tonight.'

'First I've heard of it,' said Juliet, in the background.

'Might be midnight, might be two,' said Jake. 'You be there, Celia, hmm? And I'll see you soon.'

Juliet looked up from her cigarette. 'Has he fucked off?' she said.

'It's terrible about the oil,' said Celia, putting on the television. '*Exxon Valdez*.'

'Seal,' said Juliet, 'Jake really is a shit, honestly, he is, he doesn't care about anyone else. Don't get a pash on him, Seal, honestly. Listen. I'm giving you advice.'

'Look,' said Celia, pointing at the telly, her fluffy head trembling like a dandelion on its stalk. 'Gulls.'

'Poor sods,' said Juliet. 'Turn it over, Seal. You know I can't concentrate on the news. There's too much of it.'

2

In 1989, there were just crazy amounts of news: news from all quarters of both hemispheres of the globe; news of the very meatiest, most ideological, melodramatic sort — the *Exxon Valdez* was a popped pimple to most of it. Merely in the months Phillip lay in hospital, moving from Intensive to Critical, Critical to General, learning to slump in a wheelchair and sip from a spoon, Poland held democratic elections, the Ayatollah Khomeini died, the Americans went into Panama, there was a massacre in Tiananmen Square, and Mrs Thatcher introduced the poll tax in Scotland. So much news: so much of it, like the sunny weather, so unexpectedly gratifying to the English spectator, so fully supportive of the notion that he had been right all along, right since Hitler — you'd never have thought a playwright's stroke would make the papers.

But there were also so very many papers, then; and the papers were so fat; and written almost entirely by people who had been obliged to read Phillip's epoch-making play, *The Pit and Its Men*, at school, and to include it in studies of Angry Young Men at university; that the stroke did feature in the news. And not just the *Ham and High* either ('Local Author Phillip Prys "Stable but Critical"') but also a paragraph seven pages into the *Independent*, and a small article in the *Los Angeles Times*, which linked Phillip (incorrectly) with Richard Burton, and said that he was dead.

It took yards of Giles' fax to sort out the *LA Times*. Meantime, in Britain, English teachers weary of revision, sick of marking exam-practice essays with variations on *Describe the dilemma Pip faces in The Pit and Its Men. Does he make the right choice?* (GCSE) or *In its original production, The P&IM was described as 'amoral, communist and justifying matricide'. Do you agree?* (A-Level), happened upon the *Independent* notice and told their pupils about it, even as far as Pontyprys, where Phillip grew up, and Cuik High School, Cuik, Scotland, where the young English teacher, Mr Fox, had unconventionally opted to teach *The Pit* for Higher. Mr Fox had thought, in this breezeblock lowland town crouched among orange bings, that the play would reflect the kids' mining background and *set something alight*, but, as his colleagues had predicted, none of the kids doing Higher actually had mining backgrounds, those ones all left after Standard Grade, and several of the Higher students were insulted by the mere idea. Of the thirty pupils in the Higher English set, in fact, only Struan Robertson reacted to the news of the stroke.

'Would that be an embolism, sir, or a thrombosis?'

Struan worked part-time in an old people's home and intended to be a dentist. He was also that exotic thing, an orphan, though his dad had died of MS, not a thrombosis.

16

'I have no idea,' said Mr Fox.

'Well, I'm sure we all wish him well, sir,' said Struan. 'Either way. I'm sure we'll be thinking of him, as we are writing about his play, sir, and wishing him the very best.'

And thus, tranquilly, in the mild early summer, Struan took his Higher English, and aced it. In England, meanwhile, Juliet made an utter arse of her GCSEs, and Celia was hospitalized with jaundice but came out in time to sit her Maths. Jake Prys phoned his mother and told her he was taking his *Two Gentlemen* to Edinburgh, the post-modern, Tiananmen one.

On the last day of June, Giles went to visit Phillip, and put Wimbledon on the radio: 'There's a terrific young chap playing,' he said looking anxiously at his inert premier client. 'German. Like a ploughman out of Breughel. Listen, off he goes, biff boff baff! Terrific. You should see him. Calves like hyacinths in sport socks.' And then there wasn't a lot else to say, really: it wasn't as if Phil could talk. So Giles said, as everyone said, on their way to the door: 'You'll be out soon, old chap. Can't quite believe it.'

Because there was another thing about 1989, in England. Hospitals had very surprisingly stopped being places of recovery, where nourishing meals were served at regular intervals to persons on plump pillows and floors were scrubbed by junior nurses. Hospitals instead had become tense, dirty, over-crowded warehouses where anyone able to breathe independently, let alone sit with assistance and eat from a spoon,

17

was sent home. It had taken ages for this change to occur, people had voted for it, and it was very well documented, but somehow, most people went on believing in the Former Hospital, in the matrons, pillows, and scrubbing, until the moment they actually found themselves genuinely on the pavement with a real, incontinent, elderly relative in a dressing gown, in the actual act of hailing a minicab. Even then, as they often said to anyone who would listen, they simply couldn't believe it.

'I simply can't believe it,' said Myfanwy to Shirin. 'I can't believe that they are going to send him home. In that state. With a nappy.'

'There is a district nurse,' said Shirin, 'twice a day. For the rest, I can buy private help.'

'And what,' asked Myfanwy, 'is the hourly rate on that?'

★　★　★

But a lot of the time it wasn't at all bad. For a start, the sleeping thing. How many hundred nights had Phillip spent stalking sleep across the dark moors of the small hours, or tracking it on the flickering dial of his Roberts radio? How many bunches of hops had he shaken at it, how many cups of hot milk had he abjectly offered, shivering in the doorway in his dressing gown and slippers, only to have it shake its flanks and evade him at the last moment? It was a satisfaction, then, to have it curled up so, plumply on his plumped-up pillow. All Phillip needed to do was shut his eyes (he thought he

18

was learning to move one eyelid. No one had noticed) and sleep would cover him with its scented mink, release him into spectacularly liberated, near-hallucinogenic dreams.

Even when he was awake, memories seemed near, and enormous: meringues from his fifth birthday party, warty with burnt sugar; his great-aunt's fruit cage in supernatural 3D Kodachrome. And they weren't static, these visions, they weren't photographs, oh no. They moved, billiard balls on an infinity of baize. You could travel with the croquet ball, smack through the butterflied hoop, chase its textured scarlet roundness through the tunnel of long grass. A lot of the visions had to do with tunnelling, in fact, a side effect, surely, of the black cone which seemed permanently round his eyes (he did wish he could move his head), but a pleasant one. Like being a camera. You could home in on that greenfly on your great-aunt's raspberry bush, on the very bulbous fruit. Spectacular. Smashing. Everything there but the smells.

3

Literary Giant seeks young man to push bath-chair. Own room in Hampstead, all found, exciting cultural milieu. Modest wage. Ideal 'gap year' opportunity. Apply Prys Box 4224XXC.

It was Mr Fox who passed Struan the ad. He had been handing Struan things at the end of class, all year, ever since Struan had taken 20 out of 20 on the *Macbeth* Test. Books, mostly, but also newspaper articles, also flyers for poetry readings in strange Edinburgh pubs. Struan took it, as he had taken all the others, slowly and courteously, pausing to put his sports bag on the floor and rest his great length on the foremost flip-top desk, to turn the paper over in his extra-large, spade-shaped fingers. It was clipped from the *London Review of Books*, a journal he had not previously encountered.

This, on Struan's behalf, was pure philan-thropy. Cuik Library was well stocked, and Struan's card well dog-eared. Struan had read *The Outsider, Huis Clos*, and *Franny and Zooey* (though not, it is true, *Portnoy's Complaint)* well before Mr Fox handed him his precious paperbacks. Nor had Struan, appreciative though he was of poetry, any wish to go in a pub before he was of age, or indeed to journey twenty miles to Edinburgh on a week night. Struan stayed and talked to his teacher because outside the

20

classroom you could hear the engine growl of tall fifth-years talking from the bottom of their newly broken voices, from the bases of their acned throats. You could hear the chafing sound of third-years kicking the corridor wall. Almost, you could hear the spit they were saving, gargling from one side to the other of their mouths. Struan stayed to keep his teacher in the class-room where it was safe and warm, where the sun was coming briefly through the too-large win-dows. Struan stayed because he worried about Mr Fox.

He had done so from the first minute, when Mr Fox had bounced into their Higher English class waving his Bog People poems and his unconventional hair. Mr Fox was undersized. He was English. *English* English: a voice like the telly. He was filling in for Mr Nicholl, who had taught twenty-five years at Cuik, and who had recently suffered a heart attack — an actual, red-faced, groaning, gratifying heart attack during which had shouted at his third-years and clutched at an imaginary tawse. Mr Fox was at most twenty-one. He was keen on *acting out*. He was a ditcher of worksheets, an importer of photocopied poems about blackberries and frogspawn, poems by Catholics, or folks at any rate with Catholic names, and he believed Shakespeare was gay.

In such circumstances, there was very little Struan could do, but he always wiped insulting graffiti off the board before his class, and regularly removed toilet rolls and once a turd from the teacher's chair. Struan had the authority to do this. No wee guy, young or old, had bothered Struan since he got his height and his dad had died, which had happened at the same time, two years ago. Overnight, his identity as one of a beleaguered group of skinny swotty third-years with overloaded bags had disappeared into an aura of peculiar, lofty virtue. Now, he was a sort of Lazarus figure, six two in his nylon socks, his grey jaw and set green eyes gazing into another country. It was to Struan, not the staffroom, to whom the third-years ran when they had driven Mr Nicholl to apoplexy, and Struan, not the staff first-aider, who had administered the kiss of life and heart massage and saved the bristly old man's life. Struan read the lesson at Prize-Giving. He was mentioned in Talks to prospective pupils, and in dispatches to the Council. His outlandish good marks were popularly forgiven as a sort of excess of grief, like his height, rather than a hideous striving after distinction. So Struan could afford to throw the heron's wing of his protection over his small fluffy teacher as he bounced down the corridor, and he did, as often as possible.

But none of this, he could see now, had done any good. Mr Fox's hair had declined, flat to his scalp, and his friendly beery eyes had retreated into his head. He had developed a cower. His original nickname, *Mr False* — a tribute to his accent — had given way to the simple *Turdy-Man*. And now he seemed to be telling Struan he was quitting altogether.

'You're going back to England, sir?' said Struan, as kindly as he knew how.

22

Mr Fox started, blushed, then shook his head. 'Oh no,' he said, 'I wasn't thinking of me, Struan. I was thinking of you.'

'Me?' said Struan.

'You're the one who works in the old folks' home,' said Mr Fox, who had been horrified when he realized Struan had kept up this job, all weekend and three evenings, straight through his exams. 'I think that's what 'bathchair' means.'

'Bathchairs are wicker, are they no?' said Struan. 'They cannae seriously be using equipment like that.'

'It's a joke,' said Mr Fox. 'An old literary guy. And look: *Prys Hampstead.*'

'Oh,' said Struan. He crumpled the piece of paper over in his hand. A flush of blood spread up his strange, grey complexion, highlighting his freckles. 'It wouldnae be Phillip Prys, though.'

'Why not?' said Mr Fox. 'He had the stroke, remember. We read about it?'

'Still,' said Struan, 'it wouldnae.'

'They do exist,' said Mr Fox. 'Famous people. So does London.'

Struan knew that. He had taken Standard Geography. He knew Newcastle was there, beyond the great orange bings that surrounded Cuik, over the vast emptiness of the Borders, and York beyond that. He knew Paris was out there too, and New York, somewhere, full of masturbating Portnoys and Woody Allen, and California, and Lanzarote, where he'd been with the Sunshine Promise People and sat with his dying father on a hot black beach. But London was different from these other places, and Struan felt irritated with his teacher for ignoring this self-evident fact. Plenty folk in Cuik had been to Spain, and even Portugal, and come back burnt red, and settled back down to their Cuik lives. No one assumed their journeys had put them above themselves, or made them homosexual. But no one Struan knew had ever come back from London.

'You could send your CV,' persisted Mr Fox.

'Ma curriculum vitae?' said Struan.

'Yes,' said Mr Fox. 'Just — speculatively, you know.' He liked saying that. CV. Speculative. In 1989, CVs were in the air. All of a sudden, everyone had one and was sending it somewhere, by fax. Mr Fox had whizzed his own off that morning, as it happened, to a London publisher's.

'Actually, sir, I did a CV, last week, in secretarial studies,' said Struan. 'I'm taking a module, you know, now I've done my big exams. We had to pretend we were applying to the Council, for a summer job.'

'That'll do, then,' said Mr Fox. 'And you know, it wouldn't affect your dentistry application, Aberdeen would hold your place.'

Aberdeen had already asked him to delay a year, in fact. Struan should have told his teacher so. But he didn't. He was thinking about his CV, and the loathsome, pallid person who had somehow emerged from his busy clack-clacking. He had nothing to put under 'other interests'. Not Duke of Edinburgh, not Drama, not Sport. You couldn't put Death, or The Elderly, or Gran in any of those lists. 'Badminton,' he'd lied, in the end. 'Current Affairs.' That meant telly.

'It's a good idea,' said Mr Fox, as he had been saying for months, 'to get some life experience. Seventeen is too young for university.'

Struan gulped. 'They'd feed me?' he asked. 'It wouldnae be just the room?'

Mr Fox nodded. 'It says 'all found',' he said. 'Anyway, Struan, look, you're just applying, right? You're just shooting off an arrow in the air. Who knows where it will land, mm?'

Struan closed his eyes momentarily. He clenched his fists. He pictured that arrow, buffeting merrily across a blue, English sky, its feathers fluffy and nonchalant as Mr Fox's former quiff. Then he pictured his grandmother at the kitchen table with her cup of tea. She wasn't saying anything mean, that was never the trouble. She was saying, 'I'm that proud of you, son,' and her pebbly green eyes were watering as they did so often now, since his father died. He didn't want her to wipe her hands on her pinny because of the rasping noise it made. Would she be proud of him if he did this? Would she mind? He could say, 'Look, Gran, the Uni want me to take the year off, and there's no work here,' and she'd know that was true. There had been no work in Cuik for a decade, since the mine closed. Not even the old people's home could give Struan more hours for the summer. If he did this thing, went to England, he wouldn't need to ask Gran for anything. He'd saved up his money from the Home, he could get his own clothes and ticket, he could even leave her a bit of cash, just take maybe £50 with him, as a starter.

25

'It's only England,' said Mr Fox, 'in the end, just a few hours on the train. You can always come home.'

'Ah've never been though, Mr Fox,' said Struan, 'never been South.'

'Then you should,' said Mr Fox, nodding emphatically, 'then you really should. Everyone should travel, at least a bit. Broaden the mind. I went to Thailand, you know.'

Thailand, Struan wanted to say, was one thing. Mr Struther's new wee wife came from Thailand. Hampstead was another. But:

'Uh-huh,' said Struan. 'OK. Thanks, Mr Fox. I'll give it a shot.'

4

July 1989. The news continued strange and beautiful. In South Africa, President P. W. Botha met the imprisoned Nelson Mandela, face to face. In Siberia, three hundred thousand coal miners went on strike and were not attacked with tanks, or forced into gulags. The first President Bush visited Poland and Hungary, and was not attacked, either. In London, the summer continued equally lovely and unreal: each day, a sky like a dazzling silk tent; each night, breezes hot as breath, and spurts of stink like steam from a ham-bone.

In Yewtree Row, the long, closely placed sash windows had been open for weeks, their hand-blown glass flashing in the sun, their shutters pulled half across. In the black-and-white shade behind them, the rooms sighed, and rustled, and smelled: tar, teak oil, polish, dust, the very bricks seeming to give up the last whiff of the horse shit they'd been mixed with two centuries ago.

On the first floor, Shirin was at work in the en-suite bathroom. She had taken to spending most of her time, when she wasn't with Phillip, in here. Cramped — but that wasn't much of a problem, for not only was Shirin herself very small, but she painted miniatures, postmodern Persian ones, in acrylic, on boards as big as her hand. The bathroom light was good: high and a little diffused, and one could run a little water in

27

the round grass-green bath for background ambience. If you shut the bathroom and bedroom doors, you could not hear the nurses come and go at all; or Myfanwy, using her key with abandon, banging economical, self-righteous brooms.

At the moment, Shirin was simply letting her. She had an opening in a week, on Cork Street; it would make the papers because of the Iranian election, and her Khomeini/Father sequence was not even half done. So she'd let Myfanwy put an ad in the magazine, instead of employing a professional nurse as the hospital had suggested. She'd accepted that it was necessary to think of the children's trust fund. She'd insisted on knocking through from the study to the loo under the stairs to make a sort of bathroom for Phillip; but she'd let Myfanwy veto a ramp to the front door, on the grounds that the door case was listed, agreed that a bit of plywood would work quite well instead. She'd let Myfanwy run through the CVs, pick out the Scottish boy; she was currently letting her sort out the room. Shirin had no idea if this was wise: it had not happened to her before that her semi-paralysed husband was returned to her care within six months of marriage while she was preparing for her first major show. Shirin would consider wisdom later. In the meantime, four pieces were still in gesso. One was actually wet.

As it dried, she was gilding: the scimitar of a prince leaning from a black car against a textured silky red and purple background which on closer inspection seemed to be either a gathering of blood corpuscles or a crowd of cowed, veiled heads. Shirin breathed on the foil to make it stick, licked it down with an infinitesimally tiny sable brush.

★ ★ ★

Struan had been on the overnight coach, bent up like Meccano. The bus had disgorged him at Victoria and he had drunk his bottle of water and eaten the egg roll Gran had mournfully packed for him right there in the coach station. Then he got out his map and the compass he used for orienteering, and found his way to the Tube station. It was a fine, blue, airy morning, and as he walked, swinging his sports bag, his spirits rose. After all, nothing bad had happened to him on his journey, and no one was now questioning his right to be on this pavement smack in the middle of London. He had a job, and directions to it in his pocket.

Soon, he thought, he'd see London. Something shockingly stylish, something chrome, a name off the Monopoly board. But there was nothing so far but a big road, and at the end of it a station, not as big as Edinburgh Waverley or as fine, but more crowded, filled with more people than he'd ever seen in his life and moving together like a river as he struggled down the stairs to the ticket hall and the Tube.

At the bottom of the stair, Struan held on to the rail, back against the tiled wall, and gazed. He wanted to be dazzled, outclassed. He wanted the London folk to dress in some completely alien way, he wanted the Adidas sports bag and jacket he'd saved up for to be lost in translation, but he couldn't see anything: just hundreds of suits, and women in cotton jackets and printed dresses, and a couple of Goths maybe, but nothing you wouldn't catch any Saturday down Rose Street.

★　★　★

Myfanwy was in the attic, clearing out. To Myfanwy the hoover, to Myfanwy the mop, the duster, the black bag! Well, what else? Myfanwy's practicality had kept brick mortared to brick since the day she made Phillip buy this house, a genteel wreck, in 1967. Myfanwy's ingenuity had curtained it in damask from condemned country houses, furnished it with bargains from the Portobello Road. Despite the divorce, and Linda's execrable taste in cream paint, and Shirin's neglect, it was still lovely and as a top-flight Hepplewhite, and Myfanwy was engaged in saving it for her children.

She had picked Jake's room for the Scottish boy — it was larger. Besides, Jake hadn't really stayed here since he was fifteen: just brought back the occasional girl when his father was away. There were never-worn clothes in the wardrobe, ends of spliffs under the floorboards, candlesticks and ashtrays across the windowsill.

Myfanwy fiddled open a black plastic bag. Plop, plop, plop: in went the candles, the mouldy toothbrush, the tuna-can ashtray, the Aertex shirt for a twelve-year-old. The shorts could stay, though, hanging in the closet: the poor Scottish

30

boy might appreciate them. The books on the shelves, too: *Franny and Zooey, Huis Clos, The Outsider*, a full set of *Tintin, Asterix* in Latin. They would be an education for the oddly named Struan. He would not mind having the guitar case in the corner, either, or Phillip's National Service rucksack and cot occupying the eaves cupboard.

Air. Myfanwy opened the Velux above the bed and remembered that the window only had two settings these days: fully open with the pane suspended on its broken hinge, or locked. It was an early Velux, that was the problem. What an exotic item it had seemed to be when Myfanwy had ordered it, back in '78! But then, so did the Jack and Jill bathroom, with its shiny red taps, now rather limescaled. The whole extension was one of Myfanwy's early triumphs of interior design; one that had set her, you could even say, on the path to her current successful career as a property developer.

For who would have thought you could carve two rooms out of that top storey, with its rickety floor, and maids' grates, and crumbling ceiling? When they first moved in, you could see straight through to the slates. A poet had stayed on the bare boards for nearly a year, and the shagging he had done! A wonder the floor had survived. But even then, you see, Myfanwy had thought *practically*. He had got a cheque, suddenly, at the end of the year, from Faber and Faber, and Myfanwy had totted up what he owed them, walked him along to the bank, and sent him on his way with five pounds change.

31

It would be preferable, decided Myfanwy, to leave the window open: it hadn't rained for weeks. She hopped on the bed, carefully rewound the cunning little hook of garden wire around the hinge, braced the window in her hand, then let go. The sheet of Perspex hung vertically a clear three feet above the bed and only shifted slightly in the wind. The chances of the wire snapping were small; and the blind had never worked in the first place. And you could still look out the window, in the manner of *A Little Princess*. Myfanwy tried it out: stocking her bosom under the slope of the roof, spreading her arms on the hot, historic, chipped slates. She sighed with satisfaction. She loved to make small economies: they gave her a virtuous, cosy feeling inside, like a smile from Grandma Davies, her long-dead mother.

Myfanwy shut her eyes, opened her hands, and welcomed her mother into her mind: breathing deeply the while as Zbigniew had taught her. Ma Davies, with her wide arse and wide eyes, her rage against her wayward daughter softening rapidly into pride. Ma, with her brooms and brushes. Ma, who Phil, come to think of it, had banned from this house for exactly this: cleaning. Or whitewashing, to be more precise. The larder. He had called a taxi and made her get in it, squeaking and still spotted with caustic lime. Myfanwy closed her hands and opened her eyes. Well, she said to the broiling sky, there would be no more of that for Phillip Prys, no more drunken phone calls, sudden confiscations, double-crossings of bank managers, no more shouting, no more *language*. Phillip Prys was stuck inside himself, breathing. *No more than he deserves*, hissed Grandma Davies, in Myfanwy's head.

He won't last, Ma, Myfanwy smiled back, confidently. And when he finally went, she would get this house back — this house which she still thought of as hers, the one where the authentic slim Myfanwy was still running down the stairs in her knickers, where Cecil and John were demanding coffee after a long night's frotting and fighting on the hearthrug, where the *Daily Mirror* was on the doorstep, hoping for a snap of the star of the latest West End smash — and she would whitewash the larder herself in her mother's memory. They were coming back, such retro touches. Myfanwy wished she had kept the original, enormous, cast-iron range.

★ ★ ★

In the study, Phillip heard the bangs that meant Myfanwy, Myfanwy doing something with brooms. He betted she was wearing one of her Finnish outfits: Narda Artwear, and a Laura Ashley apron over it. Phillip was glad he could not see her: muscly fat hips in all that sofa fabric. Perhaps it was spring-cleaning: something very like sunlight was cracking the brown curtains of the study. Had it been there yesterday? He had no idea. Time was still liquid at present, but he had hopes that it would solidify. He needed to remember events, put some posts in all this marsh.

He had an idea, for instance, that at some

point in the past he'd divorced Myfanwy: he could see the decree nisi at the bottom of a long dark telescope. In which case, what was she doing in the house? The beautiful girl had come to see him this morning, and had fed him, and he was fairly sure that he was married to her now, and not the girl in between her and Myfanwy, who had been called Linda, and had a horse. Had he married Linda? Had he ridden the horse? Myfanwy was his second wife, not his third. His first was in Wales, enormous, still angry about the botched abortion. He couldn't remember her name. It was not possible that she too was called Myfanwy.

The Girl would know. Shirin, Sharoon, Rose of Sharon, her. He wished she would come in, prise his head from the pillow, put her cool fingers on the itch. She understood it all, perfectly. He could tell just from the way she grouped herself exactly in the circle of his vision: her tiny polished limbs, her long layers of black, thick hair, her wonderful sulky mouth. This morning, when she gave him his breakfast, she'd been wearing her tunic and roman sandals too: a martyr, painted by some fabulous Victorian pervert. She had tipped back his head and spooned peach juice into his mouth. His taste buds were working perfectly. He wished he could tell her that.

★　★　★

'Jake will be mad if you clear out his room,' observed Juliet to Myfanwy, wandering into the attic, sucking her hair. Reluctantly, Myfanwy got down from the window and considered her stout and unbrushed daughter.

'He'll shout,' said Juliet, mournfully, 'Jake will.'

'But,' said Myfanwy, still thinking of Grandma Davies and the brooms, and putting on her best *How Green Was My Valley* chapel lilt, 'we have the young man arriving today to take care of Daddy, and I think he needs somewhere to sleep, don't you?' And she ostentatiously busied herself with removing a poster stuck on the sloping ceiling. When Myfanwy had been sixteen, she'd been living on the King's Road, high on diet pills and well into her first *affaire* with an older man. She'd been skinny as Brigitte Bardot, had black Capris like Audrey Hepburn, and would never have left the house without her eyelashes on.

'He doesn't need to go in Jake's *room*, though,' said Juliet. 'You could put him down in the collection rooms. It's mad, those rooms being there with no one in them.'

'Those rooms are full of Daddy's things,' said Myfanwy, reprovingly. In fact, the rooms on the second floor had been hers, for the last years of the marriage. The wallpaper was still her grey sprigged dimity, the curtains early era printed-cotton Laura. Phillip had started filling the rooms with junk the day she moved out, hauling stacks of books and paper up from the cellar, the study, the shed, springing past her on the stairs with crates as she tugged her suitcases down. Myfanwy didn't even know exactly what was in there: Linda had kept her out. And now, they were not only full, but locked, with new, neat, aluminium locks. Shirin's work. Myfanwy would pick a quiet moment, and search her bedroom for keys.

'Besides,' she added, still tugging at the hardened Blu-tack on the poster, 'Jake is twenty and he will see that we have to put Daddy first. And he can always spend a night or two in your room.'

'No,' said Juliet. 'No he can't. And he really won't see that.'

'He's not coming home, anyway,' said Myfanwy, 'not this summer. He's doing his play, isn't he?'

'*Two fucking Gentlemen meet a Tank.* Edinburgh really needs him. That poster's going to bring the ceiling down,' observed Juliet. 'I should leave it up there,' she added, 'the poster. The boy will like it. Everyone likes Aztec Camera. Everyone *young.*'

But Myfanwy kept pulling, and a good bit of the ceiling came down, coating them both in choking fine dust.

'That's totally your fault,' said Juliet, 'I'm not going to help.' And off she toddled, hardly able to move her fat arse in her too-tight jeans.

★ ★ ★

There were hundreds of foreigners on Struan's Underground train, every colour of black, brown, and yellow. Were they all tourists? They didn't have maps, the most of them, or cameras, the way the Japanese did in Princes Street in Edinburgh, taking a million shots of the castle.

Lots of them weren't dressed up, either: they looked like working people. On the way to Hampstead he was rammed up against a young woman in an African-print headscarf and dress, like someone out of a geography book, and Struan flushed scarlet with the strangeness of it, because there were no black people in Cuik. There was no one, in fact, who was not pale as a potato, though when he was young Struan had once been treated by a Nigerian student in the Dental Hospital. He had been fascinated by the pink undersides of her fingers. He tried, now, to see if the woman in the African headscarf also had pale palms, but the Tube stopped at Swiss Cottage and she got out.

★　★　★

Juliet's room smelled nearly as bad as Jake's. She opened the Velux, put a record on the old mono record-player, looked inside the wardrobe, and pulled out the summer dress she'd left there last year: pink, and short, with buttons. Top Shop. Celia had persuaded her to buy it. She looked thin in it, Celia said, from the side.

Celia. Juliet had been round to see her, in Highgate, last night, and Celia had said: 'You can't stay. I'm expecting someone. I'm expecting my lover. I'm in love.'

And of course Juliet said, 'Don't be daft,' but Celia wouldn't take it back, not for anything. She said he came up the garden, and got in the window, every night. She said Juliet couldn't meet him, not yet, it was too new, and then Juliet said, 'What about Italy?' But Celia didn't care, and Italy was off, and she made Juliet walk back home alone through the hot stinking streets of London, barefoot, because her flip-flops were broken.

Round and round went the little fat record, making its thin song. Lloyd Cole and the Commotions, singing about a girl who looked like *Eve Marie Saint, in 'On the Waterfront'*. That was Celia. Celia wearing a white vest and thin little pants and a bracelet, perched on her window seat, her hair was all brushed and shiny. Thin looked better than fat, thought Juliet. It just did, and being jaundiced or dead or infertile or any of the other things they said about Celia really didn't matter a button by comparison. Seal looked like a photo, with her thin flat sides of hair and thin flat thighs and the way her pants fell in on her belly, and that made her look real, that was what. Like a girl should look.

Myfanwy banged the party wall, meaningfully. 'I'm busy,' shouted Juliet, 'do your own housework.' And she squibbed herself out of her jeans and into the pink dress. It had shrunk. The armholes were too small, and her arms bulged out like balloons, and the waist wouldn't button, and her shins looked like hams and her knees like pillows stuffed badly into their cases. In the mirror over the dressing table she did not look thin from the side.

'Mum!' shouted Juliet. 'Mum! What did you do to my dress?'

★ ★ ★

38

At Hampstead, Struan got out and was hustled into the lift. It was astonishingly hot. He was disappointed how old the machinery seemed, how low-tech and undersized. The air inside was like the steam from his Gran's pressure-cooker. If it was as hot as this in Cuik, no one would have mentioned anything else. The whole town would have been out talking about it, as if a flying saucer had landed. Surely, even here, it had to be unusual, had to be worth mentioning. 'Boiling, isn't it?' essayed Struan to the lift, and no one replied.

★　★　★

'I didn't touch your dress, Juliet,' said Myfanwy, on her knees on Jake's floor, dustpan in hand, vast arse in the air. She sat up, took an inch of the hem in her fingers. 'Shrunk, has it? Cheap, was it?'

'You washed it!' said Juliet, fat tears welling in her fat black eyes. She sat on the bed, raising more dust. 'You shrank it just to make me feel bad, you're always doing things like that. And now I've got to spend the whole holiday with you, because Celia's cancelled Italy!'

'Oh,' said Myfanwy (pleased, as she had been putting off paying Celia's mother the air fare), 'that is disappointing. Is that because of her health?'

'She's fine!' shouted Juliet. 'She's fine, she's just got a boyfriend and wants to go on shagging him!'

'Well,' said Myfanwy, 'natural enough. When I was your age — '

'Yeah, you were shacked up with a fifty-year-old pervert, bully for you, and I'm letting you down because I'm not shagging anyone, well you can shut up, OK! You can put a sock in it. 'Cos I'm not shagging anyone and probably I never will, and anyway, I'm probably a lesbian, I keep thinking about Celia's hips.' And Juliet collapsed on the filthy bed, and sobbed.

(Actually, this last bit was sort of put on. Juliet thought it would be horrible to have no clothes on with Celia, so scratchy and bumpy and yellow. On the other hand, it would be lovely and silky with someone like Shirin, like getting into a freshly made bed.) Myfanwy sat down beside her.

'You can't,' she said very certainly, 'be a lesbian, Juliet.'

'Why the fuck not?' asked Juliet.

'Because,' said Myfanwy, 'you're too fat. You can't be a fat lesbian, see, because people will just think that's why you are one. Because you can't get a man, you see. Lesbians don't want lesbians like that.'

Juliet took one hand, then another, away from her face, and looked at her mother's pink plate of a face, angled towards her, perfectly sincere. It came to her very clearly then that Myfanwy had said a terrible thing.

Juliet got off the bed and backed across the room. She put her hands on her hips, wrinkled her nose up to her eyebrows, and her eyebrows to her forehead. She scrunched her shoulders like a small pig about to spring over a high wall. Myfanwy, recognizing the signals, stood up in a

40

demonic cloud of plaster dust.

These were their starting positions: identical to the blockings of mother and girlfriend in Act 3 of *The Pit and Its Men*, arguing over the put-upon Pip. (Myfanwy had been the girlfriend in the original production, and had reprised as the mother an alarmingly small number of years later.) Now there was going to be a row.

★   ★   ★

Struan emerged from the Tube, consulted his map and compass. The air was shimmering and a snake of sweat crept down his back. He passed a shop called Whistles with women's shorts in the window, coloured ones, and silky halter-neck tops, no more than scarves. No one wore that sort of stuff in Cuik, those were abroad clothes, holiday clothes, but he could see that here, in the heat, they were maybe necessities. Down the pavement came a girl in just such an outfit, a girl with a little dog and a dandelion of gold hair, but when she passed Struan he saw she wasn't a girl at all: she was old, and her legs were wrinkled and orange as a party balloon gone down.

Then he started to worry about his own clothes. He'd no shorts. He'd grown out of the ones he'd taken to Lanzarote, and hadn't needed them since. He had a pair of PE shorts, but he'd left them in his drawer at home. Maybe Gran could post them.

★   ★   ★

The great thing about rowing frequently is: you speed up. In the attic, Myfanwy was already asking for the one thing that Juliet's father had ever done for her.

Juliet had been working on the answer: 'Sports Day, when I was six. I lost the egg and spoon, and I really didn't want to do the sack race, and Daddy came and got me and took me to the pub instead. He got me chocolates.'

'And drank himself into a stupor in a corner,' said Myfanwy, 'and I had to come and get you. Did you forget that bit?'

'Yeah,' said Juliet, 'but you didn't. You're so bitter, it's just sad.'

'Your father doesn't know how old you are, Juliet,' said Myfanwy. 'He doesn't know what school you go to.'

'He's ill,' said Juliet, squeezing out a tear. 'Of course he doesn't.'

Suddenly Myfanwy put down the bag of ceiling and sat on the stained bed. 'He's ill now, Juliet,' she said, without acrimony, 'but he didn't ever know. He didn't ever care. Not about you. Especially since you turned out so plain.'

This was a new one. It made Juliet sit down. She looked down at her belly, sticking out over her jeans, and her tiny silly fat hands. She remembered her father saying, 'Get her out of here,' at the dinner table. She couldn't remember why, or even how old she was at the time, just the bald head shining, the yellow eyes looking anywhere but at her.

'Look,' said Myfanwy, 'at Shirin. That's the kind of woman your father can see. He can't see

42

the others. No body older, no body younger, no body fatter: we don't exist.' And for a bleak little moment, Juliet saw that was true, and, looking at her mother's matching belly and matching fat hands and matching despair, that her mother felt the same way. About women. About Juliet. About herself, too.

'I can't stay with you though, Mum,' she said, 'can I? Not all summer. Now I'm not going to Italy. We're driving each other nuts. I'd better stay here, with Dad.'

They both stared at the plaster dust, settling in the shaft of sun from the Velux. Often as Juliet had volunteered to move in with her father, it had never before been a real idea. Now Juliet said, frightened:

'I could try and help, with Dad. I couldn't do the nappies, though. But I could do walks, maybe. Look, I'll sweep up the ceiling. I'll get the vacuum.'

'Shirin doesn't want you here,' said Myfanwy ritually. 'You'll cramp her style.'

'You haven't asked her,' sniffed Juliet. 'It's not fair, you should ask her!'

And Myfanwy bustled past her out of the room, and leant over the stairwell.

'Shirin!' she called. 'Shirin!' until the door below sighed open, and Shirin slipped out, white as a candle, and gazed up the stair.

⋆ ⋆ ⋆

Struan reached Yewtree Row. Mr Fox was clearly wrong about it being a grand address. The

43

houses were half the size of the Edinburgh lawyers' where his dad's will was read, and were made of brick, not granite. Some of them even had iron 'S' braces on the brick and were surely near to being condemned.

Struan checked the number on the door against the note in his hand. He put the note in his front pocket. He put his sports bag on the steps. He took a hankie from his back pocket, and carefully wiped his hands: there was black on the white cloth, shiny, like boot polish. Struan thought about *Our Mutual Friend*, and *The Pit and Its Men*, and dust heaps, and the Chernobyl disaster the year his dad died, the radioactive birds flying in from the West. He thought about Cuik, so clean since the mines closed, and how fast the air moved there, dashing between the bings like Gran's feather duster. He thought about his life so far and the worn place in the doorstep and the squintness of the step and the heavy, overbearing smallness of the door case. And Struan stretched out a clean Scottish finger towards the tarnished bell.

5

The lady who answered Struan's ring was wearing a tiny dress, ruched like the bathroom curtains, and she had gold eye make-up on though it was only the morning. 'Tarty,' said Gran in his head. But this lady was grown up, and she didn't look tarty, she looked foreign, the most foreign person ever. She was looking up at him with a pursed, firm, shiny gold mouth. She was holding a paintbrush.

'Mrs Prys?' said Struan. And, when she nodded, he held out his hand. 'I've come to help with your husband. I'm Struan.'

The lady placed her hand, golden, be-ringed and tiny as child's, momentarily in his white fist. Then she retreated inside the house, calling, 'Myfanwy!' And a much larger woman with plump, pale, freckled arms waddled down the stairs, struggling with an immense dusty bin bag. A wee fat girl appeared at the top of the stairs, said, 'I am too staying, Mum, so triple bollocks to you!' in a voice carrying as the radio's, and disappeared again.

The next bit was in slow motion. The large lady shouted, 'Juliet!' and twisted up the stairs to shout louder, but the bag over-balanced her and she was precipitated suddenly forward, plaster and dust fountaining up the stairwell. Struan hurdled over his sports bag, and caught her, his two huge hands on her tweed bosom. Those were

45

Struan's first handfuls of breast, and they felt like a settee. Hastily, he moved his hands under her arms, lifted her clear of the stair, and set her on the floor.

'Sorry,' he said, 'sorry, I was aiming for your oxters.' Both women stared at him, bemused. They didn't seem to understand him. 'Armpits,' he essayed, remembering his English.

'Peits?' said the pretty lady. 'You are Dutch? I thought your name is Strew-anne?'

'Uh-huh,' said Struan, 'Struan, that's right, Struan Robertson. From Cuik. Ah've come to help out?'

The pretty lady nodded at him, blinking in the sun. Her eyes were long and amber-brown, and it wasn't just gold painted round the edge of them, the backs of them were gold too, textured, like the foil from a packet of cigarettes.

'Super,' said the fat lady, dusting herself down. 'Super to meet you, Struan.' And she held out her fat hand.

The beautiful lady waved her paintbrush. 'My gesso,' she said, 'will over-dry.'

The fat lady smiled. 'Let me make Struan some coffee,' she said.

And she shouted up the stairs, 'Fresh sheets, Juliet!' Then the fat lady opened a door, and ushered him through it, and the beautiful one disappeared like smoke.

★ ★ ★

The sunlight was in Phillip's eyes. No one had come, after the doorbell rang. He could hear

46

voices from the kitchen: Myfanwy, setting someone straight, someone else joining in. *Juliet*, Myfanwy was shouting, *Juliet*. Or maybe it was the radio, or a dream of the radio. He had written a play like that for the radio, once; mother and daughter, having a fight. Women all hate each other, like cats. He'd said that at how many parties, got a laugh, usually, lots of laughs. *Juliet, Juliet*, said the radio. His daughter was called Juliet, but she wouldn't be old enough for such a part, not yet, she was a little thing in a round school hat, and he'd said to Melissa, what about a part for her in the films, you know, child star, and Melissa had said, too stout, darling, not enough range, and it was quite true, quite true, you could see the stiffness in her little face. Looked just like her Grandma Davies. Silly bitch, that one, he was fairly sure she was dead, her.

Phillip wasn't dead, him: he could still hear. *Juliet*. Banging on. *Juliet*. They were still banging on. He wanted them to come and move him. He wanted a cigarette. This was the bit that was a damn nuisance, the itch in his eyes, and not being able to do anything about it, the not being able to say. All the words accumulating like pee in the bag.

★ ★ ★

The fat lady made Struan a coffee in a fancy metal machine, but not a sandwich. Then she talked. Her mouth was very small and pink and her face very big and loose and the one wobbled the other. Her eyes were huge and a hard shiny blue-green, like glass beads. And her voice was sharp-cut too: big round 'o's like an elocution teacher. She kept referring to herself in the third person. Mrs Prys.

She was saying the nurse was in the house 7:00 am to 9:00am, and 6:30pm to 8:00pm, for getting Phillip up and putting him to bed. Apart from that, Struan was in charge, though he would have help at meal-times from Mrs Prys and generally in between from Mrs Prys who would be just upstairs, so nothing would really be at all burdensome, there was no need to really do much except keep Phillip clean, and Phillip was honestly not sentient, and of course Struan was absolutely free to amuse himself when Phillip was asleep, he could really do anything he pleased, except, that is, go out unless of course an adult, Mrs Prys for example, happened to be around and he'd asked and Mrs Prys didn't mind, and Struan could have Saturday evening off by arrangement and she expected that he could just make his own meals from what was in the fridge or the larder, and that the room was nearly prepared upstairs, a couple of things just being sorted out, Struan wouldn't mind helping. It was a lovely room, it belonged to her son really, but she expected Struan wouldn't mind camping out for a bit in the sitting room if Jake wanted to stay, that wouldn't be for a while and she was sure meeting Jake would be a real thrill, Struan could receive phone calls by prior arrangement but should make outgoing calls from the box on the corner —

48

Then she said, 'I'm sure you've got a lot of questions for me.'

Struan put the earthenware mug back on the table, leant back on his Swedish chair. He was a terrible long lad: it was all he could do to stop himself swinging backwards on two legs, the way he did at home. There were so many things to wonder about, he hardly knew where to start.

'Do you have a toasted-sandwich maker?' he asked.

'No,' said Myfanwy, 'but you may use the grill if you wipe it.'

'Who's the lady who answered the door?' asked Struan.

Myfanwy smiled horribly.

'Mrs Prys,' she said.

'Oh,' said Struan. 'I'm sorry. I thought you were Mrs Prys. Are you the housekeeper, then?'

And Myfanwy smiled that lipsticked smile again. Her wee pointy face and pop eyes looked odd, Struan thought, over her huge bosom: like a hand-puppet, Mrs Punch, talking over the curtained stage of her chest. The clacking pink mouth was saying all sorts, stuff that Struan had never heard in his life before: apparently the young Mrs Prys, Shirin, was the latest and last of a long line, a very long line, of mistresses (she used that word) superseding a girl called Linda who really, said Myfanwy smiling martyrishly, she had got quite fond of. Shirin had insisted on marriage, she said for the immigration status, though really, in Myfanwy's personal view, she should have gone back to Iran, there was no genuine problem there, she had family there.

49

Struan said he saw all that, and Myfanwy mustered herself and said, yes it might strike some people as odd, how generous Myfanwy was with her care and time, the way she insisted on caring for the house, and caring for Phillip and allowing the children to keep rooms here, but really when the chips were down and backs to the wall it was down to one to pitch in and do one's best and she and Phillip had been married for twenty-five years —

'My heron-winged, grey/My blue true wife,' quoted Struan, suddenly, in his impossible accent. Myfanwy was quite touched.

'Yes,' she said, 'that's about me.'

'It's set on the Higher,' said Struan. '*Supplementary Material* to *The Pit and Its Men*. I was awful keen on my English you see, even though I'm going to be a dentist.'

Struan was thinking: he had found London now, right enough. The kitchen was painted a shade of pink he'd never seen on a wall, a sort of sticking-plaster colour. The sink was round and steel, hi-tech looking, but the dresser had had its paint stripped off it and not put back. On it was a plethora of *Alice in Wonderland* equipment: thick, wibbly glasses, plates too large for anyone to use, cups that were as much too small. There were steel knives stuck to the wall on a magnet, and sausages and something like pine needles hanging from the ceiling, and a huge cheese grater, and a wee brass colander. None of this would have done, in Cuik: but then, in Cuik, it would not do to make arrangements for your ex-husband, or to sit in the kitchen of your

50

ex-husband while the new wife was in the room next door. Struan thought it was terrible, and it was grand, both at once. He asked:

'Who was the wee girl on the stair?'

'That's Juliet,' said Myfanwy, 'Juliet Prys. Mr Prys's daughter. My daughter. My daughter with Mr Prys.'

'My tight-green bulb in rich black earth?' asked Struan, returning to the *Supplementary Material*.

'Actually, that's Jake,' said Myfanwy, 'Juliet's older brother. By the time Juliet was born Phillip Prys was, how shall we put this? Through with the muse.'

'Oh,' said Struan. 'Does Juliet stay here?'

'No,' said Myfanwy. 'Sometimes. It is possible in fact that she may be staying for a short time just now. She may be here for a week or two this summer but you shouldn't leave Mr Prys with her. She doesn't count as an adult.' Myfanwy smiled tightly. 'In fact, she often acts much younger than her years. Anything else?'

'Could I meet him now?' said Struan. 'Mr Prys? See the set up and so forth.'

So they went into the study. The room was as large as the Cuik School Library, and held more books. There was a hospital bed in one corner, and French windows to the garden on the other wall. In the middle, in a shaft of sun, lay a bald old man in a wheelchair, his body slack in a way familiar to Struan from the Home. The young Mrs Prys was sitting beside him, drawing with the same slim hand she had rested in Struan's when he arrived. She was the first foreigner

Struan had ever knowingly touched, and he would have stared at her contentedly for some time, but —

'The sun's in Mr Prys' eyes,' said Struan, 'that cannae be comfortable; Excuse me,' and he strode over to the wheelchair, unclicked its sticky brake, and moved it into the shade. Shirin stopped drawing, and gazed at him. Struan knelt down in front of the old man. 'Mr Prys,' he said.

Phillip could open his eyes, now the glare had gone, and he did. A bony boyish face and long neck came into the circle of his vision, monochrome, like a plaster bas-relief of an early emperor. Augustus, probably, with that pale, curly, close-cropped hair. Eyes grey as river-pebbles locked with Phillip's.

'Meestahpreese,' said the face. 'Avecomtayelp. Ah'm Strewn.'

The language was mostly foreign, but the last word was very clear. Strewn. He was Strewn. Indeed he was. Phillip was strewn to the winds, and a new Phillip must be gathered. And how marvellous, simply marvellous, to have found someone who understood.

'Blink,' said the head, shutting its own eyes. 'Canny blink?'

Blink? Well, why not? Mustering all his resources, Phillip did.

6

Here are the reasons why, despite sleeping virtually next to him in the hot attic rooms and sharing the Jack and Jill bathroom, that Juliet doesn't fancy Struan, not at all:

Number 1) Struan's clothes: Struan owns one pair of high-waisted Lee jeans, and one pair of BHS pleated trousers. Both skim his ankle bones. The pleated trousers, in particular, give him a strange sexless blank fold round the crotch. Whoever Celia's lover is, Juliet is sure, even if he is a grown-up, he has 501s. Struan also owns, for hot weather, one T-shirt, plain white, and one checked shirt with short sleeves (C&A). He is currently washing one of these garments each night and leaving it to drip over the tiny bath in the attic, thus allowing Juliet to inspect their labels and their cheap stitching. She has never seen anything like either of them, and both are out of the question.

Number 2) Struan's hair. This is mouse-coloured, coarse, and not so much styled as chewed off close to the scalp. In a world where hair mousse has just been invented, and there are pop-bands called Haircut 100, this is tantamount to a tonsure.

Number 3) Struan's toiletries. Struan uses cheap razors which he wipes and leaves on the windowsill, prissily on a piece of toilet paper. Struan uses unscented Men's Deodorant from

Boots, Juliet hears it schooming from the can every morning. It smells of something crude and anti-freeze-y, and the smell clings to the drip-drying shirts. Struan uses the word 'toilet' freely, instead of 'loo'. All these things give Juliet a creepy little feeling she is unwilling to name.

This is a disappointment. Nevertheless, Juliet has little to do in the week she and Struan move in, because Celia is more or less not speaking to her and nor is her mother, so she takes it on herself, in between afternoon reruns of *Dallas* on the tiny front-room telly, to take Struan about a bit, and explain things. He's never been to London.

And so it is that on Struan's fourth afternoon, which is demonically hot, and humid, as Juliet remarks, as having a whole live Labrador on your head, that she leads Struan to Hamptons Estate Agents in Flask Walk — Phillip Prys, disappointingly inert, between them in the wheelchair — and attempts to explain the London property market, which after five seasons of freakish growth, during which graveyards in Westminster and council estates in Clapham have been converted into luxury flats, and carriage lamps and tie-back curtains have frothed like algae over Fulham, is currently enduring a little local difficulty.

'The prices,' Juliet says, 'are coming down now, because of the economy, so we should look for a bargain, especially if it's got original features and it's in an edgy area, and then we can buy it and do it up and make lots of money when the prices go back up.'

Struan peers, and says there do not appear to

54

be many bargains on offer.

He also thinks the agent should change the bottle-glass window. It sags. He peers harder, and wonders if the people in the agents have misplaced the decimal point in the prices, or if mebbe, for some London reason, dollar signs are being displayed as pounds.

'Like that wee house,' says Struan, putting a large spade-shaped finger on the curved bottle-glass, 'that one is four hundred thousand pounds, and that cannae be right. What does mews mean?'

'Small,' says Juliet. 'But look, you see, it says reduced. It's a bargain.' We should remember at this point that Juliet is predicted to get E in GCSE Maths. She is preoccupied, moreover, with her reflection in the window, tastefully obfuscated by the curving glass, floating over the bijou interior in her white frock, like a double negative on an album cover. She doesn't look too fat.

'My gran's house has three bedrooms,' says Struan, still staring at the window, 'and when she bought it from the council it cost two thousand pounds.'

'Really?' says Juliet. 'You're really lucky, Struan. Is it an edgy area of Cuik? Does it have original features? Could you strip the floors?'

'No,' says Struan. 'It's got contour carpets.'

Struan's family house besides is harled, small, and perched on a landscaped slag heap. Already the good neighbours are dying off, mostly of emphysema, already the house three doors down has been empty a year. In fifteen years' time, Gran's will be the only net curtains in a street of boarded-up windows, and it will be all that Struan can do to move her out to a wee flat —

'My mum,' says Juliet, 'does up houses for a job. That's how I know all this. She's done four now. She started with this vicarage in the Gower Dad threw in with the divorce settlement, then she did a garden flat in West Hampstead, and Grandma Davies' cottage in Cardigan, and now she's got these railway cottages in Cricklewood. They're really cute, actually.'

The cottages, Myfanwy would say, were *rather a romance:* an irresistible bargain at auction, a matching, adjoining pair with simple smiling faces, low roofs, and clapboard doors. Myfanwy has restored them gently, treating them to Laura Ashley feature walls and expensive retro taps, polishing up the original, matching iron stoves. They are so petite, so dainty: each a perfect honeymoon nest for a young (very short, very tidy, without need of storage) couple.

'Soon,' says Juliet, 'she'll sell them for loads more money. Then she'll do another one. That's why I'm looking out. She says the secret's all in the paint. You've got to use pale paint, magnolia, and neutral carpet, beige. She has all these little men that work for her, Irish, they're all brothers actually, one's a bricklayer, one's an electrician. Super.'

'My uncle,' says Struan, 'is an electrician.'

And there, in a nutshell, is the reason Struan doesn't fancy Juliet. She is strange to him as a Martian. She might say anything at all in her rushing, husky, posh English voice, things like, 'Come and watch *Dallas* with me, Struan, this

56

one's got Dwarfish Lucy in it, she's my all-time fave,' or 'little men' for a whole category of adult, and not be at all ashamed of herself. She regularly slings out questions such as 'Don't all teenagers have homosexual phases?', and other statements which would have silenced and divided Cuik, casually as yo-yos, leaving Struan open-mouthed in her wake. Though he has resolved to do better to keep up.

'If the prices are going down,' says Struan, now — and he will take an A in Higher Maths — 'will they no go down on the railway cottages too?'

'Maybe,' says Juliet, 'but they were still very cheap, so we'll still make loads of money. You see, Cricklewood is a very edgy area.'

About this Juliet is entirely wrong. Myfanwy has put all her profits into the cottages, and borrowed on top. And now interest rates are rising and the wisteria Myfanwy planted in the cottages' gravelly little garden has withered and died, and the young couples who do come round to look remark on the railway (still there, still noisy) and have no deposits. The cottages are lingering on the market, and only this morning, the newly dug pond has turned an unpromising shade of purple. This is very much on Myfanwy's mind as she meets Giles in the Hungarian Tea Rooms at the top of Hampstead High Street.

★ ★ ★

Giles, of course, always seems embarrassed. His diffident, unworldly manner, so agreeable to artists, is partly what has kept him at the top of the literary game for so many years. But he also, generally, thinks Myfanwy, gets over the arty bit and stabs in there with a ray of strong commercial sense. A figure. A bottom bloody line. Where is it today? He has been moseying his way round a tray of flaky pastries for nearly twenty minutes, fussy as an Arctic yak nibbling linden berries. He's been on and on about the piece in the *Los Angeles Times*; how he faxed over a correction soon as he heard of it; but what with the time delay; shades of Mark Twain, and now he was bleating on about Phil's state; wouldn't he be better in a nursing home —

'Well,' said Myfanwy, 'possibly, but the royalties from *The Pit* would keep him there for about a fortnight, and after that it's the children's trust, and I'm not having that. Unless you've got any brilliant ideas, Giles?' Now Giles sits up in a way she recognizes.

'Actually, Myfanwy,' he says, and he beckons her to his whiskers, and flakily whispers the name of a Literary Giant, a proper one, a Great Dane to Phillip Prys's dachshund — did Myfanwy remember?

'Of course,' says Myfanwy, dusting pastry from her cheek, 'he visited Yewtree in '79.' She'd worn a blue silk catsuit, poured the Giant bourbons on the rocks, and Phil had slipped away, screwed horsey Linda in the larder.

'He's put in an offer,' whispers Giles.

'An offer?' asks Myfanwy, still seeing Phillip's hard hairy bum out beneath his shirt, pumping away at silly Linda's palazzo pants, both of them

58

squeezed into the narrow space between the tins — 'For *The Pit?*'

'No,' says Giles, 'for Yewtree. For the house.' And Myfanwy stares.

'He heard,' says Giles, 'that Phillip was, you know, and I explained he wasn't, you know, but he asked me to put it to you anyway. In case Phil was, you know, in the future. Soon.'

'Dead,' says Myfanwy, flushing. 'How much?'

And Giles names the sum.

'Oh,' says Myfanwy, and Giles nods. O. Such a lot of Os.

Then Myfanwy gazes for some time out of the window with her strange round marbly-blue eyes that were once so famous. That were once thickly fringed, snapping, full of fun, in the days when Myfanwy offered tea and rounds of toast among the bare boards and threadbare armchairs of Yewtree Row. Giles remembers that Myfanwy, lush on a dirty hearthrug: he blames Phil for her slow demise, to be quite honest.

'I hadn't thought of it,' says Myfanwy, at last. 'I'd thought of selling Finchley Road. If, you know. Renting Yewtree, at most.'

'It's a lot of money,' says Giles, 'enough to take care of Phil properly. If Shirin agrees. I haven't spoken to her yet. She's busy with this show.'

'Could she block it?' says Myfanwy.

'Yes. Her settlement entitles her to live in Yewtree till Phil dies,' says Giles. 'All found, effectively.'

'Well then,' says Myfanwy, 'she'll have to have something as good. I'll put it to her, Giles, leave it to me.'

It is starting to rain, hot drops falling on Phillip's linen shirt. Struan turns the chair and starts to walk home, chin down, silently.

'Just the weather,' says Juliet, hopefully, 'for taking off all our clothes and rolling round the garden.'

'You're joking,' says Struan, pushing faster. Briefly, he wonders if there is something wrong with him, if he ought to want to join Juliet, nude in the mud. Because Struan hardly ever thinks about stuff like that, somehow. Fancying, all that. Mud.

Probably, there is. The years most boys spent, according to *Portnoy's Complaint* and the rest of Mr Fox's dirty books, in a sweaty masturbatory frenzy, Struan spent tending his father's withering body, and after he died, other withered bodies in the old folks' home. Struan has learned to pour himself into this work with perfect concentration, exactly as he poured himself into Mr Fox's English essays, or into a Maths problem or the Periodic Table. If you looked at anything fully, he had found out early in his father's illness, if you gave yourself over to thinking about it, then all of you went outside yourself and nothing stayed inside your head to mourn or rage. Now, nothing disgusts Struan: not his father's shit-covered arse, not his English teacher's bristly mouth into which he poured his own breath, not Phillip's slack mouth nor the bubbles coming from it. But in order for nothing to disgust him, he has had to turn something else off, the bit that might have appraised Juliet, and her swelling little body, outlined in her damp dress, stumping crossly ahead in the hot, thickening rain.

★   ★   ★

In the tea room, in the sudden dark of the storm, Giles says: 'About Phil. You are sure there's no chance of recovery, aren't you? Certain?'

Giles has lived with Phillip's rage for thirty years, a rage the size of an ocean liner: he can't quite believe it has gone, lost for ever in a slumped old man in a wheelchair. 'Because,' he adds, 'he'd be hopping if he, you know, woke up.'

Myfanwy remembers the blink. That was four days ago, though, and there has been no repetition. She thinks, with sudden dislike, of the Scottish boy, and his ostentatious way with Phillip, moving him out of the sun. She hopes there will be no trouble from that quarter.

'He's never going to hop, Giles,' says Myfanwy. 'You can be sure of that.'

And they sit on, in the cosiness of rain, watching the street decompose on the window.

Myfanwy says: 'I don't want to lose it, though, if I'm honest. Yewtree. I love that house.'

Her eyes are sort of balding, now, thinks Giles, that's the problem. Maybe Myfanwy overdid the false eyelashes, back in the Elizabeth Taylor days, and pulled out the real ones. Or maybe it's her jowls, dragging the bottom lid too far down. Whichever, what with that, and the bosom, and the purple drapes, and the tummy, and the arms residual at the sides, one can't help thinking — O, bad, bad Giles — of Humpty-Dumpty. And with that pen-and-ink, Victorian thought comes a vision of the soul of Phillip Prys, small as a figure from a playing card, brown as a walnut, armed with a spoon, demanding why Giles had sold his beloved Yewtree to an over-rated drunk American with no feel for the plight of the working man. Giles shudders in his gilt chair, just perceptibly. He says:

'No need to go out, not just yet.'

7

But there was no sign of improvement in Phillip.
None. The blink had been a week ago, and he
hadn't done it again, had he? No. Not exactly.
Not, as Myfanwy pointed out to Juliet with an
ostentatious flourish of her dishcloth (she was
clearing the kitchen in Yewtree Row: no one had
asked her) at all.

'Struan,' said Juliet, 'says that people don't
recover from strokes in a straight line. He says
it's one step forward, two steps back, quite often.
He says Daddy's eyes follow him sometimes, and
that's a good sign. He says he's quite hopeful.'

'Struan,' said Myfanwy, 'is an unqualified
seventeen-year-old.'

'No,' said Juliet, 'he's eighteen in October, and
he got all As in his Standard Grades already.
That's like O-Levels. GCSEs, I mean. And he
worked two years in an old people's home. A lot
of the old folks had strokes, Struan says.'

'Marvellous,' said Myfanwy.

'I'm going to take Daddy for a walk,' said
Juliet and even her voice had gone odd. Sweeter.
'Struan says it's a good idea. He's going to push,
and I'll show him the way. We went out the other
day but it rained. Why are you here, anyway,
Mum?'

'I've come to see Shirin,' said Myfanwy.

'Well, you'll have to wait,' said Juliet, 'she's
gone into town. Her paintings are a really big

success, didn't you know? They're in the *Standard*. She's done a whole load of them, they're called *stroke/revolution*, with a sequence called *Father/Khomeini*, it's a meditation on grief and political change, it says in the catalogue and she's having an opening of them, it's tonight, it's Cork Street, that's good isn't it, Cork Street, and I shouldn't think she'll even be back, I wouldn't be.'

'She will be back,' said Myfanwy, coldly, 'at half-past five, for a quick meeting. I made an appointment.'

'It's only five o'clock,' said Juliet. 'Why are you always noseying around here? It's really weird of you, you're divorced, it's not your house.' And off she went, in a white dress with tie-strings at the back. She'd clipped up her hair in combs on either side, noticed Myfanwy, and crimped her fringe into a floaty pouffe. *Angel of the House*, decided her mother, *A Nun's Story*. Juliet was too stout and pop-eyed for either role.

★   ★   ★

Getting the chair out of Yewtree Row was a ticklish business at best. First, you had to tug the improvised plywood ramp from the basement area and lay it over the five steep irregular steps. Then someone, preferably Shirin, but today, Juliet, who had just disappeared yet again to do her hair, had to stand at the head end of Phillip and gently tip him back, while Struan straddled the pavement, leant forward to grasp Phillip's armrests, and used all his strength to brake the wheels' downward hurtle. A lot depended on

64

the speed at which the brake was released, but even if it was Shirin at the controls, each impact hurt his back round the tops of his kidneys, let off another thin pinched signal of pain, adding to a chorus from his body which Struan was finding harder and harder to ignore.

He was hungry, for a start. He'd been hungry since he'd finished his egg roll at Victoria coach station, a week ago, since Myfanwy had given him coffee and no sandwich at twelve o'clock in the day, Gran would have died rather than do such a thing. There were no meals in Yewtree Row. One Mrs Prys puréed food for Mr Prys and stored tiny pots full of unknown, terrifying green and brown substances in the fridge, the other Mrs Prys told him there was plenty of stuff for him and Juliet in the larder, Pot Noodles and beans, and he knew there had been on Tuesday, he'd seen the box, but there wasn't just now, there really was not and he didn't know what to say about it because he didn't really believe Juliet could have eaten the lot, it didn't seem possible, even though she was on the round side, and odd about her food.

It was too hot, though, that was the big thing. Each day in Yewtree Row the heat had reached further and further into his resistance. It was hard to sleep in the tiny attic, under the broiling slates. His deodorant can was nearly empty. His trainers were untenable. As soon as he got his money, his £20, which he hoped would be tonight, because he'd been here a week now, he was going to get some sandals, even just flip-flops. Everyone he passed had sandals, and he envied every naked toe. And shorts, he needed shorts.

There was a pair of shorts hanging in the tiny attic wardrobe. Denim cut-offs. Jake's shorts. Photos of Jake adorned all corners of Yewtree Row, many of them in silver frames, and though in all of them he was smiling, there was something about the smile Struan wasn't happy about, something that stopped him borrowing the shorts, even though they did fit, he'd tried.

So Struan stood at the bottom of the steps in his hot trousers and let drops of sweat accumulate on his inner thigh and snake to his trainers, and the shorts hung in his mind in the cool of their cupboard, and taunted him.

'Ready then, Struan?' said Juliet, reappearing behind her father's slumped head, her fringe freshly puffed and a flower behind one ear.

'I've been ready a while,' said Struan, 'are you ready with the brake?' Juliet smiled dimly.

'What?' she said.

Struan wiped his brow with the back of his hand. Juliet was so defiant and bouncy with her mother, but when anything practical was required, like picking up her wee pots and damp towels from the bathroom floor, like tipping a wheelchair, she'd go boneless, she'd slump like a glove puppet with no hand.

'There's no point getting cross with me for being crap, Struan,' said Juliet, 'I'm even more hopeless if you shout.'

'OK,' said Struan, carefully. 'Like last time? Brake, align, release, take the weight? Ready?' and Juliet smiled, and released the brake, and sent the whole weight of her bald slumped father,

66

the whole future of English literature as was in 1959, hurtling down a ramp toward Struan Robertson of Cuik, who took this blow, as so many others, full in the guts without flinching.

'Oops,' said Juliet, 'sorry.'

Off they trundled.

'All right there, Mr Prys?' said Struan. 'We're just going to the Heath. Off for a bit of air.'

Air. Struan had never appreciated the stuff when it came whistling past him in Cuik, but here, in London, he was desperate for it. It was clear to him that the sheer number of folk who lived hereabouts depleted the oxygen, so that what you breathed in was mostly waste product. All the staying in with the wheelchair didn't help. He felt so confined, he had even taken to long dashes round and round the block in the dark after ten o'clock at night wearing only his swimming trunks and trainers, like one of those American jogger types. He had instituted these walks to the Heath because Myfanwy said it was like the country and so airy, but the wheelchair was heavy, and somehow, Struan hadn't found the country bit yet.

⋆   ⋆   ⋆

In the kitchen, Myfanwy heard the crunch and thump of the exiting wheelchair. Immediately, she checked the larder. Either Struan or Juliet, she thought, and probably both, ate too much. Myfanwy had supervised the shopping last week and laid in plenty of Pot Noodles and beans, and here was most of it gone. Myfanwy didn't see why she should pay for Phillip's nurse from her own purse. The sensible thing to do — she'd mentioned it to Giles, he'd nodded — would be to make Juliet's educational trust into a more general House Account — especially when Juliet was actually living here.

Struan had drunk all the orange juice too — and eaten the strawberry yoghurts. Probably, he ate too much because he was too tall. That grated on her too, actually: the way he silently appeared, stooping in doorways; or suddenly unfolded himself from corners of the room, pale and birdlike and flapping. *Sad body shapes*, as dear Zbigniew would have said: drooping neck and sagging arms.

Myfanwy filled a glass with ice. The angostura bitters, at least, were untouched in their sticky bottle at the back of the larder, and there was enough gin left for a moderately stiff one. But there wasn't so much as a Twiglet left in the biscuit tin. Well, she wasn't going to rush to replace them. Shirin's job: and anyway, Myfanwy was truly pressed for cash. The agents had rung this morning: a young couple had been round the Cricklewood cottages that morning and been put off by signs of squatters. Squatters! The agent had called the police.

★   ★   ★

Struan was thinking: if he didn't get his money today, maybe he could get some cash out the bank tomorrow and then go down the High Street and buy some food and keep it under his

68

bed in his sandwich box. He was thinking: maybe the Royal Bank of Scotland on Hampstead High Street would be air-conditioned, and no one would mind if he went in there and lay on the floor. He worried that he hadn't seen any ordinary shops on the High Street yet, anywhere you could get a loaf of bread or a malt loaf. A tin of pilchards maybe. He liked mashed pilchards and tomatoes, on a piece of hot toast. There was a van parked on the verge by Jack Straw's Castle. But the chips cost £1, twice what they would at home, and he didn't have enough money to treat Juliet, and last night, she'd eaten more than half of his. Struan had £60 in his bank account, but that was his emergency money and if he spent it on chips every night, he'd save nothing at all.

Juliet was thinking: Struan did have a nice way with the wheelchair. Gentlemanly. And another good thing was that no one, seeing him with the wheelchair, could mistake him for anything other than a wheelchair-pusher. Anyone watching, anyone from School, would know that he was the carer and she, the slim, dark-haired figure in white, was the Daughter, care-worn but lovely. She was pleased with her new hair-clips, and it was nice walking along in the hot swollen evening, the sky a yellow colour, like abroad.

★   ★   ★

Over her gin, Myfanwy Prys surveyed the kitchen. *Her* kitchen, still: a succulent little place with its country accoutrements. Linda had made some inroads, added the fancy hand-built

69

cupboard, painted the walls that sticky pink, but Shirin had done nothing to the place other than leave some odd seeds in the larder and let a pestle and mortar camp prettily on the dresser. Rubbish, just left about, the way Shirin herself was always lounging on tables, cross-legged, pointlessly, ostentatiously, young.

The dresser was Myfanwy's, spotted by Myfanwy in Portobello market and stripped and polished up by Myfanwy on the very cusp of the trend for stripping and polishing — but it had been too heavy to move, at the divorce. She wondered, once again, if it could be sawed down and brought to Finchley Road, and concluded, as usual, that it could not.

What she could do, though, was insist that it was cleaned up and brought to the fore when the agents came round for the valuing — for Myfanwy had already determined that the American Literary Giant was not going to get away with a paltry first offer. It would probably be worth hinting that the dresser was an Original Feature, made for the house, circa 1710.

★ ★ ★

'My friend Celia went into that hospital just down there,' said, Juliet, chummily, as she and Struan effortfully arrived at Jack Straw's Castle. 'The Royal Free. For her anorexia, but in the end she ate enough to do all her exams. It's pioneering for anorexia, though, that hospital. Pioneering is a funny word, isn't it? Like covered wagons, setting out over the yellow desert of

70

Seal? Because she went such a colour you know, when she was ill? Like you know, that marzipan layer when you do the rat in biology? Did you do the rat? I thought that was really weird because you know, that subcutaneous stuff was fat and Seal didn't have any, but she still went yellow.'

'I never knew England was so hot,' said Struan, contemplating the bouncing strips of grey road and green heat haze, 'I really didnae.'

'You keep saying that,' said Juliet.

'I keep thinking it,' said Struan, testily, 'and you keep talking about your pal.'

'Yes, of course I do,' said Juliet. 'She's my friend. Don't you talk about your pals?'

'No,' said Struan, 'I don't, actually.'

'Why's that?' said Juliet. 'Don't you have any?'

Struan gazed out at the amazing amount of traffic. They had to cross the road and there was no gap. He thought about Archie, his best friend in primary school. They had never quarrelled or anything like that: but they hadn't managed to stay close, either. The week his dad died, Archie had asked him to go orienteering.

'Not pals like that,' he said. Who would ring him up at midnight, the way Juliet did Celia?

'Why not?' said Juliet.

'I just dinnae,' said Struan. 'Mebbe it's a lassie's thing,' and he started out determinedly through the traffic, one huge hand held out to oncoming cars. Juliet trotted after him.

'My brother Jake,' she said as they reached the other side, 'has so many friends, you can hardly speak to him. He says his friends are like his family.'

'That's daft,' said Struan, firmly. 'How can friends be your family?' He started to march towards the gate to the Heath, rather fast.

Juliet trailed behind. She was used to having this particular cliché affirmed. 'Well,' she said, to Struan's sweaty back, 'because he likes them. He likes his friends much more than he likes me. Though I hate him, of course. I like Celia much better. Even if she has been a bit weird lately.'

'It's not about liking, though,' said Struan, 'family.' He pictured his gran in her kitchen, sitting at the table with her cup of tea. He wished he was back there, and she was making an omelette and tipping potatoes from the pressure-cooker. ' I mean,' he went on, 'Celia can go off any time. Family can't.'

'If Celia died,' said Juliet, 'I'd be just as sad as if it was someone in my family.'

'Has anyone in your family died, then?' asked Struan.

'No,' said Juliet. 'But.'

'Then you shouldnae speculate about such things,' said Struan, severely, and then, more kindly: 'Anyway, why would Celia die?' Celia had come round for tea, or rather Diet Coke, the other night. A silent wee lassie, and on the skinny side, that was for sure.

'Of her anorexia,' said Juliet. 'You saw her. Do you think she might die?'

'I wouldn't know,' said Struan, 'I worked in an old folks' home, no a hospital.'

'You must have had anorexics in school, though,' said Juliet. 'In my school, half the girls have anorexia, it's the thing to do. Loads of them

72

were more anorexic than Seal, she was kind of Junior League. I mean, I'd definitely be anorexic, if I could manage it.'

'Not in my school,' said Struan, with finality. 'Not in Cuik.' The business of getting the wheelchair round the lychgate to the Heath was enough to make you weep, enough to make you consider leaving the damn thing there, in the netting cage, and returning for Phillip in the night, when it got a bit cooler.

★ ★ ★

In fact, thought Myfanwy, wandering up the narrow kitchen stair with her gin, the best plan for Yewtree Row, the way to get the very best offer, enough to put Phil in a Home and restart her property business and set Jake up in some pleasant little flat and send Juliet to Tutors for the Terminally Thick; the way to do *that*, whether from the Transatlantic Literary Giant or other buyer, or buyers — come to think of it, Myfanwy fancied an auction — would be to have the kitchen/cellar reshaped as a little service flat with separate entrance, and make over the study into a large family room/kitchen with top-quality hand-made units and dining table in the bay overlooking the garden.

Some sort of formal terrace could then be constructed outside the French windows, and the little room at the front, the one currently used for nothing but telly, the one which Myfanwy privately thought of as the parlour, could become a little formal dining room perhaps painted in a

73

bold shade. It was crying out for panelling! One could do all sorts of clever things these days, with MDF and paint effects. Myfanwy had a new book, *Your Georgian House Restored!*, and was dying to do stippling. She'd even bought a couple of sea sponges, cheap, in Boots, in case the opportunity arose.

★ ★ ★

Struan had told Juliet a few things about Cuik now, and she was beginning to understand, though the eighties were a poor era for learning geography, and Juliet a poorer student, that it was not a village up a mountain, and it did not have a castle or even a nearby loch, was nowhere near Balmoral, and that no one wore tartan there. 'That's the Highlands,' Struan kept saying, 'Cuik's the Lowlands. It's in the Central Belt. Have you no heard of the Proclaimers?'

Struan had a Central Belt himself, thought Juliet, a striped, woven cotton one with a snake buckle, tenuously holding up the terrible trousers. She was going to ask if the belt came from Cuik, and if everyone in the Central Belt wore central belts, because on the whole Struan appreciated her whimsy, and had even consented to watch *Dallas* with her one afternoon, but he didn't seem in his best mood this evening: his great grey jaw set, shoving the chair through the lychgate with such a shove, it nearly upset it.

★ ★ ★

Myfanwy wouldn't mention stippling to Shirin, of course. This was going to be a business meeting: clear and simple. Myfanwy was not going to be so silly as to underestimate Shirin's business capacity, not when Shirin had moseyed in so successfully on poor old Phillip! Cosying up to him at a party when Linda was off seeing to her dying mother! One could almost feel sorry for Linda, the silly old cow. And as for getting Phillip to marry her — that was truly a coup. Myfanwy had barely accomplished that herself, back in the sixties, when everyone got married. Linda never got so much as a ring, never mind a settlement.

So, first she would point out what Shirin must have noticed, really: that Phillip's illness could only end one way, and that a nursing home was much the best place for him until that happened. Then, on to the deal. The sale of the house would entail a loss to Shirin, that was true. Shirin would lose accommodation and a studio for Phillip's lifetime, Myfanwy could see that; and she could offer an excellent solution: a delightful railwayman's cottage in Cricklewood, rent free, for the duration. She'd brought the estate agent's pack with her, and a few colour photos.

★ ★ ★

Struan and Juliet reached a big clear bit of heath covered with young people on rugs, all bathed in the thick dusty light. Juliet was reminded of the *La Grande Jatte*, and having to copy all the dots

75

for Art. She was going to ask Struan if he had to do that too, but reflected that he probably didn't, in Cuik.

Struan positioned the wheelchair carefully in the shade, and clicked the brake. Then he flung himself to the ground. 'Scuse me,' he said, 'I have to, I just have to.' And he threw off his sweaty shoes and socks. His huge greenish feet spread on the parched grass. Juliet sat down, upwind of the feet.

'You'll get athlete's foot,' she said primly, 'if you keep wearing trainers in hot weather.' Struan started to unfasten Phillip's hand-made leather shoes, peel the cashmere socks from the hard white feet. Juliet could hardly bear the sight.

'Why are you doing that?' she said.

'Why do you think?' said Struan. 'It's hot, so he needs his socks off.'

'How do you know?' said Juliet.

'Because that's what I want,' said Struan, 'and he's a human being too.' Juliet was struck by this notion.

'What else does he need?' she asked.

'Maybe to see you,' said Struan. He was always doing this, trying to get Juliet in Phillip's sightline, which he was beginning to suspect was only on one side, the left. 'Why don't you come round here?' Juliet wrinkled her nose.

'You don't know that, though, Struan, do you? That he wants to see me? The thing is, the thing you don't realize, is that my dad wasn't all that keen on seeing me when he was well so I don't really specially see why he'd want to see me now.'

76

'For Christ sake,' said Struan, 'because you're his daughter, that's why. Just be normal, why can't you?'

Juliet was miffed. This was the first time Struan had spoken to her as her brother always did: as if she was thick. 'Well,' she said, 'actually, you may not have noticed but we're not all that normal in our family. We're Bohemian. We just don't fit into the ordinary rules.'

'Right,' said Struan, folding one sock carefully into the other, and tucking it into Phillip's shoe.

'So maybe,' said Juliet superbly, 'just maybe, you shouldn't boss.'

Struan staggered to his feet and sat down heavily on the end of the bench.

'I wasn't bossing,' he said, 'I was making a suggestion.'

'Yeah,' said Juliet, 'for the zillionth time. You keep telling me to do stuff for Dad. Why?' Struan looked out at all the brightly dressed English people out there in the light and tried to remember the answer to Juliet's question, which was a long way behind him, in a grey corridor, in Cuik.

'People bossed me, Juliet,' he said, after a while. 'My dad couldnae speak for six months, and the last two of those he couldnae open his eyes, and I wasnae exactly sure if he could hear me, but what the doctor said to me was, you've got to take a punt on it, you've got to talk to him all the same. He pushed me to talk to him, and I did, and now, now I'm really pleased I did it. Do you see what I'm saying?' Juliet looked at Struan again, knees wide, huge knobbly feet in the dust.

'Did he get better?' she said, suspiciously.

Struan smiled. 'No,' he said. 'No. He's dead, my dad. He had multiple sclerosis.'

'Really?' said Juliet.

'Uh huh,' said Struan. 'Sorry. Did I no mention that before?'

Juliet didn't know anyone dead, except her guinea pigs, and Granny Davies.

'Is that why you're so old?' she asked.

'Am I old?' said Struan, rubbing his toes in the dust.

'Totally,' said Juliet.

'Aye,' said Struan. 'Well, mebbe. Mebbe that's why.'

★ ★ ★

But she should just mention to Shirin, thought Myfanwy, contemplating the sad wreck of the study, its hospital bed and wrinkled rugs, its unfortunate medical odour — she should just point out, without, obviously, going into any detail about paint effects, just very simply *indicate* to Shirin, who could hardly be expected to be *au fait* with such things, that the current layout of Yewtree was really the equivalent of lighting the fire with five-pound notes.

That even for the simplest, quickest, private sale, just going straight for the Literary Giant, they should get Myfanwy's little men in to tidy up a few things. The sash windows, for example, were absolutely flaking — doing those could hardly be seen as controversial. It needn't cost Shirin! The money could come from the new

78

House Account, the one she was going to set up tomorrow when she saw Giles. Giles was trustee, and would have to be signatory — but he wouldn't mind signing a few little cheques for her in advance, or to cash perhaps. Not when this sale was his idea in the first place. She'd specify uncrossed cheques — so handy for cash, and all the little payments inevitable in a renovation, and which were so awkward just now with the Cottages unsold. The account should be pleasantly full: Phil had stopped paying Baker Street after Juliet failed her mocks.

Once the Little Men were in, panelling the parlour/dining room would be a surprisingly quick job! As would stripping the floor, and putting up some curtains in Laura Ashley Regency Stripe. Myfanwy would be happy to lend back the chaise longue she had impulsively removed at the time of the divorce, and *voilà*, there it would be, a perfect little period showcase for the house, right by the door.

Myfanwy imagined it all in place — panelling, curtains, bold shade, and chaise longue — and entered the house as it were from the front door. In one went, straight past the open door to the evocative little dining parlour, then up to the staircase — the dear shining curving period staircase, in need of just a little refreshment, a new runner perhaps, and then forward again to the delightful kitchen/diner opening on to the garden ... Sold! Sold without a doubt. The grandfather clock heaved wheezy applause. The quarter hour. Myfanwy's glass needed refreshing. Shirin was running late.

'I mean,' said Juliet, 'for instance. Look at you sitting up there on that bench. That's a really old way to sit. Get off, and come and lie here on the grass. Go on. Dad's OK.'

So Struan did, stretching himself at full length beside Juliet, clasping his hands under his head. It was more comfortable.

'Maybe that's why you don't have any friends, either,' continued Juliet, speculatively, 'cos you're too old for your years.'

'I have too got friends,' said Struan, raising his head irritably. 'I was very well respected at my school.'

'Respected,' said Juliet.

'Aye,' said Struan, 'I was. Is that funny?'

'No,' said Juliet. 'No, that's good probably. I mean, I've got friends but definitely absolutely no one respects me.'

'That,' said Struan, 'is a terrible thing to say.'

'The thing is,' said Juliet, gazing at the strange, mucky sky, 'I'd rather be funny? Because one of the easiest ways to make people laugh is to make fun of yourself. Like as soon as ever I got to Baker Street, the very first morning, I started going on about the F-Plan diet and farting and everything and that was it really, for that school. I was a fart joke. No respect, you see?'

'Maybe they did respect you, and didn't notice,' said Struan, reasonably, 'because you were so busy putting yourself down.'

'No. You don't know that school. It's a Lady Di school. Really, really Sloane Ranger. They're all twelve foot and blonde. That's why I made the fart jokes in the first place. Because I felt like

80

a fat Welsh dwarf. Then I became a Welsh dwarf who makes fart jokes. Brilliant.'

'Now you're trying to make me laugh,' said Struan.

'Yeah,' said Juliet, 'it's compulsive.'

'Well,' said Struan, leaning up on his elbow, 'I don't not respect you. I appreciate how friendly you've been to me here. I think the person who makes the joke, that's quite a brave person often. Breaking the ice? There was loads of ice up at home, in Cuik, you know, and not many people to break it. I often wished I had the guts to have a wee crack.'

And Juliet was suddenly terribly pleased. She sat up.

'Do you think,' she said, 'do you think my dad would really want me to talk to him? Really?'

'Aye,' said Struan, 'of course. He's your dad.'

Which was all very well. Before he was dead, Struan had probably liked *his* dad. *His* dad had probably never chucked him out of the room for being boring, or blatantly preferred his older brother. Nevertheless, being in the presence of a genuine orphan changed things. Juliet stood up and shuffled into her father's sightline.

'Hi, Dad,' she said. Then she worried Struan would look up and be able to see her knickers through her dress. Leaning forward like that, her bum would look huge. So she knelt down by the chair and picked up her dad's hand, flaccid as a rubber glove, and gazed into his fixed jelly eyes.

'He's not doing anything,' she said. But Struan's eyes were shut, too.

'I would kill,' he said, 'I would absolutely

murder, for a swim. In cold water.'

'Oh,' said Juliet, 'didn't you know? There's the Pond, the Heath swimming ponds, there are three of them. And the Lido, that's totally freezing.'

'Really?' said Struan, sitting up. 'A real pool, you can really swim in?'

And right then, with the clarity and deliberation of a dirty old man in a pub, Phillip Prys winked his bloody, bleary, brown left eye at his daughter Juliet.

8

Phillip hated the long tracking shots, the lights in the eyes, the lurching forward at the last minute. He hated the way he had to sit silent so much, and watch the rushes. Undoubtedly, they were overusing the extreme close-up, the face from the odd angle, underneath. The grainy stubble of underchin of the Scottish boy. The spot on his Adam's apple.

He had to remind himself: it was that kind of film. Art house. Phillip had written it that way. It was modern, and that was why it took you so long to realize what was going on. Phillip had scripted this one, he should know. He remembered why the boy was Scottish — it was because the film boys had said they couldn't do another Welsh Lad in black and white, and the North of England was pretty much taken too, what with Bleasdale and so forth —

But the Scottish Boy was tremendous, he thought, grainy and sensitive in the big close-ups, always bending over him for notes. He'd tried to applaud, that scene about the heat, and the dead father, and it had got stuck in his head, a long singing note like the alarm on his mother's kettle. As if Phillip were that kettle and all the words were the steam. All the words running through him mouth to arse, and leaking out the bottom. Because that kept happening. That had happened again. He hated that.

In Highgate, late at night, Juliet advanced into Celia's room with a futon in her arms.

'Don't start, Seal,' she said, 'OK? I mean, just don't start? Because I am staying the bloody night, OK? Your mum says it's OK, and I also have basically no choice. I was out on the Heath, yeah? With Struan and my dad, and my dad winked, my mum doesn't believe me, but he did, it was just when I said about the ponds, you know swimming? Well, he wanted to go the ponds, it was obvious, and I said to Struan, OK, let's go along there, we can go right now, it's just over there, yeah? And so we went, and we got a bit lost basically, and we were a bit late, and my dad kind of went to sleep and, what was really bad but not exactly his fault because he'd had a suppository, he crapped himself, and then we belted back over the Heath, and we were late for the nurse, and my mum was there, still in my dad's house, and Shirin was still there, and there were these estate agent's pictures, Mum's cottages, thrown all over the place, so obviously they were having a row, but it's no excuse really, because she went mental, like totally ballistic, she said I had to go home, go back to the Finchley Road, and she went mental at Struan as well, which is totally out of order, he is really nice and his dad is dead, Seal, did you know that? And so out we went, me and Mum, and we were going to the car and I said I've changed my mind I'm going to Celia's, and my mum said you're not, and I said actually I'm too heavy to lift, Mum, and I started walking and she tried following me and I said I'll do you for soliciting, Mum, and she was really angry but basically too embarrassed to do anything about it and here I am and I'm staying, no matter how many lovers are coming up your garden, Celia, because I need a place to stay and you used to be my friend. Are you wearing eyeliner, Seal, you shouldn't you'll muss the pillow.' Then Juliet unrolled the futon and sat on it, fatly, and started to peel off her jeans.

Celia was lying on her front. She raised herself on her long thin arms, eyes burning fashionably from her minimal face.

'That's OK,' she said, her cheekbones glowing in the last evening light. 'He's already been.'

★ ★ ★

In Hampstead, in the boiling study, Phillip Prys lay under a cotton blanket on the raised surgical bed, remembering the film. *Shallowcast*. That was the name. He had written in it '69, just after the film of *The Pit*, back when they still made decent films in black and white about kestrels and rugby and working men. He could see the pages of the script, scattered over his study floor, and smell the carbon paper and feeling of disappointment that went with them: it had all come to nothing, the whole damn thing.

But now the pages were flying back into his hands, one by one. Now they were making it, really making it, that film, and how splendid that was. Giles would be delighted. They were still at the rushes stage, and that accounted for all the bad editing and jump cuts; but it would all come out in the wash. And to think Juliet was in it too, playing the girl lead, or was it the girlfriend left behind in Scotland, anyway, the girlfriend who wanted the boy to go down the shallow-cast mine, or along it, maybe. The girl who got pregnant just to hold on to him, the boy, that was right, she was *shallow-cast*, that was part of the meaning of the title.

Because it was good to have Juliet around now, he was glad of it. He had to admit he'd never liked her much, from a baby, she was noisy and an awful bore too, so much around Myfanwy's neck and looked besides exactly like his own mother. And she cried so, a terrible thing, she cried every time he roared at her and she couldn't grasp at all that that made the whole thing worse, it practically forced him to shout at her, little wet thing, so clammy and ice-creamy and smelling of wee. But she was finding herself now, though, he could see that, she was shining in this film, in the part he had made for her. Funny how it came through, eh, the writing gift?

Jake was jealous, thought Phillip, that was the problem. That was why he only came in at night, and looked at him without smiling. When Dad favoured Juliet, when he bought her an ice-cream, Jake was jealous. That would be why Jake was angry, why he rifled the desk, looking for something. Probably, he wanted the part the Scottish Boy had, maybe his accent hadn't come up right at the auditions.

Well, Phillip would write Jake his own film, that was what. Phillip's star was rising now, that was clear. He could do whatever he wanted, the film boys would be after his used hankies after this one came out. Everyone had been so excited, out there under the lights, it was a huge event. Tomorrow, Phillip would start the new film, the film for Jake. Tomorrow, after the scene at the Ponds.

★ ★ ★

Upstairs, in his hot bed, Struan reflected that he should have stopped Juliet at Phillip's wink. Because up to then, everything was OK, even quite nice, and only after that was the disaster. He could have stopped it, if he'd tried, that was true enough. He did, just as Mrs Prys said, know better than to let Juliet set off across the Heath in search of the Mixed Bathing Pond. He did know she'd get lost, and that they'd get back late and miss the evening nurse, because, just as Myfanwy had said, all of that was typical of Juliet. But it was not fair to say that he knew that Mr Prys would soil himself, or go to sleep, or that he was lying or 'sentimentalizing' when he confirmed the wink. It really was not right of Myfanwy to have said that.

Actually, Struan thought the two Mrs Prys were maybe having a wee ding-dong themselves, when they got in, something about Cricklewood, which was where the Goodies came from, as far as Struan was concerned. *Lassies' business*, his father would have said, shaking his head. After all, Struan reminded himself, he'd never known anyone divorced, and no doubt it did leave you awful angry.

But not as angry as that, surely. Struan sat up in the bed, remembering the scene: Juliet shouting, 'Mum, he winked, right at me.' Myfanwy shouting back, 'I have had enough of your fucking Florence Nightingale fantasies, and if Struan can't stop pandering to them, he can go back to Scotland.' On and on they went, the language was terrible, and then Myfanwy had taken Juliet off back to their flat in the Finchley Road. Struan couldn't think what good that was supposed to do. He had been intending to talk to Shirin about it, but she had appeared for only a moment in a blue shining full-length dress, and gone out the front door. 'My opening,' she said, 'Cork Street. I am late. Sorry.' He didn't think she was back yet. He thought he was all alone in the house with Mr Prys, and he was not at all sure, suddenly, that this was a safe or usual arrangement for a stroke patient.

Struan checked his watch: eleven o'clock at night, and him still awake in his bed. His sheet was a damp rag across his chest, and if he lifted his hand to the sagging ceiling, he could feel its heat too, steady as a radiator. He'd removed his pyjamas already, something he had never previously had occasion to do at night, and had taken the precaution of leaning Jake's guitar case against the door, under the lock, in case anyone should come in and catch him like that.

He was too hungry to sleep, that was the truth. In all the rush across the Heath, there'd been no chips. There was a can of tuna, he knew, in the larder downstairs, on the top shelf. A square gold one instead of a round steel one, but it definitely said tuna. He would just eat that, and if there was trouble, he'd replace it tomorrow. If he could find a shop. There must be a shop. He could ask Juliet where one was. He could take Phillip, even, swing the chair down air-conditioned aisles. He might enjoy it. Struan could fill a wee wire basket with pilchards, baked beans, Mother's Pride, Frosties, eggs. There were things you could do with eggs —

At that moment, the Velux window fell straight down from its frame and struck Struan across the knees with its edge, then fell forward across his stomach and lungs, taking all the air out of them. He couldn't even yell. It felt like a rugby tackle, a vicious one, in the corner of the field, away from the ref's eye: a pure insult.

It changed Struan's mind. Suddenly, he was perfectly certain he was entitled to the tuna. When he got his breath, he stowed the window behind the bed, put on the shorts from the wardrobe, and went downstairs.

He was standing in the darkened kitchen draining the oil from the tin when he saw the half-basement window start to move. The bottom sash creaked in its old frame, and two muscular hands appeared underneath it, pulling upwards. In a moment, Struan slid across the kitchen tiles, and crashed the window down on the fingers.

'Ow,' said a posh voice from the other side, 'that hurts. Is that you, Juliet? Raiding the fridge

89

like Porky Pig? Let me in, won't you? It's Jake.'

Jake Prys. And Struan was wearing his shorts. But there was nothing for it but to let go of the window and watch as one tanned leg, then another, then a quiffed head of golden hair eased themselves through the window.

'Cool,' said Jake Prys, 'excellent. Sorry to have alarmed you. You must be the nurse, hmm? Stru-anne?'

'Ah'm Struan,' said Struan, hearing his own accent, suddenly. 'Sorry about your fingers. I thought you were an intruder.'

'Me,' said Jake Prys, 'an *intruder?* How funny.' Jake was Struan's height and build but tanned, and with his hair pouffed out and bleached at the ends like a porcupine. He had long eyelashes and a loose plump mouth and high-arched feet in deck shoes. He had shorts, all right, white ones, and a white collarless dress shirt with the sleeves rolled.

'Have you come to see your dad?' asked Struan.

'Well,' said Jake, 'could do, Strew-anne, could do. Pay my filial respects, all that. Came to get supplies, actually.' He took a bottle from the fancy wine rack under the countertop, the one Struan would never have touched, and a corkscrew from the sink, and a large, heavy goblet from the dresser.

'Have a glass?' he said.

Struan shook his head.

'Do carry on with the tuna,' said Jake.

'I'm starving,' said Struan, abashed. Jake had surely already noticed the shorts.

90

Jake took a gulp of the wine, then opened the larder door and came back with the box labelled 'Juliet'.

'Empty,' he said. 'Goodness. What a little piggy my sister is. And of course, it takes an awful lot to feed a growing boy.' And he tossed it on the floor, and took a fork, and dug it into Struan's tin.

'I thought you were in Oxford,' said Struan, 'doing a play.'

'Was,' said Jake, 'was. Will be again. Just a few problems with, you know, logistics. Supplies.' He caught the last decent morsel of tuna on his fork, and swallowed it. 'Truth is, Mercutio got arrested, the silly man. Possession. Left us in a bit of a fix.'

'Are you back in London, then?'

'I come and go, come and go. Got a comfy little berth on the other side of the Heath, actually,' said Jake, 'young lady.' And Jake raised his eyebrows and moved his hips in a way that made Struan shudder.

'You're not staying with your mum, then?' said Struan.

'My mother's nuts,' said Jake, 'you must have noticed. Nuts and very unpleasant. Bitter. You know?' He opened the fridge and found a packet of waxed paper at the back of it, and half a pint of milk, and put them on the counter. 'And her attitude to me? Sick, my dear chap. Just sick. Beyond Oedipal, into, well what would you call it? Chap who ate his children? Cronos? Fancy my sister much?'

'What?' said Struan.

'Juliet,' said Jake. 'Fancy her much? Or too

much of a lard-arse for you?'

Struan thought about Juliet, trying to talk to her father on the Heath. She had a huge bum, all right.

'I like Juliet fine,' said Struan. 'She's a nice wee lassie.'

Jake unrolled the paper and a found a layer of thin dried meat, something like bacon, at the bottom. 'Shirin, then? Now, there's class, eh?' He proffered a shred of the meat on a serrated knife. 'Prosciutto? Strew-anne?'

'Struan,' said Struan, waving away the knife.

'I'm sorry?' said Jake.

'My name,' said Struan. 'Struan, like you know. Strew-in. No Strewanne. It's a trochee, no an iamb.'

'Nicely put, Strew-anne,' said Jake. 'I didn't realize you were a student of the arts.'

'Actually, I'm going to be a dentist,' said Struan, 'but I took an A Band One in my Higher English mock.'

Jake shook his head. 'Sorry, my dear chap,' he said, 'just don't think you're what the company is looking for, on this occasion.'

'Look,' said Struan, 'you've clearly no come to see me. Shall I call Mrs Prys for you?'

'She's not here, Strew-anne,' said Jake, 'is she?' And Struan dropped his eyes and wondered how he knew.

'Are you going to wait?' he said. 'She won't be long.'

'Oh no,' said Jake, dimpling, 'can't wait, can I? Can't stay. Cos you're in my room, Strew-anne. Aren't you?'

This had never properly occurred to Struan. He was in Jake's place. He was doing for Jake's dad what he had done for his own dad. He was stopping Jake from doing it. No wonder Jake was being funny with him.

'I do believe,' said Jake, 'you're even wearing my trousers.'

'Look,' said Struan, 'I'm sorry. I'll move, I'll go home. I was just thinking about it anyway. You have your room back. You take care of your dad.'

Jake slapped his hand on his skinny white-clothed thigh. He actually laughed. 'Change Dad's nappies?' he said. 'I couldn't do that.'

Struan's eyes stung. He turned away. He picked up the serrated knife and put it in the dishwasher. He started to wrap the ham in its waxed paper. He thought about his own father, at the end, stranded and hairless in his wheelchair, and of the vast, insuperable difference between himself and this gilded wheeling stranger. He could only say it in his native tongue.

'How no?' he asked. But the window was wide and Jake was gone.

★　★　★

At four in the morning, Juliet was sitting on Seal's window seat doing her thigh-pinching. Each pinch drained the flesh of blood, turned it the new fashionable colour; the one Mum had done the living room in the flat, magnolia. Juliet pinched harder, then let go, and surveyed the red line. It would show in the morning, but it didn't matter. No one saw her in her swimming costume anyway. No one saw her without her clothes. No one ever would.

She wondered if she should do the cutting yourself thing, she'd read about it in *Cosmopolitan*, but then she thought how much fat she'd have to razor through to reach a vein. Like slicing a French Fancy for the jam. And it just wouldn't look right, anyway: razor cuts on fat arms. Like so many kinds of rebellion, tattoos, and leather, and transvestism, like going to the comp or losing your virginity, you just had to be thin to pull it off. She wished it wasn't so hot. Dawn, and hot enough for her fringe to stick to her forehead, for a single drop of sweat to run down her back.

Silent and light, Celia slipped from her bed and sat beside her on the window seat. She laid a slim flat paw on Juliet's shoulder.

'Are you OK?' she said.

'I'm in love too, you know,' said Juliet, 'me and Struan. At it every night. He's gorgeous you know, he's really tall.'

In the half-light, Celia unzipped the cushion cover, and slid a hand under the cushion, and pulled out a blister-pack of pills.

'Juliet,' she said, 'listen. I've got just the right thing for you.'

9

The next morning, Struan overslept. It was nearly nine when he staggered downstairs, his ribs bruised from the assault by the Velux, his tongue dry in his mouth. He was prepared to resign if there was any funny business: that was what he was thinking. He could just go back to his gran, and start over. He could get another job. He'd found a magazine called *The Lady* lining the vegetable box in the kitchen, and it had ads in the back, stuff he could do, no problem. But here was Shirin, neat in white jeans in the hall, picking up the estate agents' brochures that were scattered all over it and rolling them up in her hands. She turned to him and smiled.

'Struan,' she said, getting the stress perfectly. He loved her voice. Her accent was hardly foreign at all, just had a little fur and creak to it: chamois leather over glass. 'I hope you're OK.'

'I overslept,' said Struan. 'I'm sorry.'

'You've been getting up too early,' said Shirin, 'there's nothing to worry about. I got Phillip up and now the nurse has been. He's in the study, and he's clean and fine and comfortable. And in the shade, Struan, I promise, hmm? Now, you need some breakfast.'

She led him down to the kitchen. There was an omelette at his place on the table, rolled and on a china plate, and round flat breads and a napkin beside it. Under the plate were two ten-pound notes, fresh from the bank. 'Sit down,' said Shirin. She was wearing a wee gold belt with the jeans, and it was really made of metal: the links clicked. Struan didn't normally notice belts and so on, but he liked this one. Shirin was tiny, not much taller than Juliet, but half her width. 'I'm going to make you a coffee,' she said.

She used the wee metal contraption to do that, while Struan tucked into the omelette. It was cold, but that was all right, Struan thought, in fact it was nice, sort of pancake-y. And there was green stuff inside it which wasn't parsley. It was a bit nutty, a bit peanut-buttery, but crunchy, not greasy. Peanut butter with pine needles would be the best way to describe it. It was good, but.

'Is this Iranian?' he said, gesticulating with his fork, and trying not gobble.

'I suppose,' said Shirin. 'Eggs are international, aren't they?'

'I never had this in Cuik,' said Struan. 'And that's awful nice coffee too.' Shirin had warmed the milk for him, and stirred in a sugar.

Shirin came and sat opposite him at the table. 'I'm sorry,' she said, and her eyes were such a beautiful shape, and wetter than other people's, clean brown and white, like a child's, 'I should have done this before. I have been putting my show together, you see. But I should have made you a meal. My grandmother would be ashamed of me.'

'Ah've got a gran like that,' said Struan, grinning. 'Soon as you get in the house, she's got

96

the kettle on and she's feeding you a Mars Bar.'

He leaned back on his seat, legs pushed nearly to the other end of the kitchen table. He felt OK, suddenly. The window was closed: he could hardly believe the adventure of the night had actually happened. He didn't know whether to mention it to Shirin. He didn't know how much Shirin knew Jake, really. He hoped it was not at all.

'Was it good,' he said, 'your opening?'

'Very good,' said Shirin, 'And now it is done, that is the best thing, and we are going to push the wheelchair over to the Mixed Bathing Pond. That's where Phillip wanted to go, isn't it?'

'Uh-huh,' said Struan, sitting forward, startled. Shirin believed him about the wink; she did not think he was a fool. 'The swimming pond. I think so.'

'The Mixed Pond,' said Shirin, 'is not the best pond, in fact. Phillip used to like the Men's one, but I am not permitted there. I can take you to the Mixed one this morning, and show you where the Men's one is — it is very near — and then you can take him another morning. And I'll point you to the Lido, too, if you like lane swimming. Did you bring a swimming costume?'

'I did,' said Struan, 'it's upstairs.' He rose to get it, but Shirin picked up a bundle from a chair and held it out to him.

'I thought,' she said, looking at his soap-stiffened T-shirt and grass-stained trousers, 'that you did not pack for the heat? So I went through Phillip's clothes, and here are some shorts he cannot use, and some vests too, and a shirt?

They will be OK for you. Traditional British brand. Nice quality, and quite trendy, I think. Especially the shorts, they are exciting. Sixties. Like, you know, Doctor No.'

And she smiled at him suddenly, a chummy smile, as if she were just his own age, and Struan wondered how shorts could be exciting, and he remembered that film, Bond, with the blonde girl on the island. Shirin wasn't like that, like Ursula Andress, she was more like one of the perky clever dark girls Bond usually runs through in the first half of the film: the ones who wear white coats and are doctors, sometimes; the ones who are often spies.

★ ★ ★

One of the main effects of Celia's pills, Juliet discovered as she bounced off the little train at Finchley Road, was springiness. The platform sagged beneath her feet as she disembarked, then threw her back against the already burning sky. The pills sent her tripping and grinning past the ticket inspector, and goofily trotting through the barrier. It was like wearing rubber high heels. Also, there was an airy gap where her knees usually were, and a googly effect round the eyes: a sort of rainbow edge to the world.

Other than that, they made you feel terrific. Or maybe they just let you get in touch with how terrific you'd usually feel all the time if it weren't for your mother who'd blighted your life by bringing you up completely wrong and with a whole mess of body issues. The pills lifted you above all that. They made it easy to plan. For instance, this morning, Juliet planned to: give Myfanwy Celia's copy of *Fat is a Feminist Issue;* tell her all the things she'd done wrong; walk out with a suitcase of all her possessions; and go back permanently to Yewtree Row. She'd also have a real go at Myfanwy for being so pointlessly mean to Struan.

Struan didn't have much money, she'd suddenly realized last night when Myfanwy was shouting. He was the first person she'd ever met who really was poor. That's why he had nasty trousers. Even if he bought 501s, though, Juliet would not be kissing him. She'd be kissing someone else, maybe several people. The new Juliet, the springy, wobbly, clear-headed Juliet, was going to jump out of her fat like a jack from his box, and kiss simply loads of boys in 501s.

But Myfanwy's flat was empty: just a whiff of 'L'Air du Temps' and a gap where the shopping basket should be. Juliet had a quick prowl round: a Slimfast box on the kitchen table; a Narda Artwear bag in the bedroom, some new documents on the desk, mostly about the Cricklewood cottages, and, on the kitchen worktop, a letter from Jake's Oxford college, which Juliet read in case it was something useful, hurrah, like Jake overspending.

It was better than that. The letter was *personally* from the Rector, signed *personally* in pen. It said: Jake was expelled. (It said 'rusticated', but it meant expelled, you could tell from the rest of it.) Jake had failed his Collections (exams). He hadn't resat them when he ought to have. His conduct to his tutor was unacceptable. His arrest for possession of drugs was in the hands of the police. He couldn't go back to college for a year. He couldn't go within a mile of Carfax, whatever that was.

Juliet stood with the stiff crackling paper in her hands in the narrow shiny kitchen of the Finchley Road flat and felt the meaning of the letter pulse up her body in waves, surging like the bubbling sounds of the still-boiling kettle. The long, trumpeting parade of Jake's successes, the bells and whistles and trombones of it: Jake's stage parts, Jake's essays, Jake's common entrances, Jake's O-Levels and A-Levels and what the tutors had said at his Oxford interview, all danced before in her in their shiny triumph and fell straight off a cliff into a boiling sea of 'rustication'. She thought of the glory of telling Celia about this, of rubbing it into her mother till she squealed. So what if she failed Maths now! What was a resit at the comp compared to rustication! Juliet looked at the light smashed on the window and held the letter up to it, so it got a halo. It was undoubtedly the finest document she had ever read. On the stairs, unmistakeably, she heard Myfanwy's tread.

★ ★ ★

Struan had learned to swim in the chlorinated waters of Cuik Municipal Baths, but he took to the silky mud of Hampstead Mixed Bathing Pond like one of its own ducks. He thrashed in

100

the shallows like a released Labrador. In the depths, he grasped his knees in his arms and sank like Houdini down, down in the murky, muddy centre of the pool; then came shooting to the surface and breached it like the grey whale. He leaped off the diving platform, feet down, in a pencil jump, hauled himself out, and executed a swallow dive. He pulled himself up on the central platform and fell off it, sideways. Then he sped up and down for a quarter of an hour, his huge arms seeming to span the pond, in a very creditable version of the butterfly. By the time he had showered and changed back into the shorts — white pleated knee-length Aquascutum shorts from the sixties, the cotton worn soft as silk — and the plain singlet, he felt more natural and comfortable than he had since he got to London. He loped up to the wheelchair grinning, and took Phillip's hand.

'Did ya see my butterfly?' he said, scrutinizing the beery brown eyes, both of which Phillip promptly shut and did not reopen. Struan carefully replaced Phillip's hand on his chest, and wheeled the chair back on the decking platform.

'I think he's having a wee sleep,' he said, and came and sat on the deck by Shirin's chair, leaning back on his hands. He liked the warm scratchy wood under his fingernails. He'd liked the walk to this place, too, the green and gold of the park. There were trees round the pond, even a hay-bale in the fields outside. It really was like the country, like the country in Perthshire, that is, or in books, not like the unearthly heaths round Cuik.

'How did you learn this?' Shirin asked him abruptly.

'The butterfly?' said Struan. 'It was mostly my dad, actually. He used to take me to the baths on Saturdays.'

'No, I mean, how did you learn to take care of Phillip so well?'

'Oh,' said Struan. 'Well, that was mostly my dad, too, I guess.'

'Was he a doctor?' asked Shirin.

Struan laughed. 'No,' he said, 'was your dad a doctor, then?' Somehow, he thought Shirin's dad was something like that, and that he would be dead too. She wouldn't be living with Phillip, else.

'Yes,' said Shirin, 'he was, he was a surgeon. A hand surgeon. He was the best in all Iran. The best in the region.'

'That's grand,' said Struan. 'Well done him.'

'What did your dad do?' asked Shirin.

'He worked for the Council,' said Struan, 'then he got MS. He was ill a long time.'

'And so then you learned where is the brake on a wheelchair,' said Shirin, 'and how to keep the sun out of the eyes.'

'It was just me and my gran at home,' said Struan, 'and I was a big lad already, so I did the pushing round.' He looked up at Shirin. You couldn't see her eyes behind her Ray-Bans, and her mouth was like a mouth in a perfume advert, glossy and half-open.

'When did he die?' she asked.

'Two years ago,' said Struan. 'Nearly three.'

He was going to add, don't worry, and he was

102

over it, but for once this did not seem necessary. Shirin didn't say sorry, or change the subject. She asked:

'Where was your mother?' which was the clever question, the one no one ever asked. And Struan, his elbows on his knees, his chin on his hands, his eyes on the pond, said:

'I don't know. You see, she left. She left a long time ago. Before I was three. I don't remember her.'

'And you didn't tell her your father was ill?'

'He'd have had to do that,' said Struan. 'It had to be down to him.'

'But you thought of it?'

'Oh, aye. You mean, like going to Register House and tracking her down, like you read in the papers? Aye, I thought of that, but I couldnae.'

'It was too hard?' said Shirin.

'I was underage,' said Struan, and, after a pause. 'And it would have hurt my gran's feelings, besides. My gran was very down on my mum, you see. My dad wasnae. He said, he loved taking care of me anyway, and so did my gran, and it was all for the best, and I was never to think ill of my mum, it was just that there were things she had to do. But that wasnae my gran's attitude, and I had to take care of her. I couldnae start a big detective hunt.'

'And when your dad died?'

Struan thought about that time, after the death: the state of his gran, and the funeral in the sleet and him greeting everyone, suddenly six foot in his suit, and the months following, and he said:

103

'I was too tired. After he died, I was just really tired. Every morning I'd get up, and I'd think, he's dead, and he'll be dead all day, and he'll still be dead this evening, and it was work, you know, it was like a job, like someone said, you've got to carry a sack of coal all day and never drop it. I couldnae start a hunt for my mum. I didn't have the fuel in me. Besides . . . ' Struan tailed off.

'She must have known, really,' said Shirin.

'Aye,' said Struan, 'that's right. That's what I think. Exactly. There must be someone up in Cuik she talks to. We didnae move house, we lived with my gran, so she must've known. She'd have come, if she wanted to.'

'If she's still alive,' said Shirin.

'Why would she be dead?' said Struan.

'Anyone can be dead,' said Shirin. 'I am always surprised, who is dead.'

'Is your mother dead?'

'No,' said Shirin, and almost laughed. 'My mother is in Harrow.'

'Who else is dead, then?' asked Struan.

'Two of my cousins,' said Shirin, 'and my older sister, I am always surprised by this when I think it, that she is not there. And you are correct, it is very tiring, to grieve. When my father died, I was tired for two years, I think. I did not study. I had no ideas for paintings. I could not be bothered with any people.'

Phillip's eyes were open again, watching them. As if by mutual agreement, Shirin and Struan picked up the swimming things and started the slow process of getting the wheelchair back off the decking and onto the made path.

'How old were you?' asked Struan, once they were walking across the Heath. 'When your father died, I mean. And your sister. If you don't mind me asking.'

'Nineteen,' said Shirin, 'when my father died. I had been in this country two years. Him, one year. We had some trouble arriving in the same country at the same time.'

'Is that how you lost your sister?' said Struan. 'Running away?'

'No,' said Shirin, smiling again. 'My sister died in a car accident. In Iran. Not politics — just very stupid.'

'What did your father die of?' asked Struan.

'His heart,' said Shirin, 'his heart failed. But really, you see, he died of what they did to him in the prisons in Tehran. They broke his hands, he could not work. Also, he smoked too much.'

Struan looked at Shirin's golden hand, so elegant and clever, lightly clasping the handle of her straw basket, and imagined smashing it. He churned through his impressions of Iran, which consisted entirely of black-clad women round a coffin and an Ayatollah with a beard. He knew he was going to ask the wrong question, and ruin a good impression, but he plunged ahead and asked it anyway. 'Was that the mullahs?' he said.

'No,' said Shirin, sharply.

'Sorry,' said Struan, 'sorry to be ignorant.'

'People always think that,' said Shirin. 'Mullahs. Probably, the mullahs would be OK for us. My cousins have gone back, they went last year, and so far, they are in fact OK. Before the mullahs, Struan, there was the Shah, and he was not a good man. He thought up the prisons of Tehran.'

'Excuse me,' said Struan, 'excuse me, are you Muslim?'

'No,' said Shirin, 'we are Zoroastrians in my family.'

'Parsee,' said Struan, thinking he was making rather a fine stab.

'No,' said Shirin, 'Parsees are the Zoroastrians in India. Persian, you see? Iranian. Zoroastrianism started in Iran, in Persia. I am a Zoroastrian from Iran. Or at least, my family are.'

But Struan could not help asking: 'You put the bodies on the towers, do you no, for the vultures?'

'Well,' said Shirin, for the popularity of Paul Scott was a trial to her; 'in India, Parsees still do. But there aren't enough birds, now. In Iran we usually use — '

But Struan was blundering on, his face full of joy. 'I love that idea,' he said, 'you see, I love it. That's what I wanted for my dad, sky burial, him and the wheelchair, both.'

'Did you want to set him free?' said Shirin, an edge to her chamois voice.

'No,' said Struan, 'he was dead. He couldn't be free. All he could be was dead.'

'Then bury him,' said Shirin. 'Why not?'

'Because then it's like you think he'll come back,' said Struan. 'The way they tell it. You bury folk so they can get up again on the day of resurrection. Like they get their batteries put back in them. Their souls. At the funeral the minister said the body was a container, and that

106

Dad was leaving it behind on earth. That's what I don't like. Dad didn't have a soul, he was Dad. I mean he was Martin, too, he was a person, but all of him was in his body and his brain. He didn't have another bit. Och. Am I just havering? Am I making any sense at all?'

'Oh yes,' said Shirin. 'You are making very good sense.'

'Dad's body died,' said Struan. 'It died bit by bit, and when all the bits were gone, he was gone. And then he was in my memory and Gran's, but nowhere else. Not in Heaven. He was really gone. And I wanted to put him up in a tower and leave him for vultures so it would be like us all saying that. Do you see what I'm saying? That we all knew he was dead. That bodies die. People die. I just hate the pretending people do about dying, that's all. But there aren't any vultures in Scotland.'

'Don't you have golden eagles?' asked Shirin.

'Not in Cuik,' said Struan. 'It's no the Highlands, you see. It's Central Belt.' And then Struan told Shirin all about Cuik, and together they pushed Phillip back to the house in Yewtree Row, and as they crossed the road at Jack Straw's Castle, Struan remembered he hadn't mentioned money, or the window in the attic, or even the Pot Noodle supply, let alone Jake and why he might have known that Shirin was out for the evening.

On the steps was Juliet, kicking her heels, curiously cheerful.

'Hello,' she said, rather fast, 'hello, can you let me in? I've lost my key.'

'I thought,' said Shirin, 'you have gone to stay with your mother?'

'I've sorted her,' said Juliet, 'I totally have. You'd be surprised. I'm going to stay here all summer.'

'Well done,' said Struan, nodding appreciatively.

'Yup,' said Juliet, 'I left her there in the flat like a tweedy whale with harpoons in it. I even got food money off her. And I took the Jane Fonda video and the Slim-fast. I am on the biggest diet ever.'

'Don't go like Celia on us,' said Shirin.

'Oh, Celia,' said Juliet, 'don't get me started on Celia. I went round to see her last night. Celia's got this boyfriend . . . '

'I thought she was dying of anorexia?' said Struan.

'She's not,' said Juliet. 'She's got lots fatter actually. She only cancelled my holiday because she wants to carry on shagging this bloke, that's what I think. And she can't tell me about it because it's 'too profound' and I wouldn't understand. You know. So superior, just cos she's having skinny sex.'

'This is very annoying,' said Shirin, 'don't you have another friend you can ring up?'

'No,' said Juliet, 'honestly not. I'm really not very popular. I don't know when to shut up. You must've noticed. So you'll just have to put up with me, OK?'

'Grand with me,' said Struan, grinning. He was wearing better shorts, noticed Juliet, and even a singlet, but now he was sunburned, bright red right across his back.

108

10

On the wild wet night of the eighth of August, at midnight, in the flat in the Finchley Road that she had never really liked, Myfanwy Prys came across her son in the kitchen, frying eggs.

He was in his boxer shorts. His trousers were draped on the fan oven, which was on. Myfanwy hadn't seen him for three months. 'Darling,' she said, but he did not embrace her. She was fat as an eiderdown in her silk kimono.

'I've come in for some food,' he said, to the eggs.

'Are you staying?' said Myfanwy.

'No,' said Jake, 'I'm away for a bit. Then I need my place back at Dad's. What's Juliet doing there?'

'She thinks she's helping,' said Myfanwy.

'You need to get her out,' said Jake. 'Or move the nurse guy downstairs. Stru-anne. Or out. I need my room, OK? My room in Yewtree. It's important to me. It's my headspace.' And he sat down at the table and gulped the eggs, his bright eyes with their long, starry, wide-spaced lashes fixed on Myfanwy while he ground on more pepper with the outsize grinder. Then he wriggled back into his trousers and went off into the rain, leaving the plate on the table.

Myfanwy washed the plate, tracing its egg trails for the lines of a map, but he didn't ring, or reappear at all, not all that summer.

★ ★ ★

After the storms, it got hot again. Hot, so hot, it seemed the globe had stilled on its axis, with England stuck nearest the flame, on 'roast'. The days seemed to grow no shorter: the flood of news stalled, then soured. People held hands in Latvia, did strangely civic things in Poland, and it was frankly hard to care. One night in Southwark a barge careened slowly into the cruiser *Marchioness*, and fifty-one people died, and what this meant no one could bear to say. House prices in London stagnated, like the canals.

In Cuik, the High School rejoiced in the record Higher results of Struan Robertson, and Mr Mackay, Science teacher, even pulled out the old honour board, long stacked in the staffroom cupboard, and wondered if there were some way of putting Struan's name on it. In Baker Street, the GCSEs of Juliet Prys and Celia Huntington were not anticipated with the same enthusiasm.

In Yewtree Row, neither Jake nor Myfanwy had been seen for twenty-five days. Jake had disappeared so utterly that Struan had nearly forgotten him, had decided that his midnight visit was some sort of hallucination, that he must be in Edinburgh, as Juliet said. Myfanwy, meanwhile, manifested herself only as Mr Riley, the painter, 'Come to do the window frames, for Mrs Prys.' Shirin shrugged, and said, 'If she's paying,' and it seemed she was: little packets of money appeared weekly in the top small drawer of Phillip's desk. Mr Riley made his way

110

irregularly round the house, an undercoat here, a bit of putty there: a wee, silent, grey-haired man with the knack of being in a room when you didn't expect him, curled in the pool of light from an unbuckled sash window, like a cat.

Now, waking alone, marooned in his chair, in his unstrung body, Phillip Prys saw the warm light on the study wall in the morning, and the gold of the curtains, and sometimes remembered the previous morning, and that it had been the same. Often, he remembered the name of the season, too: summer, and even his age, and that this was the year something had happened: an accident.

'You're coming back into yourself,' said Struan, settling him back into his chair after his nap, and the left eyelid twitched distinctly. The little finger on the left hand moved these days too, and the eyes — or at least the left one — certainly focused. But on the whole, for Phillip, this made things worse: sleep did not come to relieve him so easily or so often; he knew he wet himself and had to be washed; and the film script had gone, its pages falling away like petals in a wind.

'Do you think he's still in there, old Phil?' asks Giles, as he always does when he visits. Giles is a useless visitor. He does nothing but sit by Mr Prys' side looking anxious. Struan is getting ready to hand him *David Copperfield*, again, when Giles says:

'It's the idea that he's trapped in there, old Phil, don't you know?'

Struan says: 'Well, a couple of times, sir, he

111

has seemed to blink as a signal.'

'Yes,' says Giles, 'that's it. Juliet told me. She said he did it on the Heath, said he wanted to go the pond.'

'I take him up there every day,' said Struan.

'Yes,' said Giles. 'But, any sign of it, you know, happening again. The blink?'

Struan shakes his head.

'Could have been a trick of the light, I suppose,' says Giles, hopefully.

'Mr Giles,' says Struan, 'you know, children's books . . . '

'Don't deal with them,' says Giles, reflexively, 'frightfully difficult market.'

'Aye,' says Struan. 'No, but you know when they draw tortoises?'

'Perhaps,' says Giles, getting ready to leave if Struan reveals himself to be a secret author.

'Well,' says Struan, 'they draw them like the tortoise can get out of its shell. Like the shell is the overcoat and there's a wee creature in there that can take its coat off if it wants?'

'I suppose so,' says Giles.

'Well, it's not like that,' says Struan. 'The shell is the skeleton. The wee creature inside doesn't have any ribs or that. The shell *is* the tortoise.'

'And?' says Giles.

'I guess what I'm saying is, Mr Prys is a guy who's had a stroke. The stroke's no an overcoat. He cannae take it off.'

'Right,' says Giles. Phillip does look a bit like a tortoise, now Struan mentions it: the brown, scaly skull, the shell of the rug, the half-closed, yellow-brown eyes.

'So you think he won't recover, then?' says Giles, and Struan sighs.

★ ★ ★

The truth was, Struan was in no greater hurry than Giles to have Phillip suddenly semaphoring with an eyelid, or otherwise demanding change. It had all been going so well, the last three weeks, since the night of the Grand Stramash. The first week, it had been cooler, and had even rained a couple of times, and even now it wasn't so bad, because Juliet had taken him to Woolworths, which turned out to be just on the Finchley Road, and he now owned a pair of perfectly usable flip-flops, three plain T-shirts, and a collarless shirt from the Oxfam round the corner which Juliet insisted was trendy and just the thing and was OK, actually, after he'd given it a boil wash.

He wasn't even hungry any more. Shirin had instituted lunch, in the kitchen, every day after Mr Prys was fed and down for his nap. Struan, Juliet, and Shirin all sat round the kitchen table, and Shirin and he ate omelettes and drank spicy soup and stuffed pitta breads with brown and green stuff which often turned out to be really good. Struan was a convert to tomato salad, made with the skins steamed off and slatherings of pepper and oil. He got double because Juliet passed him hers.

Something had definitely happened to Juliet. She had stopped eating: she sat through all of lunch with a lettuce leaf in front of her,

113

chattering. She peeled herself ten carrots every morning, put them in the fridge, and ate them through the day, her eyes dark and shiny over her hard-working jaw. She got up early in the morning and did Jane Fonda in the front room. She accompanied Struan on his late-night jogs, though she let him do the last couple of miles on his own. She had tidied up the bathroom, arranging her wee pots on the shelf in order of size. She was visibly thinner, her legs moving more freely as her jeans bagged to the ground, a pointy little face emerging through the chins, and she talked faster than ever, so much that sometimes Struan even wondered if she was on something.

But, 'This is the real me,' Juliet had said, more than once, 'coming through,' so maybe that was it, maybe she was just better without Myfanwy always on her back, and without Celia, actually, who she had only visited the once. She was certainly less moany, and even getting quite handy with Phillip. She refused to read him *David Copperfield*, but had dragged out the wee portable telly from a cupboard in the study, and rigged it up to work, fuzzily, with a yellow-tinted picture like an old Polaroid.

'Dad always watched this,' she said to Shirin, 'didn't you know? Honestly, half the time he said he was writing something he was in here, watching the racing. When I was little, he used to let me sit on the sofa sometimes and pick the winners. I always picked the horse with the maddest name.' And now they watched the races again, Phillip and his daughter, in the hot afternoons, with the curtains closed, and, occasionally, Juliet phoned in a bet to his William Hill account for a horse with long odds and a silly name. Toobuggers had come in second at Cheltenham, and the account was £5 up on the season.

After lunch, while Phillip was napping in the study, and Shirin was working upstairs, and the curtains were drawn against the sun all over the house, Struan had got in the habit of joining Juliet for more telly in the front room. The BBC were rerunning *Flamingo Road*, and it was rubbish of course, but he liked watching with Juliet, their bare feet up on the wicker sofa, sucking ice cubes and chewing carrots and giving out points for the stupidest haircut, and shouting, 'Snog! Snog!' in the love bits. It reminded him of spending the night at Archie's, when Archie's mum let them watch *Starsky and Hutch* and made them popcorn. Years ago, before Struan had got so stupidly old.

Juliet was generally a bit quieter in the afternoons (sometimes she even crashed out gummily on the sofa) but in the evenings, when they went for their stroll with Phillip, out to the Heath in the thick warm air, she would revive, and rabbit on like she was on helium, leaving Struan to say, 'Uh-huh,' and keep the wheelchair out the ruts.

'I talk about myself the whole time, don't I?' she said, sometimes, but Struan didn't mind, she wasn't boring. She was funny about Celia and the new boyfriend, for instance, and listened with huge respect, her fringed head on one side and her pink mouth in a very serious pout, when

115

Struan opined that any boyfriend who only visited at night, who wouldn't meet parents or friends, and insisted on sex with a wee girl who was blatantly not well at all, either didn't exist or was a total shit.

'I don't think Seal's making him up,' said Juliet. 'She looks really shiny and weird and religious about it. She's even managing not to get any thinner. I don't think she could put that on, exactly. And you know she's really up for the sex bit. She says he's just, you know, uncontrollable. Got, what do you call 'em, urges.' But when Struan told her that in his opinion boys' urges were no more uncontrollable than girls' urges, she was immensely pleased.

The Pond, though, was the best thing. That was mostly why Struan was feeling better. He'd found the Men's one now, decided that the nude swimming policy did not apply to Scots, and struck up a friendship with a shaven-head New Zealander called Bill who insisted, for their first few meetings, on calling Phillip Struan's 'lover' and that they both had a thing for older guys. Bill's own lover was in the Royal Free, dying of what Bill called 'the bleeding obvious', and Bill was taking something called 'me time' every morning in the Pond. Struan worked out that Bill's 'lover' must be a man during one of his Heath walks with Juliet and so was able to leave what Juliet now called his 'Cuik face' gaping on a hillock. Bill was a serious swimmer, timing Struan up and down the pond, and insisting he join him with the free weights afterwards, but he was great with Phillip too, sitting with him

116

while Struan had his swim, and wiping his mouth and moving him on the sweaty wheelchair as easily as Struan did himself. It was Bill, not Struan, who had first said, 'He wants to get in the pool, you know, Struan, does old Phil. See the way his eyes follow you?'

And it was Bill who had turned up next day with a light tubular metal chair, and Bill, with his weightlifter's muscles and lifeguard's training, who had held Phillip's head and shoulders as they eased him onto it, and Bill who helped to carry him into the shallows. That first day, they had done no more than wet Phillip's feet. Today, they'd been further in, sitting the chair so deep that Phillip's calves were lifted and his ancient feet floated up in the healing gloop like a pale and peculiar pond weed. 'He's loving it, Struan,' said Bill. 'Loving it. Tomorrow, we'll give him a dip. What do you say?'

Struan thought about it all the way home. He could shower Phillip down quite well at the pond, he reckoned, with Bill's help. Phillip never moved his bowels before the five o'clock suppository. He didn't think pee would matter all that much. It was possible. At any rate, he could talk to Shirin about it.

So, when he got home, he settled Phillip with the racing, and made Shirin a cup of coffee. He had the hang of the wee silver gadget now, and was even beginning to prefer the result to instant. He stirred in a spoonful of sugar the way she liked it, then carefully mounted the stairs to the master bedroom. He hoped she might come out and they'd hang around on the stairs as they

117

did most days, now, for ten minutes or even twenty, talking about stuff. Phillip and Zoroastrianism, his mother and Death. All that.

'Is that for me?' said Mr Riley, by his elbow.

'No,' said Shirin, 'I am sure it is for me.' And she reached out and took the cup, and before he knew it, Struan was in Shirin's actual bedroom with the sheets turned down and the dressing gown on the bedpost, and was being beckoned past that, even, into the bathroom.

'He is such,' said Shirin, 'a disconcerting small man.' And Struan giggled. 'Well really,' she said, 'you don't find him?'

The en suite didn't seem like a bathroom, because it was full of Shirin's easel, and her tiny palettes, and miniature brushes in vials of bright liquid. There was water in the bath, and just noticing that for some reason made him blush. 'My studio,' said Shirin, and smiled. 'All this time and you haven't been in.'

'Nearly a month,' said Struan.

'Is that all?' said Shirin. 'It seems like for ever.'

The floor trembled slightly beneath Struan's feet: Juliet, on the floor below, was doing her Jane Fonda. There were pictures everywhere, stuck to the walls with drawing pins, one of top of the other. Some of them were sketches: recognizably Phillip asleep in the wheelchair, a head and shoulders which surely belonged to Juliet, but also photos, and things torn from magazines, and bits of what looked like the instruction manual of Phillip's wheelchair —

'I thought I ought to show you this,' said Shirin, pointing at the square of shining colour

118

in the middle of the easel, 'before I sell it. There has been a lot of interest, already.'

Struan peered. The picture was no bigger than a pocket notebook, and had such a smooth surface, it was hard to believe it had been painted at all. It portrayed a glittering, enamelled tower, on either side of which knelt a young knight in armour and a maiden in white. On the top of the tower lay the frame and seat of what was clearly Phillip's wheelchair, delicately leafed in gold. The rest of the chair, the brake and wheels, was being carried away by birds of prey with hooked beaks and golden wings. 'Vultures?' asked Struan.

'No,' said Shirin, 'golden eagles. Look, it is the Highlands.'

And Struan looked, and saw that the background to the picture was a tiny blue mountain range in a cerise sunset.

'It's awful good weather for the Highlands,' he said, smiling.

'We are allowed this,' said Shirin, 'good weather. In a picture. In our minds. Do you like it?'

'The picture?' said Struan.

'Yes,' said Shirin, 'I am asking because it is from your idea.'

'I thought you thought I was awful ignorant that day.'

'No,' said Shirin, 'I did not. Do you like the picture?'

Struan thought it was like having a butterfly land on your hand, when the sun was shining, and you see all the wee gleaming feathers. He

119

was going to say so when Mr Riley suddenly rose into view on the other side of the window, framed by a single astragal.

'Aye,' he said, 'I like it.' He put the painting back on its stand. Shirin was gazing up at him with her strange, foil-backed eyes, expecting more of him.

'Of course,' said Shirin, 'you could say that I simply feed back to an English audience hackneyed stereotypes of the East which they are all too eager to receive. Images made palatable with a thin postmodern gloss. People have.'

Struan opened his mouth. He was thinking about caramels with a hard chocolate coating. His tongue was sweating. *Oh*, said Blondie, from below, *your hair is beautiful*. Mr Riley wiped a chamois cloth over the other side of the curved, thin glass, and it was as if he were wiping over Struan's skin, leaving all of it flushed and alive.

And then, in a violent unzipping of the air, the doorbell rang. Struan ran down the stairs, but Juliet had already answered, Juliet in her tight shiny workout gear with her mad wee ponytail bang on top of her head. Struan stood on the landing with his mouth open, horrified. For there, in button-up jeans and sunglasses, his cheeks half-shaven and his hair flicked, resurgent, stood Mr Fox.

11

In order to get rid of his teacher, and stop him coming in the house — which was obviously what he one hundred per cent intended to do — Struan had to say he would meet him for a drink in the pub. Mr Fox said they should go to the Flask on Flask Walk, just down the road, that very evening at half-past eight. Struan was enormously bothered by the whole thing. He paced round the house with his shoes off his great feet and arms loose, hangdog.

'Shirin says it's OK. She's says she's going out at six but she'll be back by eight, she'll stay with Dad. Why do you want to say no?' said Juliet, rapidly, doing her leg lifts on the carpet. Struan sat down beside her.

'I'm underage,' he said, helplessly. Juliet's eyes were strange and shiny. It had been weird, but impressive, the way she talked to his Mr Fox. Like he was their age. Like he was a person.

'Oh, honestly,' said Juliet. 'Honestly, Struan, you're ten foot tall and nearly eighteen anyway. Jake started going to the pub when he was twelve. What are you worrying about?'

'I'm not Jake,' said Struan. 'And anyway, I've never been.'

'You've never been in a pub?' said Juliet, incredulous.

'Well, ay, of course I have,' said Struan, 'like, for events. My dad's wake. With adults. But I've never been on my own.'

'Well,' said Juliet, 'you're not going on your own. You're going with your teacher.'

'That,' said Struan, 'is what I'm worried about.'

'But he's a nice guy, this teacher,' said Juliet, 'isn't he? It's not like me going to the pub with Miss Kirwan, is it. And anyway, he's left. He said he was working in a publisher's. So he's not your teacher any more. He can be your friend. He was your favourite teacher, wasn't he?'

'No really,' said Struan. 'Not being too big for my boots or anything, I think I was his favourite pupil, but he wasn't my favourite teacher. My favourite teacher actually was Mr Mackay.'

'Why?' said Juliet.

'He was just this nice old guy who told you stuff,' said Struan, rubbing hopelessly at the Persian rug with his fist, nostalgic, suddenly, for the formaldehyde and certainty of Mr Mackay's bleak lab. Mr Mackay hadn't said anything at all to him when his dad died, not even that Struan could slack off the homework. If anything, he had set him extra. But he had got the leaflets for medicine and dentistry for the universities for him, and put them in his hand at the end of class one day, and told him he expected Struan to read them and make his choice and apply by the end of the week. He told him he should aim for the best. But Struan hadn't even asked Shirin about the pond, he realized. About bathing Phillip. He'd got too wrapped up in himself, and that wee picture.

'No,' said Juliet, sitting up and facing Struan,

122

'I mean, why didn't you like this Fox guy? He looked really young and cool to me, I never got anyone like that teaching me.'

'I do like him,' said Struan, 'and I appreciate, you know, that he tried to help me and that. I'm not ungrateful. It's just — I could never work out what he wanted. I always felt a wee bit false with him.'

But Juliet had returned to her leg lifts. She grinned at Struan from behind one thigh, just like Jane Fonda on the video cover, and even Struan realized she couldn't have done that two weeks previously: there would have been more thigh than face. Juliet must have lost about a sixth of her bulk — that couldn't really be healthy.

'Look,' said Juliet, 'I'm coming too, you know. Shirin will say it's OK. So you don't need to worry. I've been to lots of pubs. Lots and lots and lots.'

And she sprang up and danced out the room in her new, over-bouncy, Kids-from-*Fame* manner, leaving Struan to feed Phillip, and settle him and mosey down to the kitchen and eat lunch, all in that preoccupied, browsing giraffe way he had with him when he was worried, the one that Myfanwy, observing him through the basement window on her way in with Mr Riley's money, found so particularly irritating.

★ ★ ★

Phillip is taking his lunchtime nap, carefully flexed and laid out on the hospital bed, a cotton rug over his knees. He is dreaming of the Pond.

123

He can see his body, its arms outstretched, floating above him in the green waters of Hampstead Pond. Soon, soon, he will slide back into it, his arms will smooth on his hands like gloves, his legs will slip into the long boots of his shins, and then his nose will crest the water, his eyes will blink in the sun, and he will jack-knife in the brightness and he, all of him, will swim off swift as Mr Jeremy Fisher. Then the blanket itch, the trouser sweat, the aching neck will be gone for ever, and the Scottish Boy will be there at the side of the pond with a towel.

Bits of him are fully asleep during this dream, and his eyes are shut. There's a pleasant sepia wash over everything. Then he hears Myfanwy's voice, and he tries to open his eyes, but because of the trouble he has with the mechanism of the eyelids, the drawbridge system, the counter-balances, the whatever it is, rusty weights on chains probably, that pull the lids up, he can't do anything about it. She is saying: 'I haven't gone anywhere, you know, Phillip,' and all he can see is the red plumbing of his eyelids.

Not that he needs to see her, really. He knows in his bones that Myfanwy has never gone anywhere, ever, that she is the boards and attic and dust of this house and that the dreams of ponds and Scottish boys and racing on the telly and Shirin's cool hands holding his head are but shadows and the play of the light. Myfanwy is his wife, and all the others, sweet Shirin, the one with the horse, even his first love, purse-lipped Dilys of the valleys with her library card and her Da and her abortion, are fleeting dreams.

124

★   ★   ★

Juliet takes two pills (it needs to be two, these days, to get the springy-heeled feeling) and calls Celia, who she has only seen once since she went round to drop the bomb-shell about Jake being rusticated, and Celia pretended she didn't care, like she had never even heard of Jake. Celia was reconsidering Oxford, she told Juliet the next time, she thought Cambridge might be more liberal and free-spirited.

Juliet does the phoning on the stairs, while she puts polish on her toenails. The stairs: partly because she is now able to bend all the way to her feet without pushing through rubber rings of fat, and partly because it feels brilliant to tuck the phone between her chin and her shoulder, and twine the wire under her ankle, like a busy girl in a film.

'I can't hear you,' says Celia.

'A double date,' says Juliet, shouting into the receiver.

'What do you mean?' says Celia.

'You bring Mr Mystery along to the Flask this evening. I'll give him the once over.'

'He's busy,' says Celia.

'All night?' says Juliet.

'Maybe,' says Celia, 'anyway, who are you bringing?'

'My date,' says Juliet. It seems to her that Mr Fox looked at her with great approval, that morning, with his big shining eyes. He asked her if she would be sure to come, at least twice.

'Someone,' she says.

125

'Juliet,' says Celia, 'I know you're not seeing Stru-anne. You know that, don't you? You are not going out with him. And anyway, it's Results Day tomorrow.'

'All the more reason to have a night out,' says Juliet, 'and anyway, Celia, I'm starting not to believe this boyfriend of yours. I'm thinking, if I don't meet him soon, I might have to tell your mum you're having delusions. Anorexics do, you know.'

Juliet puts the phone down. Her heart is racing unpleasantly, and she is sweating all over. The pills did that, when you first took them. She untangles the phone, pulling the wire over her head. A plume of black hair falls on the stair carpet. Juliet tugs at her fringe, and more hairs come, painlessly, softly, as if they'd been loosened. She stares at them, thatching her wet palm, and thinks, quite distinctly, 'Que será será,' and stumps up the stairs humming. On the landing there is Shirin and she says: 'Juliet, do you want to go shopping?'

Oh, what a day, what a sunlit day this is turning out to be!

12

Phillip was afraid, that was Struan's feeling. Something had happened to make him afraid, something during the nap. A dream?

He'd changed him, now, and sat him up, and wiped his face down with cold flannels, and combed his grey-black hair, but still Phillip kept sweating, the droplets forming on his brown pate like dew. His eyes were open, focusing. It was a hot day, humid, but not as hot as all that. Struan remembered something he had read about cats, in one of Mr Fox's dirty books, in fact: that if they were very frightened, if you threw them off a building, for instance, their paws sweated.

Struan sat beside Phillip and took his hand. The big loose fingers were cool and hard and damp. He scootched over and got his face into the position he reckoned Phillip could see the best: high up and on the left. 'Mr Prys,' he said, 'are you OK?' and Phillip's brown left eye, isolated in its lashes, aswim in his freckled slack face, closed and opened again.

Struan breathed in. 'Can you do that again?' he said. And Phillip did.

'OK,' said Struan, leaning forward, 'Mr Prys, don't try too hard, OK? No big deal? But if you can hear me, for sure, blink, OK?'

And Phillip Prys did. He was trying to shut both eyes, Struan saw, but the muscles of the left worked better than the right, giving him a sleepy leer.

'Right,' said Struan, calmly as if he'd been doing this all his days. But Shirin and Juliet had gone off on their shopping trip, giggling. The nurse wasn't due for three hours. It was him on his own.

'Mr Prys,' he said, 'excuse me, are you frightened of something? Are you upset? Can you give me a wink for yes?'

And the beery eye opened, and shut.

'Has something happened?' asked Struan. 'Something bad, just now?' And Phillip winked again.

'OK,' said Struan, 'right, just hang on a wee mo, OK?'

Struan had recently been reading about Daniel Day-Lewis in the film *My Left Foot*, and, thinking about feet and bits of chalk, he ran to the desk. Typewriter, notebook, blotter: all as Phillip had left them on his last morning. He thought he could write out a list mebbe, or the alphabet, on a piece of paper, then Phillip could blink at the right thing, but he couldn't find any paper, it was crazy. He rummaged through the drawers and in the end picked up Phillip's big spiral-bound notebook, and flipped over the notes — *Giles 10 am* — *Boy in novel son of mine manager?* — and scatological cartoons of Salman Rushdie till he got to a blank page. In Phillip's swish ink pen, in big letters, he wrote down things he could think of that might be frightening Phillip, or worrying him, just: Dream, Jake, Death, Myfanwy, Money.

And just then there was a cracking noise, and a shaft of brighter light. Mr Riley had opened the small sash window, sideways, from outside, the way you can only open sash windows if you are a sash window specialist and have done something to the frame, and now he stepped into the room from the garden.

Mr Riley looked at Phillip, and Struan, and the desk, and the notebook which said DEATH MYFANWY in large capitals.

'The undersides,' said Mr Riley, waving his scraper. Struan folded the page over, and turned back to Phillip, but now the old man's eyes were tightly shut.

★ ★ ★

Shirin led Juliet confidently out the house. She had new sandals on, little gold strappy ones mounted on clear plastic heels. Her rapid, exquisite feet seemed to float above the pavement.

'Lovely shoes,' said Juliet, as she clomped behind.

Shirin waved one: 'So gorgeous!' she squeaked. 'So uplifting! In the sale, but you know, since this country has turned tropical, one may as well!' Then she stopped, right outside Whistles. 'Here we are,' she said.

'No we're not,' said Juliet, 'I can't fit in the door there. They wouldn't let me try anything on, I'd split it.'

'Nonsense,' said Shirin, firmly, 'come along.' And she shoved open the great glass door and sashayed along the silky aisles with their ranks of unlikely garments, and led Juliet to a rack of chocolate-coloured denim jackets with diamanté studs stamped into the collars. She pulled one out: it was tiny, barely bolero. 'This,' she announced firmly, 'is for you.'

'Shirin,' said Juliet, 'do you think it is important to be slim or is it your personality that counts?'

'For men, do you mean?' said Shirin, cocking her little heart-shaped face, her mouth briefly narrowed.

'Yes,' said Juliet.

'It is important to be slim,' she said, 'I have found this true. But look, Juliet, now you are not plump. See, this jacket will fit.'

It did. It lapped smoothly across Juliet's newly flat back. It straightened Juliet's round shoulders. Its stiff collar wrapped and narrowed Juliet's round neck. It smoothed Juliet's over-extensive bosom and made an elegant 'v' in it. It invented for Juliet a waist —

'And the colour is very good,' said Shirin, 'excellent for you. Do you have something pink to put with it perhaps? A dress?'

Juliet couldn't breathe. She nodded. She said, 'But I haven't got any money.' Shirin opened her tiny gold-chained bag, and waved a quilted chequebook.

'How come?' said Juliet.

'Well,' said Shirin, 'did you know you have a trust, Juliet? For your school fees, your father set it up — each month some money goes in?'

'Yes,' said Juliet, 'but I won't be needing that any more, it's results tomorrow, you know, and

130

I'll have failed the lot, I'll have to go to the comp.'

'Yes,' said Shirin, 'I know it is tomorrow, the results, that is why I wish to give you this information today. So you can report to your mother.'

'So we can have a better fight?' asked Juliet. Shirin shook her head briefly.

'I am telling you this,' she said, 'I am giving you this information, to make it more fair.'

'What information?' said Juliet, gulping.

'This trust,' said Shirin. 'The point of the money in this account is for you to be taught, Juliet, yes?'

Juliet nodded.

'But,' continued Shirin, 'today I found it has been used for other things. For instance, your mother she told me she paid your air fare to Italy and that it is cancelled too late for refund, and the trust must pay her, and I say fair enough, but today, I phone Celia's mother, she says the fare is never paid at all. And your school fees, they are not being paid, since Easter they are not paid, I have solicitor's letter come last week for Phillip, this started me on my investigation.'

'Well,' said Juliet, 'I wasn't going back there anyway. They kept trying to sack me, you know. I'm an awful skiver, Shirin, it's a fact.'

'But,' said Shirin, 'one pays the fees, all the same, Juliet. This is England. And, anyway, if the fees are not paid, this means there is extra money in the account. So I check, and there is no money in the account at all. So I rang your mother, she said, 'Oh well this money it pays for Juliet's food and so on now she lives in Yewtree,' and I said, 'I make omelettes what are you

131

talking about,' and Myfanwy said, 'No, she has Pot Noodles.' Absurd.' Shirin was as near to worked up as Juliet had ever seen her, her little nose wrinkled, her lovely eyes narrowed.

'Struan eats the Pot Noodles,' said Juliet, suddenly worried for Myfanwy, 'but she did buy some.'

'And also,' said Shirin, actually starting to rabbit. 'Also, in this very same phone call, I find out Mr Riley is paid from this account. Your account. She said to me, the account is now the House Account, the chequebook is in the house, in Phillip's drawer, you can check, maybe it is you, cashing the cheques, Giles signs some in advance, but this is not an agreement, and then there are a lot of payments made for cash, hundreds, I cannot believe Giles signs off these cheques, I am not happy at all with him.'

'Oh,' said Juliet, 'well, I did wonder why she was paying for Dad's house.'

'Yes,' said Shirin, 'so did I.' She pursed her lips, looked down at her chequebook.

'Sorry,' said Juliet, desperately wanting the jacket, 'that's really bad of her.'

'No,' said Shirin, 'it is not for you to be sorry.' And she turned her attention back to the jacket. 'There is a stain, here, see?' she said, pointing to the collar. 'I will have ten pounds off.' And Juliet and she proceeded to the till.

Where Shirin smiled, and said: 'This jacket, it is educational, is it not?'

'Yes,' said Juliet, 'if I had this jacket, I could go to the comp.'

'Yes,' said Shirin, 'I should think you could.

And so, I will buy it, and when I am on the telephone to Giles, I will say, Juliet's money, back in her account, and twenty-three pounds to me too for the jacket while you're at it, OK?'

'Yes,' said Juliet, 'that's OK.'

'Besides,' said Shirin, 'it is in the sale. Tremendously marked down. A bargain. We must not let it slip by!' And they didn't.

★ ★ ★

Phillip wouldn't open his eyes again, at all, not even when Struan begged him. He was keeping them shut, he was sure — he was still breathing quickly, still sweating. 'Is it him?' he whispered, when Mr Riley left the room. 'Is it the painter, bothering you?' But Phillip wouldn't respond.

So in the end, Struan heaved him out the door in the chair and walked him up to the High Street and back. He thought he might see Juliet and Shirin, and explain everything to them, get some help, but he didn't, of course. London was too big for that, even a wee bit of it, like Hampstead. The whole way Phillip's head stayed at its broken, lolling angle, and his eyes open, but fixed on the wheel.

Mebbe, thought Struan, turning into the bank, mebbe London had addled his brain — the heat and watching *Dallas* and the coffee and the rest of it. Fried it, like one of Shirin's omelettes. Struan took out ten pounds for the pub. He mustn't spend more than that. He looked down the High Street again for Shirin's glossy head. Nothing.

The problem, he thought as he pushed Phillip home, was that if he told Shirin all about the wink and so on, she might not believe him. He had no evidence. She might even think he was making it up because he was after something. Another nice pair of shorts, maybe, or a wee picture. Attention, that's what.

And so it was that when Shirin came into the study, flushed and shining in a tulle blouse, aerial in the gleaming sandals, saying Struan must go out, out, he worked too hard, out with him to the pub to see his friend, that his courage failed him entirely and he meekly agreed and went up to get a shower and his clean shirt on.

13

Juliet's hair really was falling out. Some more strands came out on the brush, long ones, and then dozens of others filled the plughole of the bath, and when she came to look in the mirror, there was actually a completely plucked patch just left of her ear, where the hair-clips pulled it. So Juliet rubbed in lots of mousse, so as to glue the rest of it in, turned her head upside down, and blew it dry into a vertical column. Hair falling out was the kind of thing that might happen to a kooky girl in a Lloyd Cole song. *On account of all the rattlesnakes.* Celia's hair was all wispy, after all.

And now, on this late August evening and for the first time in her new body, Juliet pulled the pink dress out of the drawer, the one that made her look thin from the side, and shook out its knitted silky folds, and put it on, and slowly and ceremonially approached the dressing-table mirror to see how it looked.

Meanwhile, in the Finchley Road, Myfanwy Prys was preparing for a session of *reverie.* For Myfanwy might be a property developer now, but she also had trained for the theatre with the Polish avant-garde, in the days when you gave up your body and your blood for the craft. Intimate and daring experimentation in free association (guided by Zbigniew) had allowed her to find within her that fallen angel, Polly in *Milk Wood.*

Later, profound inter-generational trance work permitted her to discard little Shirley Davies of Swansea, and to reconnect with Myfanwy of the Valleys, an actress fit to play Angharad in *The Pit*. And when, as a mature actor, she had played Lady Macbeth for a famous season in Aberystwyth, it was the 'letting in' of certain childhood memories that had powered her performance: the strangling of chickens, for example, or the day she held little Tommy Jenkins in the pond till his body kicked like a starter motor.

Thirty-one years since she met Zbigniew, thirty since she had interrupted him making the beast with two arses with darling Cecil, a half-hour of free-associative thinking remained part of her daily routine. And because it was part of her practice to allow the thoughts to affect the body, to form what Zbigniew in his terrific spitty accent called *muscular vectors*, she was careful to seek out a relaxed, free-floating spot. The bath worked well; so did the floor, so did her large, well-sprung bed. Today, she was combining *reverie* with the application of anti-fungal creams to her intimate folds: the recent heat had brought on thrush.

★   ★   ★

Juliet surveyed herself in the bathroom mirror. The dress was loose. Where once her stomach had bulged like a balloon, now there was a neat drape. Where the sleeves had grabbed sausage-like arms, there were little silk puffs above slim pale limbs. You couldn't call Juliet's legs thin, not

136

yet, but they had ankles now, they had knees, and the ankles were not bad. The dress flicked up and flattered the knees. She did look thin from the side.

And now, over the transformed dress, Juliet placed the new jacket. She didn't look, all at once. Instead, she shut her eyes, bent over, swished out her hair, then stood up and opened them. In the mirror, she watched the shining mass of hair settle slowly over the diamanté collar, snugly buttoned under her new, pointy chin. The brown of the jacket was such a good brown, the very colour of her eyebrows. The pink was such a good pink: it made her skin white and her cheeks glow. Juliet was sugar-pig coloured, not a sausage at all.

★ ★ ★

To begin a *reverie* one must first release troubling thoughts, physically expel them from the body. Myfanwy had suffered a series of unpleasant events that morning, and went through them, one by one, and released each, as she had been taught, with an exhalation of breath and a raising and opening of the buttocks. (Zbigniew believed that emotion lived *all along* the gut.)

Out: the call from Giles, telling her that he couldn't stall the Literary Giant beyond the end of the week; out: the fax from the estate agent, informing her that during the latest visit to the railway cottages, signs of recent occupation had been noticed *in the toilet;* out: the letter from the bank, insisting on an interim payment. And out,

137

out, the call from Shirin Khorshidi (she was no longer using the name Prys, personally or professionally, you couldn't help noticing) about bank accounts and forgetting the sale of Yewtree. About Myfanwy's perfectly legitimate use of her daughter's trust to make the best possible investment in her daughter's future — but Myfanwy's body refused to let that one go. It was trapped in her intestine like wind. Myfanwy spread her legs, exhaled, probed deeper for the cause of her unhappiness.

Jake. Jake, of course. Rusticated! Not expelled. He could recover. His destiny was in any case in the theatre. That's why he had to go to Edinburgh. Because he had gone to Edinburgh. Myfanwy had decided that he had certainly gone to Edinburgh. She scanned the papers every morning, for the reviews. There was a *Two Gentlemen* show, with a tank, and that must be his. He had perhaps changed his name, to avoid the attention of his college. And at the thought of the college, Myfanwy became aware of tension across her shoulders: a vector, Zbigniew would say, of blame; and that her left hand had formed the vector of a fist; and that her right hand tensed and ceased its creamy ministering.

★   ★   ★

Yeah, said Lloyd from the record player, *that is perfect skin*. Juliet was a real girl, in the real world, real like Celia, the kind of girl who might really get a boyfriend. She gave a little skip. It was unbelievable, how easy it all was, once you

138

started, the journey from the non-being of fat to the being of thin. And when you got there, the minute you were even on your way, people fancied you. Like Mr Fox. Juliet clenched both her fists and promised herself she would never be fat again. She popped another pill, just in case she should be tempted to eat crisps in the pub. She wondered how thin she should get before she stopped the pills. She didn't want *all* her hair to fall out.

If Myfanwy could not rid herself of a particular thought, the correct path was to follow it to its source. Myfanwy reloaded her fingers with anti-fungal, remembered her seven years on the couch in a very full form of analysis with Ivan the experimental long-fingered Russian, and began again.

Through Ivan, Myfanwy had understood that, when it came to young men, one must remember one's Jung. Jake was in the wandering phase of life, when a young man must separate from the Father and find his own Identity. But Jake's Father had failed him and that other Father, his college, had cruelly rejected him. Jake's psychic landscape, therefore, was a blasted heath of terror and insecurity. Stumbling across it, Jake had sought to return to his First Home (Yewtree). This must have been around the eighth of the month, when he'd eaten the eggs in the Finchley Road. Stumbling through the house, he had found not only a False Mother in his Father's bed (he was surely used to that) but a False Son in his very own room. Yes, in his very own Primal Attic, he had stumbled on Struan

Robertson, with his incomprehensible accent, his horrible cheap clothes. One could only imagine the psychic damage. No wonder he was angry with his Mother! She, Myfanwy, had allowed this to happen. She had moved Struan in herself.

'An excellent arrangement,' said Shirin, prissy posh. And Struan Robertson, so grey and slow with his long spade fingers, like a great louse, leant over Phillip's wheelchair and said: 'Mr Prys signalled clearly, Mrs Prys, I saw it.' Struan Robertson, blocking the deal with the Literary Giant and Jake's future with it. By now, Myfanwy Prys' body had formed a strong muscular vector of anger: she was sitting up, in fact, flushed with rage. It was Struan and his vaunted skills with the commode who let Shirin carry on living in Cloud Cuckoo Land and Yewtree Row. It was Struan who saved Juliet from the reality of the incontinence pad and turned her priggish and cold. Struan who infected even Giles with his foolish tales, his unrealistic optimism, his ridiculous, repeated, nonsensical tale of a blink.

And just then the telephone rang, and Myfanwy answered it with a fungal-creamed hand, and on the other end was Mr Riley.

14

Struan wore his checked shirt to the pub. And his trousers with the elastic belt. Juliet said he should wear his singlet and shorts instead, but what sort of person wore their underwear outside?

In his pocket, Struan put the £10 from the bank. He had a feeling he could spend all of that, easily, this evening. Half a week's money. But his dad had always bought the drinks in the pub, carefully asking each person what they wanted before going up the bar and coming back with everything arranged on a tray and an Irn-Bru for Struan and a bitter shandy for himself. At his wake, he'd had an open bar, special instructions, though his gran had rued it afterwards.

Besides, if he bought the drinks, he could check the drinks. He himself would have bitter shandy. That didn't get you drunk. And Juliet was sticking to the Diet Coke, whatever she said. Juliet was sixteen, and she needed to remember that. He was really disturbed by the sight of her prancing along the pavement in heels and a glittery jacket and that wee pink dress. She didn't use to have that jacket. She'd put on make-up, definitely, besides, and brushed her hair all up and shiny and crimped — she looked pretty but —

'What are you so worried about, Struan?' said Juliet.

'Your dad,' he said, and it became true.

'What about him?' said Juliet.

'Just — you know. Is he getting better, and that.'

'Yeah, well I hope he does now, you know,' said Juliet, talking in that peculiar, helium way she did in the evenings. 'Honestly, I do. I quite like him now. I didn't used to, so that's good. It's normal to like your dad, isn't it? And I like living here now, with him and Shirin, so I want to carry on in the term time. I don't care if I've failed everything, I can go to the comp. You can help me with my maths, Struan, cos I've one hundred per cent failed that, you wait and see tomorrow, I'm so bad at maths it's really hilarious. Mum doesn't want me to, she wants me to move back in with her which is really mad, it's much better for me in Yewtree and I'm very helpful too, aren't I? And anyway I've got a secret weapon on Mum now, do you know she's been spending my education money on Pot Noodles and Mr Riley, and so I can say to her, Mum, you've given away any right to tell me what to do . . . '

'On Mr Riley?' said Struan.

'Yeah,' said Juliet, 'Shirin told me, it's mad, but maybe it's because of Cricklewood going pear-shaped, I reckon it is, you know.'

'Cricklewood?' said Struan. 'Pears?' And they arrived at the pub. It was right there on the street with tables on the pavement and its swing doors pinned open on its woody dark mouth. Juliet plunked herself down on a chair. 'Nice pub. Bagsie an outside seat, Struan. Outside is best.'

And Struan's wandering anxieties switched

from the question of what was up with Phillip to if it was mebbe a good idea to sit outside because then you could pretend you weren't really in the pub at all but had just paused on your way home to talk to an acquaintance, or if it was just asking for trouble because a passing policeman would definitely spot the both of them for underage.

'Struan,' hissed Juliet, 'take off your Cuik face or we'll never get served. I totally look old enough to go in.'

'You do not,' said Struan. 'No way.'

'Way,' said Juliet, her hand on his arm, and she would have pinched him, had not Mr Fox bustled out the pub in his 501s, his sunglasses pushed up on his head.

'Struan!' he said, and 'Juliet!' and most confusingly, he stooped down to her chair and kissed her on the cheek.

'You look,' he murmured, 'tremendous.'

'Mr Fox,' said Struan, 'will I get the drinks?'

Mr Fox was called Ronald. Ron. It was of course impossible for Struan to call him this, but Juliet could manage it. No problem. Juliet could ask him about his new job too, the one at the publisher's, as confidently as if she'd worked in one herself. Mr Fox was in charge of the 'slush pile' and he wasn't being paid much but it was really inspiring, he could really allow himself to be creative in an environment like that.

'And what do you do, Juliet?' asked Mr Fox. He hadn't let Struan buy the round. He'd got a jug of a browny-coloured drink instead, with strawberries in it. It was called Pimm's, and tasted of Irn-Bru and Tixylix, but Struan was worried there was alcohol in it. He was worried Mr Fox thought Juliet was older than she was.

Juliet said she was a student. On a sort of a gap year. And she saw Struan about to say something, and jumped in. 'I'm not much of a one for studying, actually. I drove my teachers wild.'

'I bet you did,' said Mr Fox.

'Not like Struan,' said Juliet.

'No,' said Mr Fox, 'Struan, now, he's a wonder. Did the Highers come out well, Struan?'

'Aye,' said Struan. 'Aye, Ah was pleased.'

'You see,' said Mr Fox, 'Struan even survived my teaching,' and there was a pause in which Struan didn't say anything at all.

'Was it really hard up there?' said Juliet.

'It was,' said Mr Fox. 'It was a hard, hard school. Rough kids. Lives shattered, just shattered by the closing of the mines.' He leant back in the chair, thumbs in the pockets of his 501s. 'Teaching, Juliet. You give out all day, and come home at night and know you've done no more than put a sticking-plaster on a wound, shone the smallest, smallest light on a dark life.'

Struan raised his eyebrows and sipped his drink. It was cold at first but had a strange burning effect in the pit of the stomach, followed by a flush all the way up the body. It almost certainly had alcohol in it. He remembered the morning: swimming in the pond. It seemed a terrible long time ago, another era. Mr Fox was still going on about Cuik.

'You see,' he was saying, 'you see, Juliet, these

144

were communities built round a single industry. The mines. The mines or nothing — '

'Dad's play is about that,' put in Juliet.

'Yes,' said Mr Fox, 'it is. *The Pit* is one of the few true works of art we have about a world like that. And that's why I chose to expose Struan to that text. But what it does not tackle — it can't, by definition — is what happens to that world when the mines go. When the spine, so to speak, is removed from that body.'

The drink pushed the blood to your nose. Like diving in the Pond full throttle. Like scanning the bottom of Cuik Baths for a rubber brick. Struan was suddenly sure of something. 'Are you,' said Struan, 'are you writing about that, by any chance, Mr Fox? About Cuik.'

'Ron,' said Mr Fox. 'Yes, Struan, I am. I am trying, shall we say . . . '

But it was Juliet who asked Mr Fox about his short stories. Struan turned his head into the cloud of lemon muddle that had appeared by his right shoulder and thought about Mr Mackay the science teacher. He'd never even written to him, after he got the certificate, to thank him. And he'd never asked Shirin yet about giving Phillip a dip. And then about Phillip, and the blink. They were all connected thoughts, all about Struan getting it wrong. He'd let Mr Mackay down, and now Phillip had asked Struan to help him and Struan was letting him down. But he didn't know how to not let him down. Who should he tell, about the blink? What should he say?

Juliet got out a packet of cigarettes and offered

145

one to Mr Fox. Mr Fox took one, got a lighter from his pocket and actually lit them both. Struan rose up in his chair and subsided again.

'I'm allowed to smoke, Struan!' said Juliet, and, to Mr Fox, 'Honestly! It's like living with the police!'

'The po-lis,' said Mr Fox, in a mock Scots accent. 'I can imagine. You know, Juliet, it's a sad fact, but everyone I've ever really liked smokes. I think it's an artist thing. A sort of death wish, you know?'

And away they puffed. Juliet was sort of waving her fag about, and leaning back in her chair a lot so that her chest popped out of the pink dress. Her wee brown jacket made her look older. Like a wee toughie. Struan swallowed the rest of his drink and felt its odd burning and bracing. He quite liked it. Mr Fox was going on about Cuik again. The narrow culture. How it wasn't just the poverty of the body but the poverty of the imagination that besieged those children.

'Even Struan,' he said, 'who goodness knows is as bright as they come. Even Struan couldn't see his way out of that trap. If there's one thing I take credit for, it's opening that door for him, forcing him out of that rut. Look at him now. Living with Phillip Prys. Eating London for breakfast. Who would ever have thought it?'

Struan thought about breakfast in London. Coffee from the wee machine in the hot pink kitchen. Juliet skipping by in her oversized T-shirt. A cold omelette. Shirin fluttering in, angelic in her painting smock. Bill and the pond. It was true that none of these things were in Cuik.

Two slim, hairy wrists with bracelets slid down on the table in front of Struan. He gazed upwards. They were attached to the heavy shoulders and chiselled jaw and blond fringe of Jake Prys.

'Who indeed,' said Jake.

'Jake,' said Juliet, 'what are you doing here?'

And then there was a pause. Struan stood up.

'You take my seat, Jake,' he said. 'Mr Fox, this is Jake Prys, Juliet's brother. Jake, this is Mr Fox. He used to teach me English. I'll go to the bar, will I? What can I get you all?'

Struan got himself a pint of Pimm's. He didn't mean to — it just came out when he was doing the ordering. The drinks cost him £9.67, including a packet of salt and vinegar crisps, and he decided that was it for the night, it had to be. What he'd do was, he'd go home and check if Mr Prys was OK, and then, if she was around, maybe in the kitchen or even if she had the light on in her room (he could knock), he'd talk the whole thing through with Shirin. It's what he should have done in the first place, probably where he went wrong. Mr Prys was afraid of something, but you could understand that. His dad had been afraid of dying. Shirin knew about all that. Shirin had made him a shining picture of it all. Shirin would understand.

Yes. That was the notion. When he finished the drink, he'd push it to the middle of the table and say, 'I'm pushing off for the night, good to see you all.' Which was what his dad used to say, on the rare occasions they'd gone into a pub on a Sunday. And then they would push off, Dad's hand on Struan's small shoulder. Except, thought

Struan, arranging the drinks on a round tray, except Dad had never had a Juliet to cope with. A wee pink sixteen-year-old pretending she was ten years older than she was and making up — he thought that was a fair enough description of her behaviour — to his former English teacher, a person of dubious provenance now calling himself Ron. He couldn't just leave her, whatever she said. He'd introduced her to Mr Fox. He was in charge of the consequences, because you shouldn't start something you can't finish. Shirin was surely relying on him. When he stood up to go, he'd have to take Juliet with him —

'Struan,' said Juliet, popping up at his elbow, 'Celia's here.'

'Is she?' said Struan. 'Well, you'll have to get her drink, then, cos I'm skint.'

'I haven't got any money,' said Juliet.

'I'll give her yours, then,' said Struan, picking up the tray.

'That's not the point, Struan,' said Juliet. 'Stop a minute. Bend down, I need to whisper.'

Struan bent to Juliet's fat shiny mouth, and she hissed, in a blast of cigarettes: 'I think my brother Jake is Celia's mystery man. You know, her midnight bone-jumper.'

'Really?' said Struan.

'Jake,' said Juliet, 'said to me, he was just passing by, he's got a job near here, and I said, why aren't you in Edinburgh, and he said he was in Edinburgh, it was huge, but he is not in Edinburgh he is in Flask Walk, and I think he is taking money from Mum and saying he is in Edinburgh and all the time staying down here

148

and shagging Celia and I said to Celia bring your boyfriend to the pub or I'll tell on you and I think Celia must have asked him to come out and not said she was meeting me, I think she did it on purpose. You see, it all makes sense.'

Struan didn't think it did, particularly. He started to walk to the double doors. Through them, lit up like the cinema in the sunset, was Celia. She was wearing a long cheeseclothy dress, with cuffs, and she actually looked really pretty, really grown-up, with her wispy hair and wee triangle face. Like a model. She was dancing, or sort of holding a pose, to some music from a tape machine someone was carrying along the street, and Jake popped up beside her, holding another pose, holding her hand.

'See what I mean?' hissed Juliet. 'They're throwing shapes.'

'Is that what that's called?' said Struan. 'I've never seen that.' It made him lonely, that dancing. He thought, you had to be English, to do that. You had to be born to it.

Then the music box walked off down the street and Struan put the tray of drinks on the table. Everyone took one and Mr Fox and Celia and Juliet sat down and there wasn't a chair over for Struan. So Struan stood behind the table, facing them, leaning against the wall beside Jake Prys, who had a cigarette in one hand and a bottle of beer in the other. Jake removed his cigarette, blew out, and said:

'How's it hanging, Stru-anne?' Then went on smoking.

'I'm grand. Thanks,' said Struan. Jake was

149

wearing a singlet and shorts, and Struan could all at once see that Juliet was right, and it was better to dress like that than it was to wear his damp checky shirt. It was a terrible humid evening. 'What are you up to yourself?' he said to Jake Prys.

But Jake wasn't really listening to him. He was listening to Mr Fox making Celia laugh, and his loose mouth was tight while he did so. Mr Fox was telling more stories about Cuik, and the girls were listening, that was what was happening in the conversation. Juliet's eyes were shining, her cheeks were flushed: she had never been so interested in Struan's version of Cuik. Jake puffed his cigarette loudly, sighed aloud, and Struan thought probably Juliet was right about Jake and Celia having a thing, and he'd probably treat her badly soon enough, poor wee lassie, but was that any of his business?

Mr Fox was going on about the mines again, and Jake leaned forward and said, 'If the mines are empty, why keep scraping them out? If there isn't any work, why keep the people there? They need to move.' And what Struan thought about that was — Struan who knew about the broken unions, the boarded-up shops, the closed clubs, about the symptoms of emphysema, about men who work fifty years underground and die in the Home a year later, about the pair of brothers who came to his school on alternate days because they had one coat between them — well, Struan thought that was a point of view.

'Jake,' said Mr Fox, 'what you don't understand is the whole mindset. This is a whole community built round one thing. You can't simply uproot

150

them. It's not just about money, it's about imagination. These are people who can't imagine themselves anywhere else, doing something different.'

Then he started telling about the High School staff-room, and how all the seats had greasy patches worn in the antimacassars and special owners for the last five hundred years, and Struan said to the table: 'Could you do it, though? I mean, if there wasn't any work in England all of a sudden? If they all of a sudden said you couldnae do arty stuff in Hampstead any more, that you couldnae do anything with words, even, and all of youse had to work with your hands in the open-cast mining. Could you imagine yourself somewhere else, doing something different?'

But the Pimm's had strange effects, and those words somehow stayed in Struan's head and didn't make it out his mouth, or maybe some of them did, but Jake didn't seem to notice, he was leaning forward listening to Mr Fox tell about the annual patchwork Christmas tree competition the women teachers had, and watching Celia watch Mr Fox and laugh her tinkling grown-up laugh. Mr Fox started telling about the Head of French who'd said, 'Och, I can't abide an orange, it's such a messy froot.' Struan knew that was probably true: she was a dull enough woman, Mme Carmichael, with her falling-forward bun of grey hair and well-filled detention book. She raffled the trees, every year, and that was for charity, but —

'The trouble,' said Mr Fox, 'is again that narrowness, that lack of experience of the world.

The children of Cuik know nothing outside Cuik, and that means, apart from anything else, that they can't see themselves. Tragic.'

Celia and Juliet looked quite cast down by this insight, but Jake jumped in, from behind Mr Fox's shoulder: 'And so you lit up their lives, did you?'

'No, Jake.' Mr Fox shook his head slowly. 'Nothing like that. I . . . I did my best for a year. You can only do what you can do.' And he shook his head, sadly.

'And do you think that was good of you?' asked Jake. 'A favour?'

'I think it was the right thing to do,' said Mr Fox, folding his arms.

'Well, I think you should have left them alone, actually,' said Jake.

'Jake,' said Juliet, 'don't start.'

'Did they want you there, Ron?' continued Jake. 'The little primitive Scottish people? Did you want him, Stru-anne?'

'We needed an English teacher,' said Struan. 'You see, Mr Nicholl, that was the Head of English, he had a stroke.'

'Did you need *him?*' said Jake. 'Did you need our friend Ron? Or wouldn't you have been just as happy with one of your own sort? A Scottish teacher?'

Struan gulped his drink. 'I liked meeting Mr Fox,' he said, calmly and firmly. 'He was that bit different.'

'Jake,' said Juliet. 'Stop being a total fascist.'

'Oh,' said Jake, 'but I am, you see, little sis? The more I go on in theatre, the more I believe in an elite. An elite of the brilliant. The truly talented. I think only a few people can make art, and life is too short. We have to meet each other. We have to get on with our work.'

'Don't you think,' said Mr Fox, 'that there might be artists in Cuik? People who just need discovering, bringing on? Like Struan, for instance?'

'Many a flower is born to blush unseen?' said Jake. 'I don't, actually. I think that's a bit of a PC myth. I think that actually the provinces are full of weeds. And that flowers announce themselves. And that Stru-anne is going to be a dentist.'

'But,' said Mr Fox. 'Your father. His background, his career. A miner's son with such a talent — '

'That,' said Jake, 'is a bit of a myth too. Dad was the manager's son. His mother was a schoolteacher. Granny Prys. Never forgave him for all the swearing in *The Pit* — did she, Juliet?'

'Washed out his mouth with soap and water,' said Juliet, in her best cod-Welsh. 'She still had us to stay though, Jake.'

'Though, of course, she can't have been much fun before that, can she? Gran. Or why would *The Pit* be so misogynist?'

'Oh, now, come on,' said Mr Fox, '*The Pit* may be rooted in its time and place but — '

'All the women in that play are nags or whores,' said Jake. 'Actually. Whores who become nags at best. Well, well, Granny Prys was a bore and my mother was a whore, so maybe that is how they all are, in the Provinces. Why don't you tell me, Ron, after your outing to the darkness? Dr Livingstone of Cuik.'

This thought went down Struan's body like an ice cube. Not about Mr Fox being a missionary — he'd worked that one out for himself, a while back. No, about the women, in *The Pit and Its Men*. Why the play didn't feel true. It was because of the women. They weren't real, they were systematically wrong. Suddenly, he was angry with Mr Fox. It was so obvious. Mr Fox should have pointed it out. Struan could have written that in the Higher exam, and not come away with the feeling of being a phoney.

'Your father's work is of a piece with its time,' said Mr Fox.

'Dated,' said Jake, 'fatal. It's a failure of sympathy, you see. Subtlety. A denial of depth.'

Struan knocked back the end of his Pimm's. It was like swallowing a pikestaff, a chilled, stainless-steel one. He put the glass on the table, felt giddy, and planted both his fists there too. The table wobbled.

'That's what you're doing, though,' he said to his clenched hands, and this time he could hear his own voice. 'That's what *you're* doing. All of you with Cuik and the provinces and that, you're not letting them be real.'

'Real?' said Jake.

'Yeah,' said Struan. 'That's it. Real. 3D. But we are real, up there. You haven't met us, that's all.'

'I think you're real, Struan,' said Juliet.

'I spent a year of my life,' began Mr Fox.

'Nine months,' said Struan, 'and you still didn't meet us, Mr Fox.'

154

'Ron,' said Mr Fox. 'Now, Struan . . . '

'No,' said Struan. 'Excuse me, you didn't.' And he stared at Mr Fox until Mr Fox dropped his gaze. 'It's OK,' he went on, 'Cuik folk are hard to meet. And anyway, it's hard to meet folk who are different, even if you are staying with them, because you bring your own mind with you. Like me. Like I bring my mind with me. I thought English people were different until I came down here.'

'We are different,' said Jake.

'Aye,' said Struan, 'you are, you really are, you're different. And what happens in my head is, I look at you and the way you act, and I want to say, that's all they are, these people, different, English. They're all the same. That's the thing that's not right. It's like what you were saying about your dad's play, Jake, I really liked what you said. About denying depth. Subtlety.'

'*You* liked what I said about *subtlety*,' said Jake, on the edge of a titter. He was squared up to Struan now, both of them standing, with the girls and Mr Fox fixed in their chairs, the audience.

'Aye,' said Struan, 'aye, I did. You see, what I think is, it's about letting folk be all there. 3D. Having all their feelings. I have to let you English people have all your feelings, not just the English ones. And you, you have to let the folk in Cuik be stupid and clever, and nice and nasty as well. You have to let them feel stuff. I mean, have the whole range.'

'They can't,' said Jake. '*Feel*. They're Scottish. They're *brutally* repressed.' Juliet and Celia laughed at this, delicately, relieved, and Mr Fox snorted. And Struan felt very angry, which he hadn't been before, he'd been trying to explain something, and he said:

'And you don't? You English? You don't repress your feelings? What about you, Jake Prys, you've never come to see your dad in his chair, since he's had his stroke. You think that's not *repressed?*'

Jake slapped Struan, then. He reached out his flat hand and just hit him. And Struan put his hand to his burning cheek, bent his head, and walked dizzily away. He thought he would just go to the Heath, then, and have a swim.

15

So now Juliet was thin, and with someone who fancied her, and walking on Hampstead Heath on a warm summer's night on an anti-Jake mission. She was not enjoying it as much as you might think.

'Of course Struan is proud,' said Ron, foraging ahead on the Heath path, his fringe bouncing in the faint moonlight. 'If your brother had ever been to Cuik, he might have had some understanding of that. It's not the sort of thing you learn at Oxford.'

'Jake actually just got expelled from Oxford,' said Juliet. Her heels were still bouncy, but her head had a bobbing, poorly tethered feeling. She wondered how old Ron was. She wondered if he had been to Oxford, and betted he hadn't, that was why he was so wound up about it. She thought how boring it was, the way people went on about Oxford, and wondered where Celia went, after the scene at the pub. She wondered, with a little hot wonder, whether she and Jake were having sex right now, and what they would look like from outside, and then she thought how totally unfair it was for anyone to think for a minute that that was normal, or that Juliet shouldn't be curious about it.

'Sent down?' said Ron. 'That's unusual, these days.' He paused at a junction, stroking his chin, like he knew.

'Well,' said Juliet, 'rusticated. He has to stay away for a year. He couldn't do his play either. He was going to take his play up to Edinburgh, but they wouldn't let him. Or maybe his money ran out, or something, I'm not very sure. To be honest that's the first time I've seen him for ages, just now in the pub, I know that's weird because we're family but it's a pretty odd relationship. Look, do you think he's shagging Celia?' Juliet was conscious that as soon as she opened her mouth, words poured out as if they'd been tightly stacked behind her teeth. That was the pills again, though combined, let's be honest, with her actual personality: the real, escaping Juliet. Suddenly, Ron grabbed her hand and fixed her with his glossy gerbil eyes.

'Is Jake taking drugs?' said Ron.

'How should I know?' squeaked Juliet. Ron pushed back his quiff with his free hand.

'He had,' said Ron, 'something strange and glittering about his eyes. I thought — just from my experience with kids, you know — that maybe he was taking something. It's all right, Juliet, you can tell me.' Juliet took her hand back, and stuck it her armpit.

'He's always looked like that,' she said. 'He was on the telly in *The Sword in the Stone* when he was eight looking like that. He was a child actor, you know, Daddy had all the connections, you know those programmes on the BBC with cardboard sets and all the acting is so crap, it hurts your teeth? I wasn't a child actor because they said I was too fat for the cameras. We should try and find Struan.'

Juliet bustled along the path. She was trying to outrun the picture in her head of Celia and Jake, throwing shapes in the street. Jake would dump Celia and it wouldn't matter, someone else would want her now, she was all woken up, she was a sex-pot, she, and not Juliet, had perfect skin. Not telling Juliet about it was weird and wrong and she should be done for it.

'How long were you a teacher anyway?' she said quickly, to Ron.

'A year or so,' said Ron, starting back along the path. He had a short person's walk: nose up, quiff a-quiver. 'What strikes me,' he said, 'just, as it were, wandering into this situation, as an outside observer so to speak, is that probably all this is about your dad. Struan, in the house, is in your brother's place, as it were . . . '

'Well, that's hardly fair,' said Juliet, 'Jake refused point blank to come home before Mummy ever hired Struan. He doesn't even visit, you know? Doesn't even come round and put the racing on the telly for Dad. Though mind you I was bit scared of doing all that, at first, if it hadn't been for Struan I might not even have managed it. My relationship with my dad is not so good, you know, he got divorced when I was eleven, I was never the favourite. Struan is a really great guy, you know, he is really kind. I think we've lost him. Do you know where the pond is from here?'

'Don't you?' said Ron, absently. 'In fact, in another way, I think you could say of Jake's action, his resentment of Struan, I think you could even say it was an anxiety of authorship.'

Juliet wished she could sit down. Her legs ached the way they always did, four hours after the pills. Maybe it was because her thighs were remaking themselves as Jane Fonda's, or Celia's. Another feature of the pills was that little sections of time went entirely missing, as if they'd been scissored out. Ron had his hands in his pockets now. His feet turned out. On he walked, hippity hop.

'Jake,' Ron was saying, 'is clearly mostly concerned about his artistic identity, about writing himself, as it were, into the world. And that leads inevitably into an anxiety around the father, or father figure, and the twin impulses to love and to destroy.'

Juliet thought she was really fed up of talking about Jake. Then she thought she had no idea where she was. Then a bench, a comfy wood one with a plaque, appeared just ahead and she sat gratefully on it and peered until the Heath clarified before her, blue and hairy in the starlight; an unearthly sheepskin rug.

Somewhere in the blue, Ron was pacing about. She wondered if he was going to kiss her. He was quite a good height for her. If someone saw them, kissing, they would think they looked all right. You wouldn't realize they were both short until you got up really close. Ron wasn't getting on with it, though. He was still talking about how young men create themselves.

'What about young women,' said Juliet. 'What about me? Don't I have an anxiety about creating myself?'

Ron sat down beside her, and grinned. A

cloud moved in front of the moon, his teeth gleaming in the moonlight. 'Tell me,' he said, 'do you?' Then he put his heavy damp arm on the top of the bench, sort of on Juliet's shoulders.

Juliet realized she had no idea. She realized that she spent so long thinking about what people thought of her that she had no idea what she thought of them. She didn't know if she fancied Ron Fox, for example. Suddenly, she worried about how old he was, and what level of sex he might expect.

'Honestly,' said Juliet, 'I mostly worry about if I look fat.'

'You've got nothing to worry about, Phillip Prys' daughter,' said Mr Fox, and then he kissed her, gummily, and their teeth clashed with a distinct little click.

16

In the study, Phillip's eyes open suddenly as blinds. It has happened again. He is helpless and prostrate and Myfanwy has come for him. He does not know if this a dream, or a memory, the afternoon or the night: all he knows is that the figure he has just in his sightline, the small, gesturing silhouette holding something glittering in its hand, is her agent.

Of course. Myfanwy, if she wished, could speak to him through the waves and streams, never mind a shadow on the other side of the study window. Myfanwy has many powers. He's explained as much to Shirin. To all the girls in fact. There isn't any point, see, in trying to get rid of her; how many times has he said that? The most you can do is draw a line in the sand, and she'll walk round it, isn't it?

The shape gestures in semaphore, but, because he'd married her, it is easy for Phillip's brain to turn the signs into speech, into Myfanwy's alto voice which only for him leaves its modulated stage-school tones, only for him goes back to its Swansea roots.

'I'm here every day,' says the shadow, vigorously waving the instrument, 'even if you don't see me. And you'll be dead soon, and then I will be here every day and everyone will see me. Then I will have this room made into the kitchen, I shall have the shelves chopped into bread boards and sell the books for pulp and when it is all done and shining, I shall sit at the table and cut myself cake, Phillip Prys, and remember every time you humiliated me, Phillip Prys, every girl you ever screwed on that desk of yours, and I shall munch up my cake and swallow it.'

Phillip's hands take hold of his wrists. His throat takes charge of his voice. His whole body is a dragnet hooked and roped to his mind. Sweat runs down the length of his spine, and he knows there will be no way ever to wipe it dry. And the shape in the window leans forward and blows out another gust of words.

'And it had better be sooner rather than later, Phillip Prys, that you push off. Each hour you live in this house is a hundred off the value. You're shitting money out your flaccid arse. I'm warning you, now, don't live too long, or I'll be back with the pillow.'

And the shadow blows again on the window and starts to shrink away, its head halving, then quartering, then disappearing entirely with a crash like a door shutting. Phillip screams then, but the noise stays stuck in his head, an awful effect, like putting a phone in a pan. He has done that more than once, we should say, to Myfanwy, to girls who kept ringing. He has often put the lid on and left them to themselves.

★   ★   ★

In the Finchley Road, Myfanwy wakes in the middle of the hot night with a burning fanny and a strong memory of having actually murdered Tommy Jenkins, who has grown to six foot tall and squalled as he went down in a Scottish accent. It takes a long drink and a lot of stroking and anti-fungal to calm herself back down. After all, in reality, she has done nothing to feel bad about.

Phillip Prys has threatened his wife with a hundred specific deaths. He has thrown his mother-in-law out of his house daubed in caustic lime. He has locked his baby daughter in the kitchen, bawling in wet pants, and gone out. He has taken his son to Brighton, gone on a binge, and left the child Jake in a hotel room for sixteen hours, to live on tea biscuits and reform his id. Also, he has shagged every mouldy slag in London. So if, that afternoon, Myfanwy allowed a few words of frustration to escape her in Phillip's study, if she directed a few colourful phrases at her former husband, then these were but Bohemian efflorescence, part of the language of their long life together. And even if they weren't, she was still allowed.

And anyway, Phillip couldn't hear. And as for Struan, she had no reason to doubt Mr Riley's word. And Tommy Jenkins had lived.

★　★　★

Because of the Pimm's, and its strangely galvanizing and yet paralysing effects, Struan can never afterwards remember the sequence of events that evening. Three episodes are clear in his mind, three silent films, monochrome and

164

jerky in the moonlight:

1: He is running along a path on the Heath. He is barefoot, and his flip-flops are in his hand. He's been running some time, and his trousers are damp, but whether with sweat or pond water he can't tell.

2: He is swimming across the black pond, his best crawl. The pond has grown a skin in the moonlight: it slides from his arms like scarves of silk: Shirin's.

3: From behind a tree, a man appears, and bends over like he is picking something up. He isn't wearing any trousers. Struan says, 'Och, I'm just here for a swim,' and the man disappears as if Struan had dreamt him.

Then Struan gets back to Yewtree Row. This memory is also silent, but this time it is in colour, and forensically clear: clear as the electric light switched on. It appears in his mind as a statement made to Police.

First off, from the street, he spotted that Mrs Prys' (Shirin's) light was on in her room. Accordingly, he walked in carefully, and up the stairs to the landing. He intended to speak to Mrs Prys (Shirin) about her husband's health. He thought about knocking on her door. He considered that it was probably late at night. He considered that he couldn't hear her in there and she was probably asleep. But the light was on. He concluded he should wait till the next day. He considered: he couldn't bear to. He thought he would just go downstairs and get a snack and that would make up his mind. He remembered a particular piece of omelette, chilled in the fridge.

So down the stairs went Struan on his great silent bare feet. Down past the framed poster of the *Pit and Its Men* revival from 1969, and the still of the set of the film. Down past the closed doors of the study and the front room, down the twisting back stair to the kitchen. But the kitchen was lit up, and Struan paused, poised on the turn, where he couldn't be seen, in case there was an intruder in the kitchen, sir, there had been before.

There he recognized Mrs Prys. It was Shirin. Shirin's blue-black hair falling down the back of her silk dressing gown, Shirin's tiny round bum and feet in ballet shoes. Yes, he was certain he recognized her, Sir, he knew her well. And he recognized him, too. The man. Yes. Grasping her by the waist, his quiff brushed back like golden feathers on a dark wing: Jake Prys.

Then Struan moved backwards up the stairs, and at the top turned and crept silently all the way up to his attic bedroom. His misery was a great bag of water which he was holding in both arms against his chest. He had to get it upstairs before it burst. But the attic landing was shaking, and there was a light under Juliet's door, and her voice said suddenly, intimately: 'Ron,' and Struan remembered that that was Mr Fox's other name, and he crept down the stairs again.

On Shirin's landing, Struan paused, looking at her closed door. He wanted to go into her studio and get out his painting, the one with the eagles. He could save that and smash the rest. Then he heard the front door click from below, and someone go out, and he backed into the sitting

166

room, which was just behind him. No one ever sat in the sitting room, even though it had a bay window over the garden: it was because there was no telly, only books and bits of china. The heavy curtains were drawn, and Struan stepped behind one. After a long while, he heard steps on the stairs, and Shirin's door open and close. In the street a car drove off. He thought she was alone, Shirin. He thought she was slipping into her room and getting into the double bed alone.

Then Struan thought he could sleep in the sitting room. He lay down on the rug, with a hard little cushion under his head, but that was no good. His head slipped off the cushion, and the rug was too thin: you could feel the boards. He tried lying on the sofa, with the rug over him, but the pile gave up dust and the sofa was too short: his legs came off the end. So after a while he crept down through the dark house to the study, and gathered up Phillip's rugs and wrappings, enough for a sort of nest, and laid them out parallel with Phillip's bed on the floor.

The room was already blue with dawn, and filled with Phillip's wheezing breathing. Phillip's hands were abandoned at his sides, and Struan pulled one out and held the stuffed cold glove to his damp face, rubbed his eyes on the leathery knuckles. Phillip's eyes opened, and then closed.

Struan lay down flat and decided not to think about any of it, and cried for nothing, therefore, for most of an hour, and then dozed till he heard the nurse at the front door.

17

Here was another rum thing about those pills: peculiar dreams. Bounce, bounce over the blue hairy Heath went dream Juliet on her rubber-heeled legs and splosh into the pond where a gigantic stone Struan sat on an island, his head in his hands like Father Time. It was essential for Juliet to tell Struan that this pond was the Ladies' one, lest Struan be embarrassed, so in jumped Juliet to tell him, but the pond was dry, a damp sheet, and all the bits of Juliet felt odd, handled and sucked. Juliet's eyes popped open, and she scanned the attic ceiling, wondering what was true.

Ron. That had happened. Heath. Struan in a huff, and lost. Had Jake hit Struan? Really? How theatrical! Ron Fox. Celia and Jake. Probably. Definitely. Maybe not.

Ron Fox. Just to review that. Juliet had definitely snogged a man called Ron who used to be Struan's English teacher, but they hadn't gone all the way. Juliet and Ron. When they'd got to the bit when he was sticking his hand into her knickers, and saying I do believe in safe sex, Juliet had suddenly said, I'm not old enough, I'm not sixteen, and Ron had stopped and said she was a little elf and walked her home, still talking bollocks about the creative mind, and then she'd said, I am sixteen really, but I'm just not up to it, and he'd been nice. He'd said OK.

Juliet closed her eyes again. There was the Heath, there was the pond, and she was just going to swim across the pond to tell the stone Struan that it was just a bit of snogging she'd been doing, and what business was it of his anyway, did he think he was the po-lis, when she heard a snore, and bing! She was awake, and there, stretched on the floor beside her, uncompromisingly short in his little jeans, was actually Ron Fox.

Golly. Juliet would have to tell Celia. Celia wouldn't believe her. No wonder. The story was very unlikely. Struan would definitely not believe her. No one, not the stone Struan and certainly not her mother, would believe Juliet about the snogging. The only way out was for no one to know. Juliet needed to get Ron unnoticed out the house. This could be complicated because Ron seemed way too interested in the house. He kept going on about her dad. And Jake, for Christ's sake. And he hadn't even met Shirin yet. He really must not, if it could in any way be prevented, meet Shirin. Juliet lay very still, and tried to interpret the noises of the house beneath her. She slid a hand under her pillow, and popped out a couple of pills, then lay still and waited for the amphetamines, and a plan, to surge through her.

★ ★ ★

Struan's heart was hurting him: a very bad pain. It didn't matter how many times he reminded himself that what a grown-up lady did with Jake

169

Prys was none of his business, he still had an ache in the chest cavity. A hollowness, as if something had been uprooted, a plant with many pink roots. Maybe it was angina. Maybe it was a hangover, from the Pimm's. Maybe he should go back to his gran. Certainly, he needed to get out the house.

Carefully, so as not to wake Juliet, Struan sneaked down to the kitchen and bolted his breakfast — two coffees, half a cold omelette, a Pot Noodle — while the nurse got Phillip up and in the chair. Shirin, said the nurse, was up and gone: Struan didn't reply. No hanging pleasantly round the garden this morning: he had Phillip draped and poised on the ramp at the front door at 9:15.

Autumn was coming, he thought. The heat didn't hurt, this morning, and the sun was just a brighter patch on the smeary sky; like the first polished spot on a Brasso'd door bell. He was just bracing himself to release the brakes and take the whole downward momentum of the chair himself, from the top, when Phillip's friend, your man Giles, appeared at the bottom of the steps, grey and sheepish in a crumpled blue suit.

'Hello there,' he said, waving his briefcase.

'Hello,' said Struan, waving back and wishing, as he always did with Giles, that he knew if Giles was his Christian name or surname.

'Going out?' said Giles.

'To the Heath,' said Struan. 'Could you mebbe just give me a hand?'

'Goodness,' said Giles. 'Well yes, all right, I'll give it a go.'

'Grand,' said Struan. 'Can you get up this end? Where I'm standing?' and Giles shuffled up, clutching his briefcase, and Struan put it in Phillip's lap and showed him the brake. 'Basically,' said Struan, 'if you can just release that lever very slowly, and take just a wee bit of the weight as it goes down, then I can take most of it from the other end, and it all goes smoothly.'

'Right,' said Giles, and immediately released the flaccid burden of Phillip Prys, his earliest and most illustrious client, full into the shins of Struan Robertson, just where it hurt the most.

'Jings,' said Struan, 'is there no an Englishman in England can operate a brake?'

'I'm most frightfully sorry,' said Giles, waddling down the steps.

'Don't mention it,' said Struan, handing him his case, which had slid from Phillip's lap during the plummet. Giles repositioned himself outside the front door. 'Had you come to see Mrs Prys?' asked Struan.

'Myfanwy?' asked Giles.

'She's no here. She'll be in her own home I'm assuming.'

'Of course,' said Giles, 'of course. Is, um, Shirin, Mrs Prys, um, up, around?'

'I couldn't comment,' said Struan.

'Of course not,' said Giles.

'She's out,' said Struan. 'Had you come to see her?'

'I don't know,' said Giles. 'Not really. No, I suppose I came to see Phillip.'

The reason he looked so young, so like an anxious small boy, Struan thought, even though he had all that grey hair, was his feet; so big and floppy and turned inward in their bulbous brown shoes. And his eyebrows: soft and furry and pushed together upwards.

'OK then,' said Struan, 'would you like to take a walk with us? I'm sure Mr Prys would appreciate your company.'

★　★　★

The sound was so comically, theatrically bad that at first Juliet assumed it was another hallucination: Myfanwy's voice, calling, 'Juliet! Juliet!'

But the wobble of the stairs and the creak of the boards were real enough, and Juliet rolled from the bed and out the door just in time to confront her on the landing. Myfanwy took up most of it, and Juliet felt very pleased that she was still wearing her pink dress and probably looked thin from the side. Myfanwy was waving a large white envelope, like a flag.

'You failed,' said Myfanwy. 'Everything but RE.'

'Oh, Mother,' said Juliet, backing her swiftly down the stairs (Ron, prostrate and miniature, was barely a foot away through the wall), 'don't you think we should talk about it like adults?'

'No, Juliet,' said Myfanwy. 'We should talk about it like a mother and child.'

'But we could pretend,' said Juliet. 'It might be good for us, don't you think? Like a drama workshop? We might behave better?' Downstairs, the phone went. 'I'd better get that,' said Juliet, dashing down, 'it's probably Celia.'

172

She picked it up in the front room. Myfanwy followed, the envelope clasped to her bosom, and settled the billows of herself in the armchair as if they were a train. Regal mode, noted Juliet: Gertrude, Hermione. Not about to weep. Not in any kind of hurry. Bad.

Juliet pulled her tummy in, and ran her fingers through her hair. Some came out. She threw it in the bin. It was Celia's mother on the phone actually, rabbiting on about Celia, who wasn't there apparently, who, if she wasn't at Juliet's all night, seemed to have got up very early and gone out already, no doubt to avoid the envelope, and in that case she was probably coming round to Juliet's and Juliet was to tell her —

'Did she fail them, then?' said Juliet, hopefully, twining the cord round her arm and peering into the street, in case Celia should be there, weeping.

'All As but RE,' said Celia's mother, 'she only got a B in RE, but really you know RE is not an important subject and won't affect her Oxbridge in any way, and of course what we are worried about, me and Celia's dad, is that a tiny, tiny setback like that might set her off her on her dieting silliness again, because you know Juliet she'd been doing so well, she looks marvellous, don't you think, these last few weeks.'

'Oh yes,' said Juliet, 'she really does. And those are fabulous results. They're really great. I'll make sure to congratulate her.'

'Let me know,' said Celia's mother, 'let me know the minute she comes round, please, Juliet, won't you? You've been so good. I know she is

173

with you every day.'

'That's right,' said Juliet, 'every day.' And she put the phone down, and turned to her mother, who arched a painted eyebrow.

'Have you noticed?' said Juliet. 'The MG's not outside. In its parking place. It's not there at all.'

Myfanwy smiled sadly: 'Yes,' she said, 'it's one of the things I've come to talk to you about. You and Struan, that is.'

'Me and Struan?' said Juliet, bewildered. 'Struan passed his exams — he got As.'

'So I hear,' said Myfanwy.

★　★　★

'Stuart,' said Giles as they strode along the path.

'Struan,' said Struan.

'Struan,' said Giles, 'you've a fair amount of experience of these cases, haven't you? Strokes, and so forth?'

'Well,' said Struan, 'I used to work in a Home.'

'Right,' said Giles, 'and I thought your analogy about the tortoise was — well, most informative, another perspective. But the plain fact is some things have come up and I wondered, what I wanted to know was . . . '

'Yes?' said Struan, stopping the chair. Giles looked down at Phillip, who seemed to be asleep, and looked up at Struan, chewing his lower lip with his brown upper teeth.

'Has he, well, blinked or anything? Recently?'

'Is there a special reason to ask?' said Struan.

'The fact is,' Giles burst out, scarlet, 'the fact is, yesterday, I had six different calls about the trust, Juliet's trust, money being used for this and that and cash. Quite a generous amount of rage and self-righteousness slopping about to be honest. It's not as if Phil cared about educating his daughter — only started that trust to avoid tax. And it's not a lot of cash, in the grand sum of things. And then, this morning, dawn, in fact, a fax. Asking me to hand over the rights to some of Phillip's stuff. Much bigger deal. His copyrights, don't you know.' Giles started to wriggle out of his crumpled jacket.

'Here,' said Struan, indicating the jacket, 'I could hang that on the back of the chair for you.' Giles looked more than ever like Billy Bunter in his shirt sleeves.

'The problem,' said Giles, 'is that this really *is* a great deal of money. The copyrights. Especially potentially, in the future, a huge deal of money. And the manuscripts. It is surprising what these American institutions will pay.' Giles got out a large handkerchief and wiped his face. 'It is really astonishing, in fact.'

'How do you mean hand over?' said Struan. 'Do you mean, like a different agent?' He started pushing the chair again and Giles followed, sweating.

'I was going to push off anyway,' said Giles, 'from the agent bit. Retire, don't you know. But I'm in the will, you see. I'm Phil's executor. I administer the trust. I can't retire from that.'

'Do you mean,' said Struan, pushing carefully up a slope, 'that you've been asked to hand over power of attorney?' Struan knew about that stuff from his dad. He'd had to do most of it, the way it worked out, the house and insurance and that. Money frightened his gran half to death.

'That's right,' said Giles, 'power of attorney during his lifetime. To her. And a request to sell the manuscript of *The Pit*. Actually, not just the manuscript, the manuscript and Phil's working copy of the first production. Both of which are in my office safe, I took them off Phil a few years ago as security, and I would like to know how she knows that.'

'Who?' asked Struan, but Giles had the bit between his teeth.

'And what I felt,' said Giles, 'with all this moral pressure swilling about, all this rather free and easy use of blanket moral imperatives, what I felt this morning, was that I just wanted to know what Phil would think about all of it. Because, to be perfectly honest, rather than sell *The Pit*, the Phil I knew would have had his fingernails removed, one by one.'

Struan pushed on a little, considering this. 'Lord Peter Wimsey,' he said, involuntarily. He'd read all those, one wet summer in the Cuik library, when he was twelve. Lord Peter was a posh detective for English people. Giles snorted.

'Jolly good, Struan,' he said, 'jolly good idea. But we haven't got a corpse, have we?'

Giles and Struan looked down at Phillip, then up again.

'I say,' said Giles, 'the Men's Pond.'

It was. Struan hadn't meant to go there, exactly. His legs had taken him. At once, he remembered Bill, and his crazy scheme to get Phillip in the pond. He thought, with any luck, it would be too early for any such shenanigans. They just could all go in and have a wee sit down. There was hardly anyone there yet.

'The Men's Pond,' said Giles, 'is actually one of my favourite spots. Do you know, I think I might pop in? Were you going to?'

'Mr Giles,' said Struan, 'was it Mrs Prys, who was asking for the power of attorney?'

'It was,' said Giles, 'yes.'

'But,' said Struan, 'how come? She can't get control of his stuff, can she? Not now. They're divorced.'

'They're not divorced,' said Giles, peering round Struan into the gate of the pond, 'they only just got married.'

'Oh,' said Struan, 'you mean it's the new Mrs Prys, that's who's asking for power of attorney?'

'Yes,' said Giles, suddenly raising a grin as the leggy figure and smooth pate of Bill glided towards them. 'Yes, that's what I can't work out. That's who's on the warpath now. Shirin.'

★ ★ ★

Myfanwy wouldn't be drawn on her cryptic remark about Struan. And she refused to be interested in the car. She was playing hardball altogether, just sitting there, smooth and pressed in bright-blue linen, nodding occasionally, eyes fixed in the middle distance, letting Juliet say again that neither she nor Struan could drive and maybe Shirin had taken the MG to be serviced.

'Shall we look for it?' said Juliet.

177

'We shall not,' said Myfanwy putting on her reading glasses. 'We shall look at this exam certificate, Juliet.'

'But,' said Juliet, 'I know what it says. You just told me.'

'Well then,' said Myfanwy, 'we shall work out together how many pounds each one of those little Ds and Es cost us — '

'I can't do that,' said Juliet, 'I failed Maths. And anyway, you didn't pay the school fees, the whole last term of it, and you've been spending my education money on Pot Noodles.' And Myfanwy looked at her over her glasses, not surprised enough.

'Only one person could have told you about your fees,' said Myfanwy, 'paid or not paid. Or other financial arrangements. I have never involved you in such things, Juliet, on principle, do you see? I don't think children should be caught up in disputes between me and your father, or me and your father's other wives. One of the things I appreciated about Linda was that she respected that.'

'Anyway,' said Juliet, 'I don't mind going to Hampstead School.'

'I was thinking,' said her mother, 'of La Sainte Union.'

'You're joking,' said Juliet, 'I'm not going to a convent. Anyway, it's miles.'

'Not from the Finchley Road,' said Myfanwy.

'I won't be living in the Finchley Road,' said Juliet, 'I've decided. I'm going to stay here.'

Then Myfanwy tapped her ringed fingers significantly on her taut lap. She smiled a pale-pink lipsticked smile, and widened her eyes. She said, 'Juliet, we agreed six weeks ago that you could spend the summer here. The summer. Because you didn't go on holiday with your friend. Now the summer's over.'

'I like it here,' said Juliet. 'I'm better here.'

'If you had passed your exams,' said Myfanwy, 'if you were going to college, that might be different. But as it is, you're going to be a schoolgirl again, and the right place for a schoolgirl is at home.'

'But,' said Juliet, 'I need to help with Dad.'

'Those arrangements,' said Myfanwy, 'are going to change.'

'Mum,' said Juliet, 'you've got to get real. We don't get on, you and me. Do we? I mean, don't take that all the wrong way, Mum, 'cos I think in a few years we'll get on fine and I'm really proud of what you've done with, you know, interior design, but right now we don't like each other, do we? And anyway, you've got Jake to take care of, in the flat, haven't you? And Jake and me *really* don't get on.'

But Myfanwy was shaking her head with a slow menace. 'No,' she said, 'I don't have Jake. That's not the arrangement as far as I know.'

'Have you talked to him?' said Juliet.

'We'll talk when he gets back from Edinburgh,' said Myfanwy, 'but the Finchley Road is not the right place for him. He'll need something more independent. That's clear.'

'But he's not in Edinburgh!' exploded Juliet. 'You must know he's not in Edinburgh. Why are you pretending he's in Edinburgh? He's living

179

round here. He must be staying in your flat. Why are you pretending he isn't?'

'Jake is in Edinburgh with his company,' said Myfanwy. She still hadn't shouted and her accent was still English. None of her was wibbling. Juliet felt a little desperate.

'But,' said Juliet, 'I saw him last night. Jake. In Flask Walk. With Celia.' And that did go home. Myfanwy sagged, just a little, and Juliet was bracing herself to go in for the kill when Ron Fox shambled into the room, in jeans and with his bare sticking-out feet in loafers. He walked straight over to Juliet and kissed her cheek.

'Darling,' he said, 'I have to get to work. Can I grab a coffee?'

★ ★ ★

Phillip Prys was floating at last. His white hairy arms and his withered hairy legs and his sagging midsection and his ancient pink dick and its straggling pubic ornaments were all free, adrift, supported by the warm soft gloop of Hampstead Men's Pond at the poisonous dry end of the remarkable summer of 1989. His head and shoulders rested on the strong tanned breast of Struan Robertson of Cuik, who had him securely under the oxters. His agent, executor, and friend, Giles, lurked just behind with his trousers rolled up, and Bill the ex-lifeguard bobbed round his feet, just in case.

'I think he's loving it, Struan,' said Bill. 'Really. Don't look so worried. You're doing a beautiful thing.' Bill had been waiting for Struan,

180

wearing an expression he recognized: the one folk wore when they came to take his dad out for a walk in his last weeks, or as they delivered a batch of scones when he'd died. The face of those intent on doing good. Bill had brought the tubular chair. He'd brought a specially fluffy towel. Struan hadn't even tried to fight it.

Even if he had, Giles wouldn't have let him. Because, though they had not previously met, Giles and Bill got on like a house on fire. They'd been at the same party, somewhere called the Lighthouse. Giles knew Bill's lover, from cottages, he said, in the fifties. This made them both laugh, and then they chatted away about someone that Bill knew, a guy called Edmund, and about something called Terence Higgins, and Bill started brandishing the chair and towel, and Giles grew so enthusiastic that Struan worried he'd take all his clothes off, too. The nudity in the pond still bothered him a lot — it was all the floating bits, in among the pond weed.

'This could be it, Struan, you know,' he'd squeaked. 'This could be, you know, a whole breakthrough moment for Phil!' and he'd started peeling his socks off. Thankfully, he'd stopped disrobing there. He was still hopping around in the shallows, now, calling: 'All right there, Struan? Any sign of, you know, action?'

'No,' said Struan, giving Phillip a bit of a swish. He thought, if there was one good thing about MS, it was that everyone knew it was incurable. People didn't turn up with snake oil and hopes too often, let alone towels and metal chairs. Strokes, on the other hand — it seemed

Bill knew someone who painted Christmas cards with his teeth as well. They both had their expectations way too high.

'Like a baptism, hey?' called Bill to Giles: and Giles nodded, more enthusiastic than ever. Quite soon, thought Struan, in two minutes, he was going to get Mr Prys out the water, and showered and dried, and then put carefully back in the wheelchair, and then he'd wheel him back home, and get himself a Pot Noodle, and *then* he was going to give a week's notice, in writing, to Myfanwy, and then after that week he was going to go home and his gran would make him a big tea. He could ask in the Home for more work, he could travel to Edinburgh, even, he could go on the dole. It might not be too late to go up to Aberdeen. He gave Phillip a last, gentle, twirl through the water:

'Is that good for you, Mr Prys?' he said.

'Struan,' said Bill, 'look.' Struan followed the direction of Bill's gaze. Phillip's little finger on his left hand, like a tiny shark, was parting the water and sinking again, an unmistakable signal. Duty opened its vast tentacles for Struan Robertson: a giant squid.

'Oh,' said Struan, 'oh aye. You see. The wee finger. Like I said. I was wondering about that.'

⋆   ⋆   ⋆

Juliet Prys took a breath and said to her mother, on the subject of the unshaven short man unexpectedly in the parlour wearing loafers on his bare feet: 'What are you going to do about

182

that, then? Aren't you pleased? How many times have you told me about when you were sixteen and playing Polly Prostitute in *Milkweed?* Huh? You haven't got a leg to bloody stand on, so don't try, you'll fall over.'

And Myfanwy said, 'Coffee? Mr? What is your name? Coffee, Juliet, darling? Let's all have one!'

'Anyway,' muttered Juliet, 'we only frotted.'

★　★　★

What Phillip would really have liked to have conveyed to Giles — who seemed all at once so interested, who was suddenly filling the tarnished circle of his vision with his round red face, whose name he could now clearly remember, together with the word 'Soho' — was the weight of the meniscus. Because that was what was actually wrong with Phillip, it had come to him in the pond. Phillip was at all times trapped under a foot of transparent liquid, a liquid which was a good deal heavier than water — something like mercury. The weight had most of his body pinned down, naturally enough, but — this was the great discovery of the pond, and he could repeat it here on the bank, it seemed, though it was harder — if he thought very hard about raising something, something like a tent, say, something also happened in the region of his hand, and Giles and the team were able to see it. It was a much better mechanism than the eyelid thing, because those weights and chains were rusted up, it was entirely hit or miss if they worked.

Giles, of course, was getting all Boy Scout

183

about it, wanted him to signal 'yes' or 'no', one lift for 'yes' and two for 'no'. And Phillip was resolved to help him out, limited though the exercise was, since it was good to see Giles, dear old chap, they went way back.

★   ★   ★

In the kitchen, Myfanwy said, 'Goodness! What a mess! All these teenagers with Pot Noodles,' and smiled at Ron and started grinding the beans in the little yellow gadget, asking Ron about his job, and saying super, how super, until really, you'd have thought she was nice.

Ron was ghastly too, he said, mmm, mmm, about the coffee beans, and their smell, and what a gorgeous kitchen, he did like crockery mismatched, and chairs, and Myfanwy said how she had bought the table at Portobello market when Portobello really was Portobello, and Ron said he knew exactly what she meant, and Juliet knew, looking at him, that he was at least eight years older than her. Juliet couldn't think of a thing to say. The sweat went drip drip into the armpits of the stained pink dress in which she looked thin from the side.

Myfanwy warmed the milk in a little pan and filled the cafetière and everyone had a coffee and Ron Fox raised the cup to his lips — Juliet hoped he had washed his hand — and said:

'And a beautifully mismatched family, too. To go with the chairs!'

'What do you mean?' said Myfanwy, slightly prim, of a sudden.

184

'Just,' said Ron gesturing at the crockery, 'that it's a beautiful thing to see the post-nuclear family in action. Here you are, your marriage with Phillip Prys at an end — a famous marriage, a wild beauty and a genius — but you don't invest in those years, oh no. You move on. Here you are, still in his life and his children's life in this beautiful way, and Jake and Juliet living in a fluid way, his house, your house — who cares? Just fluid, you know? And room for strangers along the way. Young Struan. Me. It's been sort of a dream of mine, to find real Bohemia? And here it is.' He lifted his coffee cup. 'Cheers!' Myfanwy said:

'Jake? What do you mean, Jake?' And Juliet said:

'I failed all my GCSEs, Ron, that's why she's here. She's not usually here.'

'Except RE,' said Myfanwy.

'And she doesn't know Jake's in London,' added Juliet, 'she thinks he's in Edinburgh. But he was in the pub with us last night, wasn't he, Ron?'

'I don't need to monitor my grown-up son,' said Myfanwy, smiling. 'Do I, Ron?'

Ron waved his cup.

'Of course not!' he said. 'You're so calm! Juliet, I'm in love with your mother! I'm in love with this house.'

'She's not calm,' said Juliet, 'she's threatening me with the fucking convent.'

'That's a suggestion,' said Myfanwy. 'Juliet has all Ds and Es at GCSE, Ron, you see. It is disappointing.'

185

'She should resit,' said Ron. 'She's obviously very intelligent. I've seen lives turned round with an extra year, Myfanwy, just turned round.'

'Well, I'm not going back to school,' said Juliet, 'I'm going to go on Enterprise Allowance, I just decided. I'm going to have this business where I'm going to shop for people. What I'm going to do is, I'll get the person's size, busy people who don't have time to shop, and I'll go to Selfridges and choose them ten outfits, then I'll take them round, and they can decide what fits and what doesn't and then I'll take the other outfits back.'

'Don't,' said Myfanwy, 'be completely stupid.'

'No,' said Juliet, 'and what I'm going to do is specialize in people who think they're fat, when they're not. I'm going to get clothes like jackets and stuff that really suit them, but they'd never have tried them on because they think they're fat, so they'll be really pleased when they can wear them.' Ron said:

'Juliet, don't turn your back on literature yet. There are so many books I'd love to show you.' Myfanwy said:

'And where do you think you might stay while you start up this business? Because I have to warn you, Juliet, that Yewtree Row may not be available.'

'Bloody hell,' said Juliet, 'enough of the portentous remarks. What are you planning to do to Yewtree, Mum? Bomb it?'

★　★　★

'Mr Prys is going to get tired,' said Strewn, at the edge of Phillip's hearing. 'Don't go on too much, OK?'

'Right,' said Giles.

'And,' said Struan, 'I'm really confident he's only got vision in the one side. Look — just stick your head round there, on the left — '

Giles' head came back into focus, in a grubby halo of sky. 'Hello, old chap,' he said, 'I've just got one question, really. Your rights, you know? Are you happy to have Shirin take power of attorney? To, you know, make sales and so forth? One lift for yes, two for no.' Shirin. Shirin going forth to the sales. Phillip thought of her that morning, or had it been yesterday — recently at any rate — turning her ankle for him, saying, 'Look, Phillip, these shoes, from the sales.' Little golden shoes, like a divine tiny slave girl. Clearly, Shirin should go to the sales, as many as she liked. Laboriously, Phillip visualized lifting his hand. No go, so he tried the image of the tent again — the damp canvas one he'd used on National Service. Up it heaved on the poles, and up went his finger. Splendid.

'There,' said another voice — this one, strangely, seeming to come from the Colonies, probably from the World Service — 'that's a yes.' Giles mumbled something Phillip couldn't hear. 'Just give us your opinion, Phil,' added the Antipodean announcer — it would help if they turned the radio off, World Service or no World Service. 'Being specific here. Can Shirin Zelda Pitt?' Extraordinary question. Zelda Pitt, star of vaudeville, was dead, everyone knew that. One turn too many on the vaudeville stage. Shirin didn't do vaudeville, certainly not in Australia.

'Are you happy for her to be in charge?' urged Giles. Phillip was clearly going to have to come up with an answer, or Giles would never go away. What he wanted was for Shirin to go shopping, and to come back covered in bags, little coloured carrier bags with bright string handles, and then for her to put on the outfits, one by one, before him in the Vaseline'd camera of his gaze, so he could remember her for ever.

'Mr Prys,' said Strewn, in his ear, Scottish and dour, 'are you happy for Mrs Prys, for Shirin, to go ahead and make that sale?'

And one last time, Phillip raised the damp tent of his National Service experience, and this time got inside it, stretched the khaki cover out on the army cot, and went to sleep.

★ ★ ★

Myfanwy raised a painted eyebrow. 'These are hard economic times, Juliet,' she said. 'We have to think practically. The arrangement at Yewtree is coming to the end of its practical life.'

'I am,' said Juliet, 'thinking practically. I can go on Enterprise Allowance. It's a really good idea. Loads of people think they're fat and don't even dare go into shops, you'd be surprised.' Myfanwy said:

'And in this scenario you'd be living with your boyfriend here, would you? Do you have a squat, Ron?' And Ron said:

'Steady on.' And Myfanwy said:

188

'I was living with my lover at sixteen, I'm not opposed.'

'She said she was eighteen at first,' said Ron.

'I'm just pointing out,' said Myfanwy, 'that I can't give financial support. And nor can Juliet's father. So it would have to be you.' And Ron said:

'Anyway, we only frotted.'

★　★　★

'Well,' said Bill, 'I think that's conclusive.'

'I'd never have believed it,' said Giles. 'Never. Phillip was tight as a virgin's arse all his days. Especially about rights.' Struan said:

'Sometimes when stroke patients come round, they're no the same at all. Sometimes they're terrible, to be honest. I've known nice douce wee men do nothing but swear their heads off — '

'And Phillip Prys has become a generous old dotard,' said Giles. 'Well, I'm blessed. I really think I am.'

'This is really something, though, Struan,' said Bill, 'this is a huge, huge breakthrough. You'll have to tell that consultant, Struan.'

'Aye,' said Struan, wretchedly, remembering Shirin, 'but that'll be down to Mrs Prys, no me.'

'That's right,' said Giles, 'we'll have to tell Shirin. Have to tell Myfanwy too, can't imagine she'll be delighted actually. She can hardly stick him in a nursing home now. Fortunes of therapy he'll have to have.'

'Coffee?' said Bill, getting out a flask.

'In which case, Shirin probably should sell

The Pit,' said Giles. 'Keep him at home, get him on a programme. Probably what she's thinking of. Probably saw this coming. Thinking of Phillip all along. You're right, Struan, I was playing Lord Peter Wimsey. Wise young chap you are.'

'It's all good,' said Bill.

'All good,' said Giles, grinning at Bill.

'I brought some panettone,' said Bill, and Giles took a big piece. Bill raised his coffee mug.

'Well, I'd just like to say,' said Bill, 'that this was a beautiful thing for me. This is a man healed we've seen here today. A man revived. An incredible thing to witness. And I'd like to raise a mug to Struan, here, to thank him.'

'Hear, hear!' said Giles and raised a coffee to Struan, who was stooped over the wheelchair, adjusting the wraps, the muscles of his stomach and arms showing in the gesture like the famous Greek statue of the discus thrower. Two months in the sun had expanded and joined Struan's freckles into a creditable golden tan and bleached his hair to something like brass.

'Me?' said Struan. 'I havenae done anything.'

'You're right,' said Giles to Bill. 'He is a beautiful young man.'

★ ★ ★

Then Juliet summoned herself. She said:

'Look, all I've done is fail my exams and had a snog. I've not, you know, dropped off the cliff of existing as a person. I don't want to move back with you, Mum, cos I think I'd go mad. And I don't want to go back to school. I'd be better

190

getting a job, I honestly think so. And I don't want to move in with Ron, either. I just want a boyfriend. You know. Someone who likes me and likes me rabbiting on and doesn't mind how fat I am.'

'Well,' said Ron Fox, 'I could have a go at that.'

And he turned Juliet's face to his, and smiled with his shiny eyes, and she got funny squelching embarrassed heaving feelings inside as she gazed at him and remembered about the knickers.

And Myfanwy flinched, twitched, and everything might have been very different had they not, at that very moment, heard the creak and drag of the wheelchair, reentering the house.

'Well,' said Myfanwy, 'we'll see. But first, we have to talk to Struan.'

18

Struan was on his own. Giles had pushed off. Those were his very words. He said, 'Struan, I'm going to push off now. Can't tell you how relieved I feel about you know, all that.'

'But,' said Struan (Shirin, Myfanwy, Back-up, Help), and Giles had merely waved.

'A most serendipitous morning,' he said, 'especially the dip. Very serene. I'll be in touch, Struan, very soon — take care of the tortoise.' And then he'd dashed off. Ran, in fact, to catch up with Bill, and off they went down the street, loping shiny-headed Bill, teddy bear Giles. They were suited, Struan could see that — Giles always looking for consolation, Bill to console — but it seemed miles home, and heaving the wheelchair up the ramp was no joke, solo. He was sad and bruised before he even entered the kitchen, and spotted its inhabitants, seated round the table for all the world like the three woebegone gnomes who lived in the garden two doors up from his gran, forever dining off an all-too-convincing toadstool.

'Been shopping, Struan?' said Myfanwy.

'Hello, Struan,' said Juliet, who was still wearing the wee pink dress, a bit mucky now, 'I've failed all my GCSEs but I don't want to go to the convent. I thought I might not go back to school at all. What do you think? Ron came in for a coffee. You remember Ron. Ron taught

192

Struan English, Mum, at school. You didn't see Celia out there, did you? Her mother's been calling. Shall I make you a coffee?'

Mr Fox said: 'Struan! You're back! We looked for you. How're you feeling? Quite a night, eh? Did you know you have a bit of a black eye coming up? Just a bit of bruising?'

Myfanwy said, 'No coffee, Juliet. Please don't sit down, Struan.'

'You what?' said Juliet. 'Don't be stupid, Mum.'

'Why don't you want me to sit down?' said Struan. And something about the way he said it made them all shut up. He loomed above them: his head up with the rosemary and colanders, nearly scraping the pink, beamed ceiling.

Myfanwy stood up too. She cleared her throat. She took a sip of coffee and put the cup down. She said: 'I'll get straight to the point, Struan.'

And she made her points, one by one. How it worked was: her words rolled out of her mouth and expanded and flattened and filled the bright kitchen with cold, and the Points stuck into her words and held them down.

Point 1, the MG. The car. Struan, said Myfanwy, had been driving the MG. Mr Riley had seen him in it the previous night, late, driving through Cricklewood, where Mr Riley lived. Mr Riley had thought he had seen him in it there before then, but hadn't got the registration number for sure. Last night, though —

(Struan, blindsided, groping: You're saying I was driving the car?

Juliet: Struan doesn't drive, Mum.

193

Struan: Aye, I do.

Myfanwy: When did you get in last night, Struan?

Struan: Four in the morning. And this is a tower of shite.)

Point 2. The cash (£160). Myfanwy had left an envelope of cash in the study desk the previous lunchtime for Mr Riley. It contained cash (£160 in £10 notes) for materials Mr Riley had agreed to collect from a wholesaler's in Cricklewood the next morning. But when Mr Riley went to collect it at five o'clock, it was gone. He then recalled that at three o'clock in the afternoon he had seen, through the window, Struan Robertson rummaging in the desk, and that when Mr Riley entered the room, Struan Robertson had acted funny.

(Struan: Acted funny?

Myfanwy: You had written words on a notebook.

Juliet: But we went to the pub. Yesterday. We went to the pub, Struan was there.

Myfanwy: In the afternoon?

Juliet: I was out shopping.

Struan: Oh, aye. Those words.

Myfanwy: Exactly.)

Point 3: The Bank. And then, at four in the afternoon, Mr Riley had seen Struan Robertson in the bank.

(Ron Fox: That really isn't the Struan I know.

Struan: Aye, I was in the bank. Uh huh.

Myfanwy: Were you his teacher? Didn't you write his reference?)

The bank was significant because, over the last

194

week, there had been several large withdrawals in cash from Juliet's educational trust.

(Juliet, outraged: That's you though. You did that, Mum. Shirin told me.

Myfanwy: I removed some reasonable living expenses for you, Juliet. Shopping. And some expenses for Mr Riley. Quite reasonable when you are living in Yewtree, and all agreed with Giles. I did not write out three large cheques to cash and forge his signature.

Struan: You're saying I did?)

Point 4: £1,246.

That was the total amount of cash that had been withdrawn from the trust using the cheques.

And those were the Points. When they were all stabbed in, and vibrating in their targets like spears, Myfanwy looked up at Struan Robertson, tall and grey with the tendons of his jaw showing suddenly. 'Of course,' said Myfanwy, 'I hate to make accusations. We have all been so open with you Struan, so trusting. But the cheque seems conclusive. Besides — who else would have the opportunity?'

'Your boy would,' said Struan, 'Jake Prys, that's who.'

Myfanwy smiled: 'Jake hasn't been anywhere near the house for months,' she said.

'He has so,' said Struan.

'Which is very, very painful for me,' trilled Myfanwy.

'He comes by at night. I've met him,' said Struan.

'And I am sure, very, very painful for him,' added Myfanwy.

'It's him that gave me this shiner and all,' said Struan, 'he's a wee shite, if you want my honest opinion.'

Myfanwy stepped back. Juliet squeaked: 'Jake was at the pub last night last night, Mum, I told you.'

'You're sacked,' said Myfanwy, to Struan.

'That's not for you to say,' said Struan, turning on his heel and marching to the sink, 'but as it happens, I was going to hand in my notice anyway. You're saving me the bother.'

'It's not as easy as that,' said Myfanwy. 'We will be needing that money back.'

'Well you won't get it here,' said Struan, turning on the tap, and testing the water with his finger for temperature, 'because I didn't take it.'

'We'll get the police,' said Myfanwy.

'Fine,' said Struan, filling a glass, and turning to face them, 'you do that. I'll repeat what I've said. Jake and all. Fucking druggie, if you ask me. See his eyes? Meantime, I'm giving you all notice. I'm away. I'll get the night bus this evening.' And he drank the glass of water without pausing, poured a fresh one, and went up the stairs, carrying it.

'You,' said Juliet to Myfanwy, wiping her eyes with her skirt, 'are a stupid cow.'

'I really can vouch for his character, Mrs Prys,' said Ron Fox.

'I'll have the law on you,' said Myfanwy, to Ron. 'She's underage.'

'Don't,' said Juliet, 'listen to her. I'm sixteen.'

And Ron Fox got something out of his wallet. 'My card,' he said, and gave one to Myfanwy, and one to Juliet. 'Call me,' he murmured to Juliet, stroking her cheek, 'I love sixteen.' Then he left.

'And you,' said Myfanwy to Juliet, 'you can go upstairs and start packing.'

'You must be joking,' said Juliet. 'I'm going to take Dad his lunch and make him comfortable for his nap.' Myfanwy stared, her eyes bulging from her head.

'Well,' said Juliet, 'someone has to, and you just fired Struan. Would you like it to be you?'

19

Struan was flat out on his bed. His skin itched from the pond water. Through the pillow, he heard the front door bang, then bang again. He wondered if he should go to the phone box and tell his gran all about it, then he thought of all the ten pees and fifties he had fed in that box because Myfanwy had told him to, his first day, and all the times Juliet had called Celia and stayed on the line an hour maybe, and the times when he had heard Shirin talking to people in wildly foreign tongues, probably abroad, and he thought fuck them, he'd just fucking give Gran a call from the phone in the hall. Then he realized he was shivering, and he wrapped the blanket round him tighter and thought about Myfanwy Prys saying those things with her pink painted mouth. He thought about his gran, hearing them. He thought about Jake Prys, lounging against the pub wall with his cig, and about Shirin, surrendering her mouth, her upreaching throat like a lily of the Amazon. And Struan put his pillow over his head and hoped to cease, there and then.

He thought no one would come for him, ever, but after a goodish time, he heard a heavy step on the stair and the door was kicked open, and 'Struan,' said Juliet, 'I brought you a sandwich.'

Struan lifted the pillow and peeped. Juliet had washed up; she was wearing her old white dress with the wee brown jacket on top of it. Her eyes were big and earnest over a tray bearing a large mug of tea and promising-looking brown object. He sat up.

'It's toasted,' said Juliet, 'the sandwich. Cheese and tomato. I peeled the tomatoes. And I gave Dad his soup and put his feet up and put a rug over him, but I did not change his nappy.'

'Should be OK,' said Struan, 'I washed him down at the Ponds.'

'Please don't leave, though,' said Juliet, 'I can't do nappies.'

'Incontinence pads. That's not my lookout,' said Struan, grabbing the sandwich. 'Do you want some of this?'

'No,' said Juliet, sitting on the end of the bed with a small sigh, 'I'm taking pills, Struan. I might as well tell you. They make me buzz around and not eat things. I've lost twenty-three pounds. Celia gave them to me, the pills, but now my hair's falling out.'

'Then stop taking them,' said Struan, gulping tea, 'for Christ's sake.'

'I can't right now,' said Juliet. 'There's too much else going on, but I will in a bit.'

Struan gobbled and chewed. 'Juliet,' he said, 'your dad, right? You know the wee finger thing? Your dad's definitely getting that back, a bit of control. He can signal, yes and no.'

'Yay,' said Juliet, flopping back against the wall, 'I knew I was right. Sucks and triple sucks to Mum.'

'Yeah,' said Struan. 'Look, you'll have to ask Giles about it, OK? Get him to fill you in with the details. He was there. Don't let them talk you out of that, when I'm gone. Not this time. Giles, talk to him. The wee finger on the left, OK? And you need to make sure your dad can see you, so you have to go right over round to the left, because his vision is restricted, I'm sure of it — '

'Could he do Morse Code?' said Juliet.

'Don't be daft,' said Struan.

'No, honestly, Struan, listen,' said Juliet, 'if we could teach him Morse Code, we could get him to say you were innocent! Dad's in the study all the time! He must have seen who took the money. I bet it was Mr Riley! Unless it was you. Was it you, Struan? I don't care even if it was, but was it you?'

'No,' said Struan, chewing. 'Was it you?'

'No,' said Juliet, 'but I might have taken it if I'd known it was there. The cash, I mean, I've never done cheque fraud but I might have had a go, it is my trust after all. Did you know the chequebook was there?'

'No,' said Struan, cheese strings hanging from his teeth, 'and I wouldn't take it anyway.'

'The cheques, then?' persisted Juliet. 'That's my money really, but if you sent it to your gran or something, you can tell me, I don't mind.'

'Uh uh,' said Struan. 'Wasnae me.'

'Why not?' said Juliet. 'I mean really, Struan, why not? I mean, I'm not sure that's even sensible. We owe you, don't we? We don't pay you nearly enough. Is it just because you're from Cuik?'

'Aye,' said Struan, 'probably.'

'And I failed my GCSEs,' said Juliet, 'I don't

seem to care very much, but maybe that's the pills. But I'm not going back to Finchley Road. I'm going to stay here, I thought I might get a job. Please, Struan, you stay too.'

'Don't be daft,' said Struan. 'How can I? Your mum just fired me.'

'She didn't really,' said Juliet. 'She didn't even hire you. That was Shirin. So Mum can't fire you. She can't do anything to you really, she just acts like she can.'

'Acting? Saying she's going to the police?' said Struan, and Juliet thought that even though Struan had been looking a lot better later, with his tan and everything, he didn't now. He had gone sort of yellow and his mouth made a mean line. He looked old. She ploughed on.

'You see, you're not used to my mum, Struan. She's a bit, you know, theatrical. I mean, she gets ideas. She gets on her high horse and sometimes she's completely wrong, and the thing to do is not to expect her to take it back, you just have to work round her. Like about going to the convent. I mean, I just won't go, and in a month or two she'll forget she even said it. She won't go to the police, because she'd have to tell them about taking money from the trust for Mr Riley, which would be really embarrassing. She was just making a noise. If you just stayed on, it would probably be OK, she probably would just never mention it again.'

'Juliet,' said Struan, 'I'm not theatrical, OK?'

'No,' said Juliet, sticking her hair in her mouth and starting to chew it, 'I can see that.'

'Look,' said Struan, 'you're my pal. My wee

201

pal, you know that. But your brother hit me. Your mother called me a thief. She said I stole the car, and I stole some cash and I stole a cheque-book, and that's no a joke, cos I didnae, OK?'

'Sorry,' said Juliet, and she put her head in her hands and actually shut up for a bit.

'I'm sorry about Jake too,' she said, after a bit. 'Did you really meet him in the house?'

'Uh huh,' said Struan.

'You should have said,' said Juliet. 'It's weird of you not to.'

'Aye,' said Struan, 'that's probably true.'

'I don't think it was Jake, though,' said Juliet, 'took the money. I mean, I haven't seen him at all. I think it was Mr Riley. Classic move, taking the cash, blaming you.'

'Mr Riley's no a cocaine addict,' said Struan.

'Point,' said Juliet. 'On the other hand, we don't know, do we? Maybe he's got two wives or something, and they keep demanding fur coats, and a son who looks like you who is really good at forging signatures.'

'Juliet,' said Struan, coldly, subsiding onto his pillow, 'this is real fucking life.'

'Sorry,' said Juliet. 'And I'm sorry about, you know, Ron. It must be a bit weird for you. I only snogged him though, honestly. I mean, so far, I've only snogged him, and frotted a bit, but I am going to see him again probably.'

'It's none of my business,' said Struan, from the pillow. Exhaustion swooped round him like jet planes.

'Look,' said Juliet, 'one thing. Wait for Shirin, OK? She's out at a gallery, selling something, she

202

told me yesterday. But when she gets back, she'll sort this out. She hired you, not Mum. She knows we need you.'

'Oh aye,' said Struan, 'I'm well aware of that. I'm very useful, I am. I'm a fucking genius bum-wiper.'

'Well you are,' said Juliet, 'you really are.'

'Thanks for the sandwich,' said Struan Robertson, and he put the empty mug on the plate, and the plate on the tray. He handed the tray to Juliet, and curled his long legs back into the bed. He gazed upwards at the Velux, nailed cleverly together by none other than Mr Riley, and the yellow sky above it. 'I'm going to have a sleep now, OK?'

'Struan,' said Juliet from the door, 'you know my exams? Do you think I'm stupid?'

Struan opened one eye. 'No,' he said, 'I think the only stupid thing you do is not think enough of yourself. Now go away.' And she went.

20

Juliet Prys agreed that she was clever, really. Juliet agreed that she did not think enough of herself. Juliet took a pill and a yoghurt, and decided to sort out the entire recent calamity.

First, she went into Shirin's room, knocking superstitiously on the door first. She lifted Shirin's dressing gown from the end of the bed. She picked up one of Shirin's snakeskin belts, coiled on the dressing table, and tried it on her own middle, on the loosest hole. She got out the card Ron Fox had given her, and pulled the phone off Shirin's dressing table. She looked at herself in Shirin's mirror: a small slim girl in a brown jacket, about to call her boyfriend, Ron, on the phone. She got the answering machine, but it was good to know the number was real, even if she couldn't help remembering his short bouncy walk, and the littleness of his feet in his loafers.

On the dressing table was Shirin's house address book. Juliet started work. Under 'E', she found 'Emergency nurses, turn up on spec, cost £££s,' and called them, and engaged someone to call round and clean and change Mr Prys asap, the bill to be sent to Mrs M. Prys in the Finchley Road. Then she called Shirin's gallery (under G) and got a posh girl and said, 'I'm sorry to interrupt, but there's a domestic emergency'; got Shirin, explained the whole thing, maybe a bit fast, and Shirin said for heaven's sake, and not to let Struan leave, and to give her a couple of hours.

Juliet wriggled round on the bed till she could see herself in the mirror again, firm and competent with a phone, and then she called Celia's house and let her mother rabbit on about how Celia was still missing. 'You should call the police,' said the new Juliet, and Celia's mum breathed in sharply, and said, really, did she think so? Juliet said yes, to be honest I've hardly seen her for weeks, she has a much older lover don't you know? And after Celia's mum had dashed off in a panic, she made a winsome face at herself in the mirror and pulled at a bit of her fringe and some of it came out. She thought, honestly, she should stop the pills, and then the nurse rang at the door downstairs, and Juliet let her in and then went into the front room, and put on her Jane Fonda while the nappy stuff happened, she had to do something with the twitchiness.

★ ★ ★

Struan had been had dropped from a great height onto a moor of Scottish heather. He was flat out and it was a great relief to be alive, but all his limbs were paralysed. Golden eagles whirled overhead, with intent.

'Struan,' said Shirin's voice from hundreds of feet below him, and he tried to raise his head, but the blow was too recent, and the bonds of the parachute too tight. A fold of silk touched his cheek —

'Struan,' said Shirin again, and Struan yelled and sat bolt upright, clutching the blanket to his chest. She was actually sitting, tiny and composed, wearing a pair of white shorts and tightly belted blouse, on the end of his bed. 'Heavens,' said Shirin, 'sorry to startle you.' Struan's tongue was thick as a sausage.

'It's OK,' he muttered.

'Struan,' said Shirin, 'Juliet explained. But you mustn't think of leaving. It is me who employs you, Struan, and I do not wish to dismiss you. I have said so to Myfanwy.'

'How no?' said Struan. He looked at Shirin's lovely dark head, neat as a bird's, and remembered it in Jake Prys' hand. Close to, you could see the olive pores of her golden legs. She smelled of new pencils, and she was talking on about Myfanwy, how it was all bluster and theatre and nonsense, at the bottom of it, a business venture of hers gone sour, and slackness on Giles' part, hardly Struan's responsibility, and Struan ran his tongue round his dry mouth, and said nothing, even when she stopped, and stared straight at him, and smiled, carefully.

'I said to Myfanwy,' she said, 'that there was a mistake. I said I'd cashed some cheques and used the cash to buy some necessities for the house, just as she did.'

'You took the money?' said Struan. 'The cheques and the cash?'

'I said so,' said Shirin, with a small laugh. 'She does not believe me of course, but she cannot say so. Really, this is none of her business in the first place. She does not employ you. And for the

206

cheques, she is in a bad problem herself, she has used that account for too many things to argue with me.'

'You mean you didn't take the money?' said Struan.

Shirin sighed. She pushed herself back, wrapped her knees in her arms. Her feet were bare on his sheet. She said, 'Struan, we all take things.'

'No,' said Struan, 'not me. I dinnae.'

'Me, I do,' said Shirin. She curled round in the bed, leaning on the bulk of Struan's blanketed knees. He held them stiff as he could.

'What did you take?' he asked.

'My grandmother's jewels, for example,' said Shirin.

'Aye, no, she'd have wanted you to have them,' said Struan.

'Not at all,' said Shirin — 'no, not in the least. My grandmother's jewels — you are imagining a brooch, something like that, Struan?' Struan was imagining his gran's good pin, actually, on her tweed coat, at the funeral.

'I am talking about a cache,' said Shirin, her head propped on her hand, 'it was the collection of my great-grandmother. Several quite good pieces, actually. French-made, mostly, two Russian, all pre-war. Just one big necklace — the rest, small pieces. Perfect, you see. This is a path out of the country.'

'Bribes?' said Struan, thickly.

'Exactly. They are perfect — we give one piece here, one piece there.'

'Was it your dad's mum, your gran?' asked Struan.

'My mother's mother,' said Shirin. 'My father was in England already. That was the problem. We used all our money, our families' money, to effect this. Now me, and my two sisters, my mother, we were still in Tehran. We needed to leave.'

'Would she no help you, your gran?' asked Struan, interested despite himself.

'No,' said Shirin. 'No. She told us she had nothing, it was all gone, spent. She wanted everything for her son, you see. My uncle. My mother's brother.'

'That's always the way,' said Struan. 'Sons.'

'The youngest son, too,' said Shirin. 'He was no good, but of course, my grandmother did not see that. I knew her hiding place, from when I was a child — under her bed, the floorboard lifted. A perfect little vault. And so there we were, in Tehran, waiting and waiting, and then one night, we went one night for dinner there, at grandmother's, and I excused myself, and found the vault and I put the jewels under my long coat. And then we left. I took my mother and my sisters, I said now is the time, and we went straight from my grandmother's house to Paris. Then here.'

'Were you the oldest sister?' asked Struan.

'I am the middle one,' said Shirin. 'The oldest one is good, the younger one is dead, the youngest of all is a child. So I am the one who says what to do.'

'And — what happened to your gran?' asked Struan. 'In the end?'

'She died,' said Shirin, meeting his eye, and

208

nodding, 'soon after that. Her son, you see, the one she loved? He went to prison.'

'Did you hate her?' breathed Struan.

'No,' said Shirin, 'I loved her. But we were four who were young and she was one who was old. And she lied to me too, about the jewels.' Struan looked at the gold chain lapping Shirin's neck, and then into his mind came Jake Prys' arms, with a bracelet on the wrist, and the cuffs of his shirt tucked up. And he thought what Shirin was saying, telling this story, and he thought about Myfanwy, in the kitchen, and said, coldly:

'I still didn't take the money, if that's what you mean.' Shirin stood up. She was very angry, Struan could tell.

'Very well,' she said, 'you play it that way. You didn't take the money. I'm happy with that. We are talking about a few hundred pounds to which in my view you are entitled, or which you could work off if you prefer. But not if you didn't take it.'

'I'm no staying here,' said Struan, 'I'm getting the bus.'

'Oh please,' said Shirin, 'please. Don't be a prig.'

'Come on,' said Struan, 'can we not have the truth?'

'What truth,' said Shirin, 'do you have in mind?'

'He took it,' said Struan, 'I keep saying it but you're the only one who knows it's true. I didnae take the money. Your man took it. Jake Prys.' Shirin grasped the door handle and grimaced.

She turned slowly to Struan on the bed.

'Of course,' she said, 'yes, yes I'm sure he did! Jake! That must be the answer,' and she laughed, so prettily, her jaw wide as a cat's, and went out and shut the door.

21

Juliet the ingenious, Juliet the speedy doer of good deeds, finished her high kicks and went into the sitting room. In the bottom of the china cupboard were the games they never played, bought by Myfanwy when Portobello was still Portobello. Ivory spillikins, glass mah-jong, Scrabble with a mahogany turntable. The Scrabble was what she was after. Her idea was, she could use Dad's hand signals to produce a coded message which would prove that Mr Riley or, even better, Jake, took the cash and the chequebook, thereby getting Struan to stay and her mother staked out in one elegant move. And Celia, too, because Juliet was more than ever positive that Jake was the midnight bone-jumper, and it was about time she realized who she had hooked herself up with.

But when she went into the study, her dad was laid out and clean from the nurse but wearing all the wrong clothes, stuff grabbed from the laundry that was easy to do up: Struan's T-shirt; terrible, unzipped trousers; he looked like the guys she and Jake made for bonfire nights, from Phillip's old clothes, the guy of himself. He opened one eye, looked at her, and closed it. Juliet thought: she had been afraid of her father, all her life, and now she wasn't. Now she was just sorry.

The sun was in the wrong place: in his eyes.

Juliet drew the blinds and pulled the little telly into position, switched it on for the two o'clock from Kempton. The telly did its old-fashioned warming-up thing, and Juliet took her father's hand. 'Shall we watch the racing, then, Dad?' she said, and his little finger moved, yes. 'Oh,' said Juliet, and the telly came on and the horses crashed from the gates with those terrible ankle-bashing noises they always made, and Juliet thought about her failed GCSEs and the sports day when she was six, and remembered that her dad didn't care, never had cared at all, whether she won the races, only if Jake did, and thought that maybe there was a good side to that, just a small one. Juliet swung her father's hand.

'Hello, Dad,' she said, 'whoever you are.'

★ ★ ★

This was what Struan was discovering about rage and injustice:

Even more than love, it hurt the heart. All his ribs felt bruised, as if he had recently had an operation, the kind where your ribs were raised like a car bonnet.

That, no doubt as a consequence, his circulation was drastically affected. Even though the horrible English heat was turned up high as ever again, even though the sun persisted in beaming down in a shade of foolish, cloudless, celluloid gold, Struan's feet and hands felt thin and chilly. When he looked in the mirror, he could see Scottish Struan back under the English

212

tan — pinched and grey with the freckles standing out.

That it was both flattening and motivating: rather like the Pimm's. If you allowed yourself to lie back and think about, for example, beautiful deceitful heartbreaking foreigners, and if perhaps you were a little prig, then it was pole-axing, like having an iceberg on top of you. But if you focused on your enemies, the agents of your injustice, if for example you thought about the fat Welsh woman who had falsely accused you, or her evil, insinuating seducer of a son, if you focused solidly on them and not at all on beautiful dubious Iranians stabbing into your moral universe with their disturbing stories of jewels and theft and desperation: then it was grand. Then, you could sit up, and warm fists of rage would surge through you. Then, you'd be down in the kitchen eating Pot Noodles before you knew it.

All the Pot Noodles, actually: five packets. And no intention of clearing up. By focusing on Myfanwy, Struan managed not to care about Phillip's suppository. The nurse could do that later. By focusing on Jake, Struan managed to put his feet on the table and read the *Daily Mail* till ten past six. Only the crust of the toasted sandwich, and the trace of Slimfast on the counter, got him up the stairs to the study in the end. None of it was Juliet's fault. She was his wee pal: he couldn't leave her to the commode.

But she was yak-yakking on the phone somewhere; he could hear the ends of the yaks. Her dad was asleep in the study, the telly turned to the news. He wasn't especially smelly. On the table, Juliet had set out a Scrabble set: an old-fashioned one with ivory letters and a board on a turntable. MR RILEY was spelled out on the board, but Phillip could never have done that. The board wasn't in his sightline apart from anything else and the Y was on a triple letter score. Juliet was just arsing about. Struan tipped the letters into the little green baize bag, hoping it was so, and Phillip's brown eyes opened and met his.

'Christ, Mr Prys,' said Struan, sitting down, 'I'm awful sorry. I'm awful sorry about all this.' And he took Phillip's hand, which would not be peaceful, but insisted on jerking out the fact that he was alive, like the telegraph tapping out the last messages of the *Titanic*, hours after it had gone down.

'Mr Prys,' said Struan, desperately, 'I got fired, OK? I cannae stay on after that, I just cannae. You'll be OK, you'll see.' And then the doorbell rang: the nurse. Struan rushed into the hall, switching on lights as he went. The dusk came so early, in August, in this country.

Struan let the nurse into the study. Then he went into the front room, where Juliet had stopped yakking and was curled on the sofa, and lay flat on the floor beside her.

'Struan?' said Juliet. 'If you were going to kill yourself . . . '

'I'm no going to top myself, Juliet,' said Struan. 'I'm just going home to Cuik. Christ, I'll go to Victoria and get the night bus in a minute, so I will. I'm going up to pack right now.'

'No,' said Juliet, 'not you, Celia.'

'Is that who you've been talking to?' said Struan.

'Yeah,' said Juliet, 'she's on the Heath, at the Spaniard's. You know, the pub. I rang her back on the pay phone.'

'There'll be a bill,' said Struan.

'I had to,' said Juliet, 'she's says she's going to kill herself.'

'What, with anorexia?' said Struan, sleepily. 'That'll take a while.'

'No,' said Juliet. 'In the pond. She's always had that as a back-up death plan. She's very keen on Virginia Woolf, you know.'

'Did she fail her GCSEs and all?' asked Struan.

'No. It's because of Jake,' said Juliet, and Struan sat up.

'What's he been up to?' he said, suddenly as fond of distant, uppity Celia as if she had been his own wee sister. 'Has he been upsetting her?'

'He's dumped her,' said Juliet. 'It was him who was shagging her, told you so, and now he's dumped her. Or, anyway, he was flirting with someone, but he said she was flirting, he got off with someone else in fact . . . '

'Who?' said Struan.

'Don't know. Wouldn't say — she keeps crying. Anyway, he got cross at her for nagging, he dumped her, and now she says it was all her own fault, she should let him flirt, and he only did it because she conned him into going out to meet us, he was really cross about that, but I'm telling her no, it can't be, he was going to dump her anyway, right?'

'Right,' said Struan. 'But, Juliet, if you think

215

that's true, and Celia'd really do a damage to herself, you should get on to the police, and her mum and dad.'

'That's just it,' said Juliet, 'I did. I called them, and I was really organized about it, and I told them about Jake, and Virginia Woolf, and everything.'

'Then they'll be on their way,' said Struan. 'You did the right thing. I hope they fucking lock him up.'

'But,' said Juliet, 'I've thought of something. I thought I'd done really well, but now I'm thinking, I said the wrong pond. They've gone to the Highgate Ponds. The mixed one. You know, near her house. But Celia wouldn't have gone there, not if she was at Spaniard's, it's too far. She wouldn't have gone there anyway, cos she doesn't like the changing rooms. She'd have gone to the Ladies' Pond.' Struan said:

'Do you think she'd mind about the changing rooms if she was going to top herself?' And Juliet said:

'She is nuts, you know.'

Struan stood up. 'Right then,' he said. 'We'll just go ourselves and check. It'll be as quick as phoning them. Come on, Juliet.'

Juliet took a pill from a blister pack, swallowed it, then proffered the pack to Struan:

'Go on,' she said, 'they just give you a little boost.' Struan took one, and they opened the front door.

'Look,' said Juliet, bustling across the street. 'The MG. It's back.' It was, and the cover wasn't on it, either. Struan strode over and touched the

216

bonnet: warm as an animal.

'Only just back,' he said, and he slung one leg over the door. 'Come on, Juliet, get in. This'll save us loads of time if we're going to Kenwood.' And he clambered into the driving seat and started unscrewing the ignition panel with his Swiss army knife. Juliet leaned over the other door, alarmed.

'You can't drive,' she said, accusingly.

'Aye, I can,' said Struan, still screwing. 'I got my licence on my birthday. How do you think my gran got her shopping in? Get in.'

And Juliet rolled into the passenger seat. Struan was identifying two wires, and hooking them together. 'See my gran's car?' he said, as the car growled into life. 'This is how you start her. Every time. Do up your seat belt, Juliet.'

'Was it you driving the MG in Cricklewood, then?' asked Juliet, reasonably, as Struan, one hand on the steering wheel, one relaxed on the car door, drove them, at a moderate, assured 40 mph, around the Heath.

'Nope,' said Struan, 'that wasnae me. I dinnae touch what disnae belong to me. Except in an emergency.'

'Then who was it?' said Juliet.

'It was Jake,' said Struan. 'Have you no worked it out? Mr Riley saw Jake, and cos it was this car, he thought it was me.'

Juliet looked at Struan, tanned in his singlet, his bleached hair fluffed up with pond water and sweat.

'Because you look alike!' she burst out, astonished.

'You catch on quick,' said Struan. 'Jake and me, we're exactly the same, except he's richer. Here we are.'

In the enshrouding shadows of Kenwood, Struan carefully parked the MG, then leapt out over the locked door like Starsky. It was getting dark, though it was not much past seven. The Pond, if it obeyed the rules of the Men's one, would certainly be closed.

'Juliet,' he said. 'Did Celia have a plan of how to get into the Pond to top herself or was she going to do it in daylight hours?' But Juliet was ahead of him already, talking to a couple of short-haired women with damp hair.

'Here, Struan,' she said. 'You can get in over here.'

And sure enough, there was a well-worn path through the rhododendrons, and a gap in the iron railings. Juliet squeezed through, thinking of the way Celia always hesitated at the barrier into the Tube, because she believed she would stick, and wondering if she hesitated here, too. Struan followed, hurrying, aware now of the speed in his system, surging through his fingers, constricting his lungs. He thought of Jake Prys and hoped he was in there, by the pond, somewhere where Struan could hit him. He hoped Celia *was* topping herself, he hoped she'd have to be rescued from something high or low, something big, something Struan could fling himself against with maximum velocity.

But there was nothing there: just the silvery plate of the pond, the shadow of the diving board, the fringe of trees.

'Seal?' called Juliet. 'Seal, are you here?' and they looked a long time before Struan spotted her, a thin figure in white, perched on the edge of the decking, feet in the water. 'Celia!' he called, and he ran towards her, flip-flopping along the dry smooth wood, and she turned to face him, that strange little cat face, and smiled, then slid forward into the water, and Struan jumped out of his sandals and dived in after her.

Oh, but it was dark under there, it was a heap of green velvet, it was a pit of mercury, it was black as death. His lungs were burning, and he had no idea where he was, where the deck was, and Juliet called, *Struan, Struan, here!* and he followed her voice, then her pointing hand and went down again, and this time found something white, it was Celia's dress, but it was the wrong end of it, the wrong end of her, the dress was floating round her head, and then he had to grab the rest of her which was lumpy and heavy and strange because she'd tied stones round her waist, the stupid cow, all knotted up in her jeans, brilliant, fantastically thorough fucking job, Celia, absolutely fantastic.

Struan walked out the pond with Celia on his shoulder, and shook and squeezed the water out of her, and laid her flat on her front and squeezed more water of her, and dumped her on her back and started putting air in her, Juliet squealing the while like a stuck smoke alarm.

Struan had had enough dying. He knew you stayed that way. Celia didn't know that: she was doing this whole thing for a put on, for a play, to make a point. He would have to teach her. And so Struan bore down and bore down on Celia's chest, and as there wasn't much to her ribs, he broke two of them, he heard the cracks. He didn't care, though, he pumped some more at her heart and he blew in her mouth and pumped and blew and insisted on her breathing again and sitting up and throwing up pond water and throwing up some more and yelling and fucking well joining the land of the living, whether she liked it or not.

22

It was September, and then it was October. The weather, and the news, continued mild. Ethiopia made peace with Eritrea. Norway agreed to cooperate with Russia. Hungary turned into a democracy. Apartheid began peacefully demolishing itself. In Leipzig, democracy protests were held. In Prague, seven thousand East Germans were allowed to leave for the West. In East Berlin, people began to take day trips across the West, to turn up the Western TV, to walk up to the Wall, the old monster, and give it a slap. And still, no one was shot.

Even in England, the High Court released the Guildford Four, admitting that all they had ever done to earn imprisonment was play cards and be Irish. In Hampstead, warm mornings ripened into sweaty afternoons, the sunshine was gold all day. A kindly colour, like the bright washes of early technicolour; as if London were playing itself in a movie, and needed flattering lights. But:

'I'm sick of London, actually,' said Struan Robertson to Giles, as they stood on the Heath, contemplating the yellow grass and haystacks, the amiable, puffy clouds. 'I mean,' he went on, waving at the hunkered grey horizon, 'it's just money, isn't it?' They'd just been to the Pond.

'Oh, I don't know,' said Giles, blinking, thrusting his awkward paws in his linen pockets.

'There's all sorts here, you know, Struan, all sorts of people.'

'Aye,' said Struan, 'aye, that's the problem, though, isn't it? Too many folk, and nobody cares?'

'You know, Struan,' said Giles, 'when I was your age, and came to London, I worked that one out too. Nobody cares.'

'Were you not born here?' asked Struan, astonished. He had thought of Giles as essential to Hampstead, just as bings were to Cuik.

'Amsterdam, actually,' said Giles, 'my people came to England in 1939. Saw which way the wind was blowing, you see.' He paused, stuck his hands deeper in his pockets, coughed: 'Jewish family, don't you know.'

'You havnae an accent,' said Struan, astonished. In Cuik, most folk still said 'to jew down' for getting a bargain.

'Well, no,' said Giles, 'you see, they sent me to school here. Ampleforth. Just the place for a little Jewish Dutch boy. Frightfully nice monks. Books.' And he smiled at Struan, his boyish smile with the eyebrows pushed anxiously together. 'So you see,' Giles went on, 'when, after all that, university, and so on, I came to London, and worked out what you worked out, that no one cares here, no one notices, I didn't feel bad about it. Because really, do you know, for a chap like me, that was just what I needed. That was absolutely terrific.' And Giles opened his shirt-sleeved arms in an expansive gesture, as up the path and into the arc of that arm and the warmth of his great dimpling smile, loped long-legged Bill, carrying the towels.

'Struan is tired of London,' said Giles to Bill.

'Then he's tired of life,' said Bill.

'Aye,' said Struan, 'that'd be right.' And they all laughed.

Struan knew Giles and Bill quite well, now, even though they were adults. You could almost call them friends. It was because Struan still pushed along to the Pond most mornings — the one journey to which Phillip would not raise his tiny, telegraphed, moth-on-lamp-shade objections; the one way left to get him to sleep in the day — and Giles and Bill were usually there. All the long push, in fact, Struan would look forward to seeing them, tweedy and silky, waving a greeting, ready to talk to Phillip while Struan did his weights and had his swim. They'd never actually given Phillip a dip since that memorable August morning, though: he had proper, though so far ineffective, hydrotherapy these days, twice a week in a hot chlorinated pool in St John's Wood.

'Have you told him?' said Bill, grinning beatifically at Giles.

'Not yet,' said Giles.

And Bill said, 'Struan, we heard it was your birthday. We heard you're going to turn eighteen?'

'Oh no,' said Struan, 'that'd be Juliet.' The new Juliet, that was: still very much in residence in Yewtree Row. Victorious Juliet, who only allowed her mother to speak to her on the phone twice a week. Small and nearly slim and short-skirted Juliet. Juliet with the pretty, jaggedy

223

haircut with crimped bits over her nose and mad wee plaits in the top. Juliet who only took drugs at weekends, now, at events called 'raves' in the company of Struan's former English teacher, Ron Fox. (Juliet, by her own admission, would still be on speed if it was available, but it turned out that the Lovely Pills, like so much else, had come to Celia via Jake's dealer Frankie, a connection now severed. Juliet had been very bad-tempered, during cold turkey.) Juliet with the nose piercing and small tattoo. Juliet who bossily rang people up —

'That's right,' said Bill, 'Juliet. She even phoned up your gran.'

'She never did,' said Struan, blushing to his hair.

'Straight up,' said Bill. 'Your gran can't make it, but she was pleased to be asked. And then Juliet talked to Giles, and Giles talked to me, and well — all sorts of folk here feel that we owe you, so we've organized you a party.'

'Och,' said Struan, sincerely, 'no.'

'Yes,' said Giles, 'we're going to the zoo.'

'The zoo?' said Struan.

'My idea,' said Bill. 'For tea.'

'Have you been?' asked Giles.

'We can push Phil along,' said Bill.

'Or not,' said Giles.

'Celia is coming,' said Bill.

'Jeese,' said Struan.

'Now,' said Bill, 'she's such a pretty thing, Struan.'

'She's mad as a bat,' said Struan. 'Kind of girl who likes getting her ribs broken.'

224

'Struan,' said Bill, 'you rescued her from the pond. You have to let me keep my romantic dreams alive. I love being match-maker.'

'Who else have you invited?' asked Struan. 'Myfanwy?'

'We have not,' said Giles.

'OK then,' said Struan, 'thank Christ for small mercies.'

Struan had not laid eyes on Myfanwy since Gnome Morning. Myfanwy had gone to Cricklewood, where the Goodies weren't, and Mr Riley was, and Struan did not plan to visit. She'd moved into her own railway cottage, where, said Giles, she could appreciate her own wisteria and carriage lamps, and wipe her own stains off the famous oatmeal carpet, and service her own debt by renting out the flat in the Finchley Road to an obliging family from Saudi Arabia.

In the other cottage, presumably appreciating the mirror-image carriage lamps and carpet, was Jake Prys. Myfanwy had fetched him home, battered and dishevelled and on the run from Frankie, from the Notting Hill Police Station in the middle of the Carnival. They hadn't charged him with anything, though, to Struan's chagrin: not cheque fraud, which Celia attested he'd frequently committed, not Damage to the Cricklewood cottages, not Taking Without Permission for all the times he'd whizzed the MG round town, not even Possession, though, said Juliet who went to visit, he was still bug-eyed and stoned as a rabbit if you asked her. Nothing: Myfanwy had just sent him to a clinic.

'What's the matter, Struan?' asked Bill.

'Just thinking,' said Struan. Thinking about Jake, riffling through the dog-eared hand that went: Jake the car thief; Jake the fraud; Jake with cheques in the Royal Bank; Jake in the night; Jake with coke; Jake in the kitchen; Jake throwing shapes; Jake's hand in Shirin's hair at the bottom of the kitchen stair. And with that last image, always, Shirin's elegant profile, talking to the police that night, the Celia Night, when they all got home from the Royal Free. Shirin's voice, calm as the radio, saying, 'He asked for the car key, as he had before, and I gave it to him. He said he wanted to take his girlfriend out for a spin. The car wasn't stolen.' Sticking up for him. Sticking up for him. Jake in the kitchen, saying, 'fancy her much?'; saying, 'I've got a lady,' and moving his hips. But maybe Jake Prys got the car key off Shirin, and then just kissed her, in the way he had, the way he thrust his fists down on the pub table, the way he crawled through windows, the way he reached out his hand at the pub, and hit Struan Robertson, bang across the face . . .

'Struan,' said Bill, 'whatever it is, stop thinking about it. You'll give yourself wrinkles. Are you worried about the party?'

'I'm not great at parties,' said Struan. 'To be honest.'

'The zoo,' said Giles, 'is one of my very favourite places. The black-handed gibbons. The marmosets. The Twilight World of the Small Mammal. Super. Especially on a dampish day.'

'It'll be beautiful,' said Bill. 'A beautiful thing. You wait and see.' Struan nodded, and looked at Giles' kind hairy mammalian face, and Bill's

226

smiling piscine one, and nodded again and kicked the dry earth at his feet.

'Cheers anyway,' he said. 'Thanks. It's good of you.'

★ ★ ★

Sometimes Phillip thought he was dead, and sometimes he thought he was alive. Being dead was all right, being dead was quite comfortable: they had arranged for him in purgatory a simulacrum of his study, and they let him get on with his play. It was a terrific play, not the usual sort, it was about a Welsh boy, do you see, a working boy, in the Pits, and his Da, and his struggle to get free. When he wrote it, the typewriter sang, and the words came back to him in a Scottish accent, which was an effect, he thought, of being dead, but a grand effect, part of the solidarity of the working classes. The play was green and shone on the telly, for now, it was a *Play for Today* maybe, but that was just a start, Phil would get it on the stage where it belonged, it would be at the Old Vic, it would get a crit to make old Osborne green.

The trouble was, there was no sure route to being dead. Most of the time, they made him be alive. Alive was worse. Alive was bumpety-bump in the wheelchair, light in the eyes and a close-up of Struan's spots. Being alive was Giles or some other bugger talking on the radio high above his head. Salman Rushdie, still in the sodding news, and no one to move the radio down to a decent level, where you could hear it, where you could get hold of the dial and bloody adjust it. Being alive was being hungry, or being cold, or itching in some specific part of your body, for instance, between the toes, and no help for it. Being alive was hours in the study with that chill or that itch, and no one there, having a nap the fuck he was. Alive was no way to tell anyone except twitch and typing boring typing onto a fire screen, a film, a telly, a computer for fucksake and all your words were scattered as spillikins and so, God damn it, was your spelling. Being alive was them all going away and your own voice in your own head bashing on like a wasp in a jam jar.

When you were alive, you knew your latest wife's name, and that she visited you maybe twice a day, and that you were never never going to have her again because none of the bits of you worked, none of the bits you needed. When you were alive you could not read for yourself, and when they read to you they read the wrong parts. When you were alive your son did not come to visit you, not ever, not in the night, not in the day because probably he hated you for being alive. Probably, he was in league with his mother now. Going to come with her with the thing, the square, the cushion, the hillock the billow, the bloody pillow for fucksake, he was going to hold it on your head, because she'd filled his mind with poison, she'd told him his dad was standing in his way, so he was coming with the pillow and the day they came, you, Phillip Prys, would be able to do nothing about it.

When you were alive you did try to tell them.

Tell them about the pillow the billow the murder coming. You sent a lot of messages to the Scottish boy using the plectrum, the telegram, the thumb, about Jake and Myfanwy and their intentions to do you, to have you and to bury you under the hillock, smother you in a barrow, Othello you with a hanky, a headscarf, a pillow a pillow, and you hadn't been at Bletchley Park, is it? Not a gentleman, is it. A man, a man, a bloody Welshman. No Latin at his school, no Cambridge for him. And so all the messages were in the wrong code.

Being alive was the bastard. Being alive was the pits. When you were alive you just had to close your eyes and hope you'd wake up dead.

★   ★   ★

One of the reasons Giles and Bill were so blithe about Phillip, thought Struan, as he strapped him into the chair and settled the rug round him, that they were so pleased with his restored ability to communicate, was that you couldn't bring the Amstrad to the Heath. At home, this ponderous machine with its bright green script dominated Phillip's waking hours and reduced Struan's life to an endless series of tiny adjustments — of Phillip's head in front of the screen, the pillow under his neck — and hundreds of intricate crossword puzzles with surreal, baffling, luminous green answers: *My fan concusion. Jak get late. Di I stop. She wil.*

Phillip, Struan agreed with the glass-eyed consultant and a series of therapists, could no longer spell. They all smiled encouragingly about this, as if Phillip were a slightly backward child, and said it was marvellous, the progress he had made already. But they only spent an hour with him, max. They left Struan to find out how frustrating the whole game could be: this chasing of words with a broken butterfly net; this dipping in alphabet soup with a long-handled spoon. Struan, and Phillip, to be fair.

No one but these two had to go through the leaving-the-Heath rituals: the endless finding of a yes/no question — 'Ready to go home now?'; the squatting down and the checking of eyes and fingers; the waiting for an answer like a radio signal coming in from very far away. Phillip's finger-taps had a voice for Struan now: a little, tremulous high-pitched voice; like one of the old ladies in the Home; a voice like a fish hook in his softest organ, the conscience.

Giles and Bill didn't hear that. They just sat by Phillip, holding his hand, and talked away, rubbish mostly. And there was nothing, Struan thought as he bumped Phillip over the stones, shoved him along the earthy ruts, nothing he missed as much as talking rubbish. Just walking along with Juliet, chatting, the wheelchair between them blank as a pram. These days, you couldn't do that. These days, you had to watch your tongue, because he could hear you.

And these days, anyway, Juliet was hardly ever there. Juliet, extraordinary to think of, had a job. Just two days after the rescuing of Celia, one day after the jaggedy haircut, and on the very last of Frankie's Pills, Juliet had walked into the small boutique on the corner of the High Street, the one that belonged to an eccentric friend of Myfanwy's and sold odd, elaborate Japanese clothes and super-expensive scarves, and asked if they had any hours going. Their pretty assistant had gone down with the *Marchioness*, and in the general disarray, and on the grounds of being the daughter of a local celebrity, Juliet landed three days a week, with clothes allowance. Then, inspired by the time her CV had taken to type on Phillip's typewriter — actually, she'd got completely fed up with it after three versions, and had made Struan do it, clack and clack, Struan, and stop whingeing about the fibs — she had enrolled herself on a Secretarial Skills course in the college at Swiss Cottage, using the remnants of her educational trust to pay for it.

Juliet said she wasn't sure, any more, if she was going to set up her business choosing clothes for people who thought they were fat, or if she was going to be a journalist, scribbling her new shorthand in a spiral-bound notebook. Juliet thought she might swing a job on the *Ham and High*, using her father's name. She thought she might start on the property pages, and then work her way up into fashion and make-up. She thought she could write the kind of articles where people go on a lot about how fat they feel and are funny about it. There is always a market for those, she reckoned, even if no one ever did buy another house. Juliet still talked a lot, but less to Struan, more to Mr Fox, who was around so much of the time, Struan worried about him keeping his job.

Struan was pleased for her. He liked her new haircut and hard merry manner. He didn't want to go to raves with his former English teacher, anyway, listening to him go on and on about liberation and Ginsberg. He just missed Juliet, that was all.

Though — Struan braced the wheelchair round a corner — he couldn't get to grips with the way Juliet had got over the Celia episode so quickly. The way the whole event seemed simply to have cheered her up. You should be pleased too, she kept saying to Struan, you're a hero now and we all have to be nice to you and give you pay rises. Come on, smile, you've totally defeated Jake. Which he had, in a way, and he did get a wee kick out of that, there was no denying it. But he still wished, at bottom, that none of it had ever happened. He still worried, every night, that the whole thing was a put-on, that if he hadn't come rushing along the boardwalk, Celia wouldn't have jumped in the first place, that she'd have gone home and read her Virginia Woolf instead.

Juliet pooh-poohed this, but then she hadn't done the actual saving, that was the difference, maybe. Probably it didn't just pop up in her mind, the way it did in Struan's, the whole thing, pond, and dark and ribs, suddenly beside him on the Heath path, real as an opened door. Somehow, too, the experience had liberated a host of memories of Mr Nicholl, the English teacher who had a heart attack back in Cuik: the awful smell of his breath, the prickliness of his stubble, the old man's sorrowful gratitude and lost purposelessness in his wee cottage, the day his wife had asked Struan to tea. Struan wondered if this always happened if you saved people, that you had to carry a bit of them on your belt for ever, like a shrunken head.

He thought, if this was the burden that you bore for saving a life; if just a whiff of death meant you had to carry that earthy smell on your hands for ever: then he, Struan Robertson, was through with heroism. He would not, he resolved, standing at the gate of the Heath, staring out at the stream of traffic, down at Phillip's wool hat, up at the traffic again, be saving any bugger more.

23

Juliet was in the kitchen, eating. She had arranged six scoops of ice-cream in a bowl, interleaved them with digestives, squirted honey over the whole, and was cramming it in her mouth with a soup spoon.

'Don't start,' she said to Struan as he loped into the kitchen, muscular and baleful in the 501s Celia had given him as part of her on-going, tedious need to thank him for her life.

'I'm saying nothing, me,' said Struan, picking up the ice-cream tub and starting work with the scoop.

'I'm having a crisis,' said Juliet, still eating, 'I'm thinking about chucking Ron.'

'Grand,' said Struan. 'Why?'

'Because,' said Juliet, 'I'm just not sure that it's real love. The thing is, he gives me a phoney feeling all the time.'

'He gives me one of those too,' said Struan, licking the scoop, 'he always did.'

'He's actually,' said Juliet, 'always thinking about himself.'

'Och,' said Struan, suddenly sorry, remembering Ron, crushed by the third-years, 'Juliet, but he's always round here.'

'I know,' said Juliet, 'he wants to save me.'

'Well,' said Struan. 'That's nice.'

'Yes,' said Juliet, 'it is nice, and he says nice things, but the problem is, when he's being nice, he's always in there thinking how nice he's being. That's the problem. And the way he walks on the outside of his feet. That really gets to me.'

'Aye,' said Struan, 'I can see that.' He grinned at her, finishing the ice-cream in the corner of the tub. Then he moved on to the bread bin. 'You really going to dump him though, Juliet? He'll be awful upset.'

'I am going to,' said Juliet. 'Definitely. It's a question of when, really.' Struan dropped four fat slices in the toaster.

'Now,' he said. 'You can't just keep him hanging on.' Juliet picked up her bowl and licked it.

'I can,' she said, putting it down again, ice-cream on the end of her nose. 'If I want to. If I've got good reasons. I mean, I'm not going to chuck him before the zoo — did Giles and Bill tell you? We've organized you a party! I mean, that would be socially awkward for him, and he wouldn't be able to come, and he's known you longer than anyone.'

'It wouldnae bother me,' said Struan, 'and I'm the birthday boy.'

'But,' said Juliet, getting Struan's toast out of the toaster and smearing it with butter, 'I have to do it pretty soon after, or he's going to demand full sex and I'm going to run out of excuses.'

'Och, Juliet,' said Struan, at both the sentiment and the toast theft.

'Well,' said Juliet, folding the toast and stuffing it in her mouth. 'It's true. There's only so long you can fob someone off. I made him get an AIDS test already. It's just not fair. Urges, you know. But, when it comes right down to it, I just don't want him to be the one.'

'The one?' said Struan.

'Yes,' said Juliet, 'the one you love. The one you want to, you know, lose it with. It. You know?'

'Oh aye,' said Struan. 'That'd be right.' And Struan, as he so often did these days, sank down into one of his slumped, irritating glooms when he honestly didn't seem to see a foot in front of him or remember who Juliet was. Juliet tutted and moved for the fridge. Sugar Puffs would hit the spot in the present crisis, she reckoned, a large bowl.

'Juliet,' said Struan, as from the bottom of a well.

'Yup,' said Juliet, fetching the cereal from the larder.

'Do you think honesty is important?'

'Don't,' said Juliet, pouring the puffs into the bowl, 'start on me, Struan. I'm *saying* that honesty is important. *That's* why I'm thinking about dumping him.'

'No,' said Struan, 'I wasnae ticking you off, honest I wasn't. I was just saying, do you think, if you love someone, you should just say, you should tell them, even if you know for certain that they don't love you?'

'Oh,' said Juliet, pausing with her spoon, 'like a crush?'

'Aye,' said Struan.

'Well,' said Juliet, 'I think crushes are like boils, you know? I mean, if it's a small one, and it's on your bum, then you should definitely not tell anyone, and wait for it to go away, otherwise you will be totally humiliated. But when you get big, big crushes, like as big your head, right, then you should just tell, because that's like lancing the boil, right, just letting all the pus out. Because otherwise, it gets really toxic, like you know a dream deferred and a raisin in the sun? Ron is always going on about it. Frustration, basically. It's bad for you.'

'Right,' said Struan. 'Thanks. I think I'll have a wee lie down. Your dad will be up, soon enough.' And he headed off up the stairs, leaving Juliet to finish her bowl of Sugar Puffs, and wonder who it was that Struan had a crush on, and to find the only realistic candidate to be Celia, though how he could think his feelings weren't reciprocated when Celia was round once a day, flinging herself at him like a static-filled duster, she could not imagine.

And if, thought Juliet, pouring herself a second bowl of Sugar Puffs, it was Celia, then really, she was sad. Because she had Struan in her head as the only boy in the world who saw through all that, who didn't fancy girls with triangle faces and no body and no humour. Ron Fox preferred Celia, she strongly suspected. He kept making them visit her. Celia definitely needed saving, way more than Juliet, these days, and Ron loved saving people. She betted he'd have asked her out, not Juliet, if he'd just been tall enough.

★   ★   ★

Struan sat in the study by the sleeping Phillip, whirling the Scrabble board on its turntable. He'd glued the pieces on the board: the whole alphabet, a section of diphthongs, and a 'yes' and a 'no'. You could stick it in one of Shirin's easels, adjust it to Phillip's vision, and twirl it. To be honest, he still preferred it to the Amstrad.

He wondered how Phillip would wake up: sweaty and despairing and semaphoring messages with 'Jake' and 'Myfanwy' and 'die' and 'stop' in them; or in the more placid, suggestible mood when he would tap out a word or two and Struan would turn it into a quote from *The Pit and Its Men* and Phillip would signal 'Yes' over and over. They'd retyped quite a lot of the play now, in no particular order, interspersed with bits for the *Supplementary Material*, and wee snippets from the Bible that Struan happened to know.

It wasn't so bad, those bits, typing away while Phillip blinked and twitched, watching the green words up on the screen. Struan was adjusting wee bits of it as they went along, giving Angharad a few of Pip's speeches for instance. He thought he might let her go to London at the end of the play, instead of staying in the grim village of Armprys with the baby. Phillip would be quite happy with that, he thought. Phillip was happy with all of the writing stuff, you could tell, especially when Struan set the hefty hammer printer going, with its pleasing banging typewriter noise. Struan made carbon copies of everything, sat the piles of paper in Phillip's lap, under his fingers, held the inky pages under his nose for a sniff of the ink. After a good session, he would become quite malleable and sleepy, twitch Yes! Yes! Yes! to his suppository, his snack, an hour with the racing.

The only problem was: only Struan could do it. The writing bit. The therapists were hopeless: kept trying to get Phillip to study phonics, or signal diphthongs; activities which just made him close his eyes. Giles had tried to do a shift, but couldn't get to grips with the computer; Juliet lost patience; though Mr Fox had a go, once, and did pretty well, wrote most of a scene. Maybe, if Juliet didn't dump him too quickly, he might come back and do it again, because when it came down to it, Phillip didn't need a speech therapist or a physiotherapist or post-stroke specialist, he needed someone who knew *The Pit and Its Men* well enough to get an A Band One at Scottish Higher Certificate, and that meant Mr Fox, or preferably, Struan Robertson, formerly of Cuik. And the only problem with *that*, when it came right down to it, was that Struan the faithful secretary, Struan the tender nurse, was actually a snake in the grass, fast in love with Phillip's wife.

★   ★   ★

How It Was Going With Shirin: a Review by Struan Physically: much the same. He still slept badly, felt peevish, had a bad taste in his mouth, sank readily into glooms. The hole in the chest continued to ache, though strings of sinew seemed to have sprouted across it now and these contracted painfully from time to time, pulling him

239

into a stoop. Other odd symptoms: ache in the jaw, when he saw her; mouth sweats; weakness down the centre of the body, as if being unzipped; stiffness and aches in unexpected limbs, from holding oneself up when the weakness happened; obsessive compulsive midnight masturbation.

In compensation: Struan was that bit sexier, he could feel it. He was in his body, for the first time in his life, and found he liked for example being tall, and the way his muscles had hardened from all that swimming. He liked the jeans Celia had bought him, and he liked wearing Phillip's old cashmere jumpers on top, with no collar showing. Folk fancied him, now — Celia, Bill — and that was something. Just not the right folk.

As to how it was going otherwise, as in, was he getting anywhere, did she like him, well that was a comedy, wasn't it, thought Struan, whirling the Scrabble board faster and faster. *Yes, no, a, e, i, o, u.* A joke. *Th, wh, ch, ght.* A boil, as Juliet said, on the bum. But not static, that was the thing. Things kept changing, just enough to keep him on his toes, to keep him here, in the study, enslaved, typing out versions of *The Pit and Its Men* when he knew fine he should be back in Cuik with his gran.

The first two weeks after the Celia Night had been the worst. Shirin had been so correct: explaining everything to the police and making them go away; giving him a very substantial pay rise, *If, that is, you wish to stay, Struan?;* smoothing and soothing Celia's parents, getting them out the house, off his back; saying: *I don't*

240

see *that there is any reason why you should have to see Myfanwy again, Struan,* and sorting it; hauling Mr Riley in and emphatically sacking him, leaving the windows without top coats all through the house. *Distressed,* said Shirin, *I quite like the look.*

And she had said, about the car, hadn't she, straight off? Said to him on the stair, on the way up to bed, on the Celia Night: *Struan, I did not know Myfanwy accused you of taking the car. Juliet did not mention this. If I knew that, of course, I will tell her, I have given the key to Jake.* And Struan had nodded, yes, and not believed her, no, and believed her, ae, and not, oo, all night and ever since. *A, e, i, o, u.* Oh, you.

But all the time, o, all that time, e, she was so cold. All the time, u, no omelettes or tomato salad, a, no smiles over Juliet's head, e, no walks on the Heath. And in the night, every night, oo, ee, ae, crying: Struan, in the bath; Shirin, in her bedroom, you could hear her if you crouched on the landing outside, bum on the carpet, feet on the polished wood. Who was she crying for?

And she went to visit her mother a lot, and she wasn't painting so much, and she didn't take much of a turn with Phillip, any more.

Then, one middle of the dark sad night, there were crashes from the room underneath Struan, the locked museum room, and Struan went in to investigate and found Shirin there, her hands full of files. And she said: 'Come to investigate a grand larceny, Struan?' and he said, 'No,' and then, 'No,' again and she softened and said, 'I

241

need to find something to pay the rates with,' and sat on the floor like a wee bird, her small soft head, and he said: 'Can't I help?'

And after that, since then, at odd times, evenings, mornings, he'd been going up there with her and helping with those rooms, which needed clearing, she was right. And if she could sell a thing or two for Phillip's care that was the right thing to do, he had no doubts about that, any more, there was no money coming in otherwise, Giles said as much. They were going to put *Top Girls* on the A-Level syllabus, that was the rumour. Not that Struan ever mentioned the second-floor rooms to Giles, or to Juliet, even. They only went there when Juliet was out.

What they did was: Shirin picked out the sketches and pictures she said were 'good' or 'had possibilities' and Struan wrapped them and labelled them the way she said and carried them down to the dealer's van which had come once, twice, three times now. Struan had done a lot of arranging books: pulling out the ones which were first editions, or signed, putting them in boxes for Christie's. Shirin had, he was startled to realize, only a limited grasp of English on the page, for all her oral fluency. She'd never read any of the books Phillip had in such numbers, no Dickens, Dylan Thomas, Bleasdale, Hughes, and certainly no David Storey; but she listened with great attention when Struan told her what he knew, read her wee bits, even. 'There are no women here,' she said, once, and Struan said, 'There's Sylvia Plath, look, *Winter Trees*,' holding out the dry hardback. Shirin picked it up cautiously, blew dust from the compressed pages: 'Unread,' she said, 'he thinks no women could write, you know, Struan. Or paint.'

'What about you, then?' he asked.

'It was never my work he was interested in,' she said, and smiled.

Shirin knew her way round the catalogues and big Art books, though. After the best pictures were sorted, she started on the photos, hundreds of them: black and white; signed; framed; a whole world of young men in polo necks in blackened streets; girls with stiff helmet hair and hard dark lips. She started a collage of especially unlikely images of Myfanwy on the side of the filing cabinet: in Capris; in a dance studio; in her pants, flashing a neat bum. Struan contributed a studio shot: Myfanwy dimpling over folded, cashmere arms; fluffy-eyed, insouciant, quite like the new Juliet.

'She was really something, wasn't she?' he said. Shirin took the picture and stared at it with predatory attention.

'She was tremendous,' she said seriously. 'And that is sad, because look at these pictures, Struan, this is her work, being beautiful like this, and then it is over and she is not thirty.' And Struan said:

'I was thinking, I might apply for medicine, next year.' And Shirin looked at him and nodded, good idea, then squirrelled the picture away as she did sometimes, 'to work on.'

They didn't look at each other when they were working, they looked at the photos, and that meant they could talk. For instance, Shirin said:

243

'I have photos of my mum in this dress exactly.'

And Struan said, 'In Iran?' and so Shirin gave him a good lecture on the history of Iran since 1901, and Struan, abashed, went and read about it, and then he understood a bit more, a bit more what it meant to come from a Zoroastrian family in Tehran, to trace your family back to Darius the Persian, to cook rice and almonds and wear Chanel, to summer in the mountains, and visit Europe in the autumn, clever and sophisticated as all get out. But the day Shirin said, 'Look! Polo neck! There is a fashion! Do you have this, your father in a polo neck?' he was able to explain about Cuik, the town too poor to support a branch of C&A, and she listened to that, too.

It all stayed in the high locked room. It was nothing to do with the rest of their lives and was nothing to do with anyone fancying anyone or anything that had gone before. Shirin seemed to like Struan, in there, respect him, the way she had before Gnome Morning, and that warmed him. It meant he thought less about Jake, too, remembered the kiss in the kitchen only a hundred times a day; or fifty even. He'd thought up that explanation about Jake being over-familiar, being the grabby sort, and rehearsed it to himself, and believed it, yes, and not, no.

Until. No. No. a. e. Struan was blushing, whirling the board like a motor. Until the other day. Shirin and Struan had been up there at noon — Phillip asleep, Juliet out at work — and were halfway through a heap of celluloid reels and film stills which had been stored near the window, trying to pick out the damp pieces from the ones which Shirin could get checked out by the National Film Theatre, when Struan asked her: 'Did you know about all this before you met him? About Phillip? I mean, about *The Pit and Its Men*, and all that.'

And Shirin, carefully peeling apart a batch of prints, said she had never heard of it.

'So it wasnae like,' said Struan, peering at a strip of film, a series of orange and black faces with mould on them, like measles, 'it wasnae like, he was the big star and you wanted to meet him.'

'Oh,' said Shirin, putting the photos down and looking at Struan. 'You mean, why did I marry him?' Struan nodded, dumbly.

'Well,' said Shirin, staring straight ahead of her, 'as Myfanwy says, there is a passport issue.'

'But,' said Struan. 'You could have married anyone. Anyone would have married you.'

'I could have married my cousin, in fact,' she said.

'But you didn't like him?' asked Struan.

'I liked him,' said Shirin, 'but' — her voice harsh and posh, full of water — 'as Myfanwy says, Phillip is rich, and he had a house. My cousin had no house. I needed a house.'

'Where were you living?' asked Struan.

'Uncle's house in Harrow. Auntie's house in Edgware. Cousin's house in Bushey. Sharing a bed with my sister, a bed with my mother. All the way through St Martins. Eight years, in fact, ever since we left Tehran.'

'Oh,' said Struan, 'I had you in a flat, a wee studio of your own.'

245

'Everyone thinks that,' said Shirin, 'that flat. That studio. Everyone has me in there. I think it is in Chelsea.'

Struan laughed. Shirin looked straight at him with her burning gold eyes. 'Eight years, I go to college, I go to parties, I go to openings, I have the right clothes, I have a drink in my hand. Everyone thinks, I am a city girl, I am a Western girl, I am rich. But I am not such a girl. We have lost our money. I borrow the clothes, I bargain them from shops. I never sip the drink. My father is dead.' Struan nodded, not seeing, quite. Shirin said: 'My mother lost her country, she lost my sister, she lost her husband. She cannot lose me, too. She needed me to be married, not — in that studio in Chelsea. But me, I needed that studio.'

'Aye,' said Struan, 'I can understand that.'

'Phillip didn't want children,' said Shirin, holding the piece of film very tight between her clean slim fingers, 'he just wanted me to sleep with him and stay in his house. He didn't mind if I went on with my work. This is a very, very good deal for me.'

'You didn't love him?' said Struan. 'You didn't mind?' His fingernails were working painfully into his palms, thinking about the *sleeping with him* bit.

'I didn't not love him,' said Shirin. 'When I met him he was . . . I liked how he was always cheerful. He was — like Juliet.'

'Like Juliet?' said Struan.

'Yes,' said Shirin, 'that way Juliet is? So hard and bright always? Like a strong little animal? So knowing what she likes? I like this in her.'

'I like that too,' said Struan.

'I liked this in Phillip,' said Shirin. 'There was no need, you see, ever to be sorry for him. It is being sorry for people that stops me from doing my work. I needed to get on with my work.'

And Struan — thinking about Shirin's studio, the tiny picture of the wheelchair, her tiny hands as he had first seen them, holding a pencil, scratching a picture of Phillip in a few thin lines, at this point actually raised his head and gazed at her, so beautiful, the foreign lady, and she dropped her lashes and flushed and got up and said:

'Who are you? Who the hell are you to look down on me?' and left him there.

So that was shit. That was *no, no, no, ae, oo, a.* That was useless, that was stupid, *a, e, i, o,* you cunt. That was a boil on the bum, that was a boil as big as your head. He'd pushed a note under her door the next day, 'I meant no offence. SR' but she was gone already, gone to flaming Harrow, leaving him with a series of locum nurses to help with Phillip. And that was really why Struan Robertson wasn't looking forward to his upcoming eighteenth birthday, why he was filled with sulks and tears worse, to his unspeakable shame, than he'd ever turned on when his dad died, why he didn't want a party, why he didn't enjoy being a hero, why he was as glum right now, to be honest, as he'd ever been in his whole life.

24

Juliet was in the shop, on her own. Miriam, the owner, had popped out half an hour ago, leaving her to tidy the rails, listen to Miriam's Billie Holiday tapes on the shop stereo, and contemplate Miriam's crochet, elegant and silvery on the counter. It was grey outside, it was darker than it ought to be at three in the afternoon. Juliet hated the autumn, it made her want to scream. She hadn't done much to the rails; and she was just deciding between calling Ron, even though he was having a writing day and she wasn't allowed, re-plaiting her little plaits, trying on the new underwear stock, and unravelling the crochet, when Ding Dong! in slid Celia, looking slightly monstrous in a rah-rah skirt.

'Seal!' said Juliet, who hadn't seen her for a week. 'You look like a pencil stabbed in a pie. You really can't wear tights, you know, when you're as thin as that. You've been starving again, haven't you?' Celia didn't answer, just sat down in a small portion of the shop's tub armchair.

'I can't help it,' she said, 'it's my self-esteem.'

Celia hadn't gone back to school in September, owing to having two broken ribs and an inadequate body mass. She was taking a gap. (Turning into a gap, more like, ha ha, said Juliet to Struan, but she felt a bit badly, right now.) Celia was seeing her therapist in West Hampstead twice a week, going to a support group at the Royal Free, and reading Virginia Woolf between times. And Lewis Grassic Gibbon, since the Struan obsession, though Struan kept trying to say, about the Central Belt . . .

'How is your mother?' said Celia suddenly. In the chair bought to accommodate the large arses of wallet-holding, waiting men, she looked like a dress, laid down on its arm.

'Mad as a brush,' said Juliet. 'She lost that sale, you know? She was going to sell Yewtree to a rich American, it turns out, only Shirin wouldn't let her, and now, like yesterday, all his money's gone pop. The American's money. Junk bonds. I said to Mum, 'Well, think if he had paid, he'd have paid in junk bonds and then you'd be bust, and anyway, you can't just sell the house. Dad's alive and I'm living in it,' but she's desperate to get out of Cricklewood, you see, who wouldn't be? I'm almost sorry for her.' Celia nodded solemnly, clasped her leafy little hands together.

'How's Ron?' she asked.

'Last weekend,' said Juliet carefully, because she had very much implied to Celia that she and Ron were having great sex, instead of just frotting and yelling a lot, 'we went to the Camden Palais. He bought these Es, but they turned out to be rubbish.' Celia nodded again.

'How's Jake?' she said, looking carefully at her tiny wet boots, and Juliet spotted an agenda.

'Out of the clinic,' she said. 'He's joined a thing called Ersatz, now. What you have to do is, after you join, you go on a camp . . . '

'I don't think it's called Ersatz,' said Celia, not raising her eyes.

'Erstaz! Erstaz! Is that it?' said Juliet. 'Anyway, what you have to do, is contact everyone you damaged when you were drunk or a druggie or whatever . . . '

'It's called Est,' said Celia, 'he called my mum.'

'Est Est is a kind of wine,' said Juliet, 'the Pope makes it. Can't be right. Anyway. What you have to do is, apologize to the person. Make amends, it's called.'

'He was really nice,' said Celia, 'on the phone. My mum said.'

'But what he said to me was,' said Juliet, 'that he didn't really think he had injured me, it was the other way around. He's making an exception for me when it comes to apologies. And Struan. Can you believe it? Dickhead!'

Juliet looked at Celia. Her eyes were twitching like goldfish in the tiny white bowl of her head.

'Did he call you, Seal?' asked Juliet, and Ding-Dong! a lady in a long raincoat arrived in the shop. Juliet picked up a random black garment and pushed it at her friend. 'Do try it on,' she said, shoving Celia into the tiny curtained changing room. The raincoat lady picked up one of the Miyake dresses, and started pulling it against herself. So Juliet popped into the changing room, where Celia was still in her coat contemplating the trouser thing in her hands.

'Seal,' she hissed, 'if Jake does call you, you won't listen to him, will you? He is a bullshit merchant, you know that, don't you?'

'This'll be too small,' Celia said, pointing at the garment.

250

'Bollocks,' said Juliet, examining the label, 'it's a ten.'

Ding Dong! Juliet popped out the changing room again. The raincoat lady was gone. Juliet dashed to the scarf shelves, started counting the Von Estorhofs. She thought one was gone: £150. There was a whimpering noise from the changing room.

'Help, Ju,' said Celia. 'Help me, I'm stuck.' Juliet popped in. The trousers or whatever they were stuck halfway up Celia's minimal thighs.

'It's too small,' gasped Celia.

'Don't rip it,' said Juliet. 'Stay still.' And she carefully teased the black tubes down her friend's legs. 'Lift,' she said. 'One foot, then the other.' Celia's skin was so thin, you could see the veins, like her father's feet when she put on his socks. Juliet shook out the garment and appraised it.

'But I can't get it on,' said Celia, 'I've put on weight.' And honestly, the way she said it, it was as if she expected to be shot for crimes against humanity, and Juliet even felt sorry for her. She actually thought, just for a minute, that maybe being anorexic was not so much fun. She looked again at the black thing. 'Juliet,' said Celia, 'do you remember that night in the pub, with Ron and Jake? Do you think, that night, I was flirting? With Ron, I mean?'

Ron popped up in Juliet's mind, round-eyed, cheery, and on the edge of his feet, Ron following directions to raves, anxiously and solemnly, Ron buying rubbish drugs and pretending they worked; Ron talking bollocks to the wind and passing her

251

a sandwich. Juliet thought, maybe she wouldn't chuck him, after all, or not quite yet.

'Why would that matter?' she said. 'Ron wouldn't care. I wouldn't care.'

'You see?' said Celia. 'It's true. I was flirting.' And then she came to a sort of stop, and whimpered, just once. Briskly, Juliet shook out the garment.

'It's a jumpsuit,' she announced. 'It's got a wrap top, see? It's Japanese. You had your legs down the arm-holes. Try this.' She opened up the jumpsuit's waist band, and obediently Celia lowered one long bony leg in, then the other. Juliet pulled up the odd, stiff, cottony material to her friend's waist, and fastened the elaborate soft belt.

'There,' she said. 'Loads of room. You could be an eight.' Celia whimpered again. Juliet wished she could cheer her up. She said: 'Look, Seal, what about Struan? I thought you really liked him.'

'Struan doesn't like me,' said Celia, mournfully fiddling with the jumpsuit cuffs.

And Juliet said: 'Maybe he does. Struan's told me, he's got a crush.'

'Did he?' said Celia, smiling a little, sliding her arms into the puffy sleeves. Juliet adjusted the pads on her shoulders, and started the business of wrapping up the fancy ties and pulling down the weird padded bit in the front. Ding Dong, said the shop bell, and Juliet added, all the same:

'Struan said, did I think, if you loved someone, you should just tell them, even if you know they don't love you.' Celia's eyes were sheenless as

252

buttons in her remnant of face. The jumpsuit suited her a lot, with its padding and cuffed legs and wee waist.

'So it could be you, Seal,' said Juliet, 'that Struan's keen on. I mean, I don't think he knows many other girls. Come on. You look great. Let's look at you outside.' And she took her friend's cold hand, and led her out to the big mirror.

And there was Shirin, in the shop, looking at the Comme des Garçons rail. She'd just popped in on her way back from Harrow.

'Wow,' she said, 'look at Celia, straight from the catwalk.' And they all did.

'Shall I wear it to the zoo?' said Celia.

25

And so, on the day that Struan Robertson came of age, he stood under the central signpost of London Zoo with his English friends at three in the afternoon. They were waiting for Ron and Celia. Bill was explaining they should all have a wander before regrouping for tea. Phillip's ambulance was due at five.

Bill was rather in charge. He had organized the ambulance, for instance, and a taxi for Celia, and a whip-round for the picnic, and Giles had said to Struan he was sorry if it was a bit much, but Bill had recently been entirely exiled from his nearly-dead lover's flat, life, and hospital bed by his lover's long-divorced wife: he needed someone on whom to exercise his kindness. 'And he can stay with me, of course,' said Giles, 'but I'm not sick enough, you see. Not for all that.'

And now it was raining: but only off and on, rags of rain, by Cuik standards. Struan was wearing Phillip's cast-off sixties Burberry trench coat: Shirin had come up the attic stairs with it this morning. It was short with a big belt and collar and a cold silk lining. It made his shoulders enormous and his legs very long. Struan could see that it suited him, but he felt odd in it, like someone else. He had a card in the pocket from his gran, and he fingered the edge, for reassurance.

Bill had equipped himself in a hooded

cagoule, and the wheelchair with a snugly tucked cycling cape affair. He was in charge of Phillip: Struan, he said, should have the afternoon off. Giles was beside him in an ancient fishing Barbour. Shirin was tightly belted in a transparent mac, tiny transparent wellies, and a transparent dome-shaped umbrella over her head.

'I am keen,' she said, through her screen, 'to see the marmosets.'

'Twilight World of the Small Mammal,' said Giles. 'You wait, fantastic.'

'Moonlit,' said Bill. 'It says Moonlit. They're nocturnal, you see.' But Giles refused to be disappointed.

'The small mammals are,' he said, 'for ever in the warm twilight of my heart. We'll take you there, Shirin, right after the black-handed gibbons. I also adore the black-handed gibbons.'

And here at last were Mr Fox and Celia, struggling through the gate with a large box. Celia was wound in a mohair shawl; Mr Fox was already soaked in a pakamac. Bill officiously grabbed the box and stowed it under the wheelchair. Mr Fox rushed over to Juliet and kissed her warmly.

'Elephants,' he said. 'Aren't you excited?'

All this was done so that Struan would wander off with Celia. Bill had arranged it; Juliet had agreed; but now Juliet watched them go regretfully: Struan tall and handsome in the square-shouldered trench coat; Celia trotting beside him, her shawl so huge and ruched over her thin legs, she looked like a hermit crab. She could have told Struan about the crab and he would have laughed his big snorty laugh. She missed that.

Ron, she thought, eyeing his too-short pakamac, didn't like her being funny. Or maybe she just wasn't very funny when she was with him, owing to the constant pressure of the knickers-off, sex thing. Which she would have to sort out. Soon.

Ron was ahead of her, leaning on the wall surrounding the tiger's cage. Or crouching, really, his hands arched on the concrete, his head flung back. He was feeling something sensitive and he wanted Juliet to notice, as usual, and ask what it was. She decided not to.

The tiger was pacing his cage, just up and down, up and down. He did look fed up. Juliet said: 'He's got Indian ink stripes,' which he had, they were gorgeous, black and shiny as if they'd just been applied. And Ron put a wet hand through his wet hair, and looked at her with his poppy brown eyes, and shook his head; he didn't like her saying the sensitive things, either. Juliet marched him off to the elephants before he could start going on about dreams deferred and raisins in the sun.

'Do you know,' said Juliet, remembering as they walked along the concrete path, 'I think my dad used to take me here. He had this friend called Melissa, she was a theatrical agent, she put Jake on telly, and she lived just over there, in Little Venice, and she used to bring us here and get us ice-creams.'

'Your dad wrote a story about that,' said Ron, pulling up his hood. It was starting to rain in earnest: rivulets were pouring off his nose.

'Did he?' said Juliet. 'The things you know.'

'It's actually quite affecting,' said Ron, 'about, you know, a gorilla, and cages, and marriage. It was in the *New Yorker.*'

'That's right,' said Juliet, 'Guy the Gorilla. Dad liked him. He died.'

And Ron took her hand and she let him. It was occurring to her suddenly that Melissa must have been Dad's girlfriend, a long-term one, like Linda. And that she must have been serious about Dad, because she was bothering with the children, with Juliet in particular, who was no good for BBC dramas. Buying them ice-creams. And that that was probably a poor tactic with Dad, who most likely wanted to have a girlfriend to forget all about his children, or about Juliet at least, he was pleased with Jake being on the telly, so it wasn't surprising that Melissa vanished suddenly from their lives.

When they reached the Enclosure, the elephants had all retired into their doleful, composty stable. So Ron and Juliet stood meekly in the dank observation passage, watching the creatures pacing and chewing their hay, and Ron got his cold hand under Juliet's mac. And Juliet thought that Melissa and Linda and all of the others couldn't have been so much fun for Myfanwy, not really, the poor old moo. It must've been a bit like being jealous of Celia. Melissa, she was certain, had been very slim. She wore trouser suits, like Purdey in *The New Avengers*.

'Did you look at the elephants, when you were little?' Ron Fox was murmuring. 'Did you like their trunks?'

'Did you ever watch *The New Avengers?*'

asked Juliet, and wriggled away from him, forward into the stable.

'They are cute, though,' she said. 'Look at the baby one.' For one of the elephants was very small indeed, and fluffy on top, like Ron himself.

Ron grabbed Juliet's hand back, and kissed it. The little elephant caught some hay in its clever trunk, and stuffed into its flat slot mouth. Ron pulled her hand down to his pocket, tried to stuff it in. Juliet sighed. He was always doing this, always rubbing her fingers over his knobbles, and sometimes she liked it, and sometimes she didn't.

'Do you think,' she said, inching her hand away. 'Do you think Struan really does fancy Celia?'

'You have to stop thinking about Celia,' said Ron. 'You're not Celia.'

'Well then,' said Juliet, 'you have to stop thinking about my dad. I'm not my dad. I'm not Hampstead. OK?' She'd said this before. This was their row. Ron sighed and dropped her hand. Juliet shrugged, sourly, and wandered out into the rain, thinking glumly about her fat ankles under the silly wet boots. She'd thought, if someone fancied her, she'd stop worrying what she looked like, but this didn't seem to be true. She blamed Ron. There was something so general about his lust, she just couldn't take it seriously.

The little elephant plodded out of the stable and stood in the outer enclosure, trunk down. Juliet waved to it, stared at its sad little eyes. Along the covered passage, on the edge of his feet, came Ron Fox.

The little elephant looked at him, upraised its trunk, and trumpeted, an extraordinarily loud mechanical noise, like a siren. Solemnly, Ron raised his arm, and trumpeted back: but terribly well, with such uncanny similitude that you'd think he'd been imitating elephants all his days, that that was his job. All of sudden, Juliet liked him.

The little elephant stared, and trumpeted again, and from inside the elephant house echoed the calls of his parent. Juliet started to laugh. Then lumbering out of the stable came the enormous shape of an adult elephant.

'Myfanwy Prys!' trumpeted Ron. 'Please! Let me give your daughter a poking! You know she needs one!' The mother elephant leaned over the concrete wall, stamping her feet, swishing her dangerous trunk.

'Run!' called Ron, and they dashed out of the enclosure, leaned against the railings, weak with laughter. He grasped Juliet's waist, both mackintoshes crackling, and she leaned against him, a familiar yielding.

'Doctor Dolittle,' she said, and she let him kiss her.

'Look,' said Ron Fox, 'I am keen on you, Juliet. Really. You're a sexy little thing. You drive me nuts actually.' And he put his hand back up under her mac as they walked on towards the Small Mammal House, where Giles had gone.

'I don't think Struan does fancy Celia,' said Ron, suddenly. 'I don't think you're going to get a result there. Struan is not at all stupid. I'd say he has an eye for Shirin.'

And Juliet, who knew the truth when she heard it, looked at him, amazed.

★　★　★

In the aviary, Celia's pigeon claws clutched Struan's Burberry sleeve. Her wee face peeped over the shawl, peaky and pink. Raindrops settled on the cobwebs of mohair.

'Happy birthday!' she said, and she handed him a little parcel, tied with a flat silk ribbon. 'I shouldn't open it,' she said. 'It's a book. It will get wet.'

So Struan tucked the book under his coat, next to his breast.

'It's *The Waves*,' said Celia, 'a third edition. One of my favourites — have you?'

'I've read it, aye,' said Struan, 'most of it.'

'It's so,' said Celia, in her whispery voice. 'Everything. Isn't it?'

Struan remembered the copy of *The Waves* Mr Fox had lent him, sitting on his gran's table in Cuik, the wide-eyed blotchy portrait on the front, like Celia, now he came to think of it.

'I couldnae get on with it, Celia,' he said, truthfully, 'all those posh folk. They didnae seem much like the waves to me.' And, when Celia gazed up at him, mutely offended, 'But I'll give it another go, eh?'

Then they walked on, through the disappointing, low, brown-roped aviary, the barges and cyclists of the Regent's Canal within spitting distance through the damp trees and railings.

They stopped to look at an ibis, huddled at the

260

back of his enclosure. 'He doesn't like this weather,' observed Celia, in her little voice, 'he's got his shoulders hunched up. And so have you, Struan.' She tucked her hand further into his arm. 'Don't,' she murmured, 'be sad. It's your birthday.'

And Struan probably would have kissed her, then, just because it seemed unkind not to, had they not been startled by a terrific bang from the other, wooden, side of the ibis's cage, and a cry of 'Celia!'

The bird lifted its heavy wings, flew to another perch, and settled again. Celia let go of Struan's arm and ran on to the next enclosure, which had netting on both sides. 'Celia,' cried the voice. The ibis opened a weary yellow eye at Struan, and closed it again. Struan followed.

Past the pond and the trees, filmic through the layers of rope and wire, was Jake Prys, perched on a green mountain bike on the towpath of the canal. Rain poured off his glossy handsome features and heavy shoulders and hunched thighs.

'Baby,' he was saying to Celia, now clutching the netting on her side, 'I love you. Where've you been?' A flamingo unfurled its leg, stalked to the other side of the pond. Another raised its neck from its wing, huffily.

'For Christ's sake,' said Struan, 'you'll set off every alarm in the place.'

'Stru-anne,' said Jake. 'Do go away. Celia's mine.'

'That's grand with me,' said Struan. 'Honest.'

'Struan,' said Celia, unstringing herself from the wire and facing him, wee hands clasped in the soaked shawl, 'I really care about you.'

'Thanks,' said Struan.

'Baby,' called Jake. 'You know you don't love him. You love me. Tell him.'

And Struan put his hands on Celia's damp woolly shoulders. He resisted the impulse to give her a shake. He said:

'I think Jake's got a point.'

'But,' whispered Celia. 'You saved me.'

'Aye,' said Struan. 'But you didn't think it was me, did you? You thought it was him.' Celia dropped her eyes and he went on, not angry or anything, just saying, 'When I came rushing up, that night in the pond, you thought I was Jake. That's why you jumped. Didn't you? You thought Jake was going to get you out, not me.' And he sighed. He'd been working that one out for weeks. It was grand, to say it at last.

Celia raised her eyes.

'Yes,' she said, nodding, like a little girl. Struan let her go, and she staggered away.

'Yow-zer,' carolled Jake, and he leant backwards on the bike, pulling the handlebars up to his chest. 'She loves me!' He wheelied down the towpath. Celia pursued him the length of the enclosure, little paws catching on the netting. A large white bird flapped alongside her, until Celia and bird pulled up at the end of the aviary. There was a three-foot gap where Celia could get to the fence. She ran along it. She hung on the wire. She squeaked:

'But you kissed her in front of me! And then you dumped me! You left me!'

Jake dropped the bike, hung on the fence on his side.

'Celia, baby,' he called, 'I just did it to piss you

off. She's my stepmum. I wouldn't do anything to her, that would be sick.' He looked at her and grinned suddenly, boyishly. 'You made me jealous, baby, the way you were flirting with the dickhead in the pub. You know I don't like you to flirt. I was just teaching you a little lesson. Then you pissed me off, the way you went on and on about Shirin. All day you went on about it, that and your sodding GCSEs. That's why I went off, baby. I was always coming back. I didn't know you'd jump in the pond, baby, it really messed with my head.'

In that recess of Struan's mind where lived the image of the Yewtree kitchen on the terrible night in August, the lights were going on. In the larder corner, the one you couldn't see from the stairs, the figure of Celia in her white dress appeared, mouth and eyes distended in a recognizable version of Munch's *The Scream*. And in the void where Struan's heart had been missing so long, a rose budded and bloomed in stop-motion animation, sent its intrusive bloom as far as his nostrils and fingertips.

'I'm sorry,' the real Celia was wailing, 'sorry.'

Jake said: 'You're all wet, baby, I can't get you dry.' And Celia pushed her face to the netting, Jake pushed his on the other side, and Struan looked at the pair of them, trying to kiss, and felt towards Jake Prys briefly the warmth of a brother. Then off he sprinted, towards the Small Mammal House.

'Stru-anne,' yelled Jake from the fence, 'I need to talk to you. There's things I have to say.' Struan waved.

'Be seeing you, Jake,' he called, 'you know where I'm staying.'

'I forgive you,' yelled Jake, and Struan stopped, and stared, gave him, on due consideration, the finger, and then rushed on, through the double doors of the Moonlit World.

It was dark in there, and quiet, and smelled of hamsters. The creatures lived in large concrete caves with glass fronts, like aquariums, each in their own forest of pot plants. Glittering nocturnal eyes, like sequins, caught his own as Struan strode along the smooth, sloping concrete floors, looking. Bill and Giles were in front of a big cage, Phillip between them, and Giles was pointing out favourite tamarinds, ones with whiskers and worried expressions just like his own.

Shirin was round the corner, the low lights shining on her mackintosh, staring into the depths of a cage that seemed to be empty. She looked very sad, and somehow, Struan found it easy to walk up beside her, and say:

'Shirin, I made a mistake. That night. The night before it all kicked off, before Myfanwy, the night Jake took the car.'

Shirin raised her head, looked at him, and nodded. He blundered on.

'I was coming down the stair, and I saw Jake kissing you in the kitchen and I thought — I thought stupid things.'

Shirin bent her head away. In the reflection of the double glass, Struan saw her flowerlike mouth open and close. Behind that, he saw, the cage wasn't empty at all. On its central tree was a dark-furred creature with a round head and

264

bald, much-jointed hands, gazing at Shirin with its circular eyes. After a long while, Shirin said:

'Well, that was a very terrible thing to think.'

'Aye,' said Struan, 'aye, I know. I'm sorry. I'm saying sorry. Forgive me.'

'No,' said Shirin, still looking back at the creature, which was a marmoset, said the notice, 'I was thinking, you have to forgive me, Struan.'

Slowly, the marmoset unfurled one hieratic finger and pointed it at Struan. Struan gulped.

'Why?' he asked.

Shirin stared harder into the cage.

'Because you were right. Not right about Jake, but right to doubt me. I *am* going to leave Phillip. I find I can't take care of him as I should. I don't love him, you see.'

Blood flooded into Struan's ears and nose. His chest constricted. Narrowly, he breathed:

'Where will you go?'

'Abroad,' said Shirin, 'for a while. Iran, if I can. Then I will come back to London, buy that studio, the one everyone imagines for me. I have taken some money, Struan. I want you to know this too. All the things we have moved from the collection rooms? I have spent some for Phillip, but most I have kept so I can leave. I have put it in my account. The Sylvia Plath sold for four hundred pounds.'

'Uh huh,' said Struan. The marmoset's finger was still stretched out, still pointing, controlled and theatrical as a mime artist's. Shirin said,

'Now you should reproach me, Struan. Please. Get on with it.'

Struan said, 'No. I think you should do that.

265

Take the money. I think you should do your painting. Your paintings are awful good.'

'But,' said Shirin, 'you're the man who doesn't take things.'

Struan nearly laughed. He said:

'I said that, didn't I? What a prick.' And she looked up at him, then.

'I think,' she said, 'I called you a prig.'

'You did,' said Struan. 'Prick. Prig. You were right. I was way above myself. Because I'd take the things I really want, the things I need, same as anyone else. Because I'd take you, Shirin, if you wanted me. I'd take you away from Phillip. I'd do that in a minute.'

And in the vast relief, the great splitting and budding of saying this, Struan sank to his knees on the smooth concrete floor of the Small Mammal House, and folded his arms on the concrete rim of the cage. Next to his nose, there was a second marmoset with a baby on her back the size of a mouse. It clutched its mother's back with its wee doll's hands.

Above him, Shirin said:

'Struan, you should go. Go first. Leave London tomorrow. I'll stay with Phillip until we have made a better arrangement. Don't worry about him.'

And Struan nodded. In the double glazing of the cage, superimposed on the marmoset's miniature, desolate face, he watched Juliet and Mr Fox, arm in arm, walking towards him, and, in duplicate, Shirin moving smartly away.

They had the birthday tea in the covered picnic area, in the wet and sudden dusk. Celia had made the cake: an elaborate, chocolate confection complete with icing swirls. Not that Celia herself was there, of course (Where did she go, Struan, Juliet kept hissing, what the bloody hell happened?) and the *Happy* of the white, swirly inscription had somehow got rather squashed.

'You know what it means though, eh, Struan?' said Bill, flattening down the cardboard box to make a sort of plate.

Bill's cagoule had got thoroughly soaked during his visit to the giraffes, and large drops from his hood kept dropping onto the icing. Delicately, with his large hands, he coaxed the candle to sit up.

'Charge your glasses!' he said, meaning the plastic cups, and the bubbly, courtesy of Giles.

'Anyone got a light?' he asked, and Mr Fox stepped forward with a Zippo and lit the single flame.

'There,' said Bill. 'Now, I'm from the Antipodes, and as you all know, we like to speak our minds there, so I'm going to make all you folks do something very embarrassing and say something nice about Struan here. You're all English and it will take you a while to break through your inhibitions, so I'm going to start and say, I met Struan at a very lonely, hard time in my life and he showed me something beautiful about patience, and hope. That day we put Phil here in Hampstead Pond, Struan — well, my life began again.'

He grinned, embarrassingly, straight at Giles, who blushed scarlet and said:

'Struan, yes. Struan is a very wise young man. I think, well, at least Struan will understand when I say I was, how to put this, *over-suspicious* about certain things. Having a Lord Peter Wimsey moment. And he set me on the right track. About that and — other things.'

There was a pause, and Giles took Bill's hand. Juliet gave Ron Fox a big nudge and he said:

'A beautiful thing about Struan is, well for me, it vindicates a year of my life. I had to leave Cuik to be Cuik, but I got Struan Robertson out.'

And Juliet said, hurriedly:

'That candle's going to burn out. Struan taught me loads about my dad. He's a really good person.'

They all looked at Phillip then, prone in his chair, eyes open. Juliet reached for his hand.

'Dad says so too, Struan, I'm sure of that.'

And Shirin, who had stood perfectly still through all this, holding her umbrella like another candle, said:

'Yes. Now blow, Struan.'

Struan looked round at them all, his English friends. He said:

'You're all under a grand misapprehension,' and they laughed, and he blew out the candle and it came back into flame, and he blew it out again and it reflamed again. It was a joke candle, you see, a novelty of 1989, and they were all very surprised about it, and laughed a great deal, but it got Struan down, to tell the truth, the way you couldn't get it out, couldn't end the moment the way you ought, with a wick and a wish and a smell of wax.

26

Juliet consented to visit Mr Fox's rented room, after the zoo, and remove all her clothes. Then she visited Celia, to confirm the worst about Jake. When she finally got home, Struan was packing. The cards from his birthday were already folded together and laid aside, and he was carefully wrapping a painting in layers of tissue paper and corrugated cardboard.

'Is that one of Shirin's?' she asked.

'Aye,' said Struan, 'she gave it me for my birthday. It's of Scotland.'

'She doesn't paint Scotland,' said Juliet, 'she's never been there.'

'It's sort of an imaginary Scotland,' said Struan, 'golden eagles and that. It's a braw painting all right. I just hope I willnae squash it in my bag.' He started to tape the corrugated parcel in between two hardback books — a copy of *Huis Clos* and one of *The Waves*.

'The tape'll ruin the books,' said Juliet.

'Mebbe,' said Struan, 'but they're neither of them my favourites. And look, brown paper.'

Juliet came over and sat on the bed beside Struan. The Burberry raincoat was hung between them from the Velux, drying. The Adidas sports bag was open on the floor.

'Struan,' she said, 'are you going away because Shirin doesn't love you? Were you telling her today, in the Mammal House?'

Struan stopped taping and folded his big hands.

'Aye,' he said, 'that's about the size of it.'

'But,' said Juliet, 'I love you. So does Dad.'

Struan smiled at her.

'I know,' he said, 'but it's not the same, is it?' He stood up. 'Come on,' he said, 'we'll go for a wee walk, and I'll tell you all about it.'

So they went, out in the cold dark towards the Heath. The rain had stopped and the pavements shone in the street lights.

'I thought,' said Struan, 'I'd go to Germany. Berlin. My gran sent me some money for my birthday, and I've saved up a bit more.'

'Berlin?' said Juliet, who still didn't watch the news.

'Ay,' said Struan, 'it's all kicking off out there. And I've got my Standard Grade German, I can talk to folk all right.'

'Struan,' said Juliet, 'why are you so cheerful? She doesn't love you. You just said.'

'Aye,' said Struan, 'but I never thought she did. But I love her, you see. And today I discovered — well, just that I was wrong, about something I thought. I discovered I was right to love her. And I told her all about it, and now I'm leaving. It's better than how I felt before, you know? The boil on the head?' He waved a small white envelope with a stamp. 'Post box,' he said, crossing the street.

'Why are you writing to Cricklewood?' asked Juliet, glimpsing the address as he slid it into the slot.

'I'm not writing,' said Struan, 'your dad is.

270

Every time he's written something about Jake, OK, or even something that might be about Jake, I've saved it on the computer. And tonight, I printed them all out, and I'm sending them to him. A lot of them are rubbish, mind, but at least he'll get the idea that his dad thinks about him. All the time. And his mum, actually.'

'Oh, thanks a lot,' said Juliet. 'Brilliant. Now he'll be round with his ersatz ersatz and his amends and his forgiveness and Celia right up his arse all over again.'

'I know,' said Struan, 'but Jake's Phillip's son, and I'm not. They need to be together. It'll be better, when I've gone. At any rate, that's what I'm telling myself.'

They'd reached the lychgate to the Heath. Carefully, Struan squeezed through, holding the gate for Juliet.

'It's awful dark,' he said. There was no moon. Juliet reached up and tucked her hand into his arm. Struan squeezed it to his warm jumper and they lurched on down a path that seemed, by being invisible, strangely soft, like walking through something: cold black water, or feathers.

'Did you chuck Mr Fox yet?' asked Struan, into the quiet.

'No,' said Juliet, 'but I haven't shagged him yet either.'

'Are you going to?' asked Struan.

'Shag or chuck?' asked Juliet.

'Either.'

'Dunno. The thing is, it is quite boring, this virginity business. I mean, I can't tell if he likes me, or if he really just wants to shag a virgin.'

271

'Well,' said Struan, 'I guess there's one way to find out.'

'Exactly,' said Juliet. 'And anyway, I decided, he's kind of my speed, you know? Second lead.'

'Second lead?' said Struan.

'Yeah,' said Juliet. 'If this was a play, he'd be the comic character, and I'd be the servant or whatever to Celia . . . '

'Bollocks,' said Struan.

'It is not bollocks,' said Juliet. 'It's the truth.'

'If Celia's the star,' said Struan, 'then Jake's the hero, and I'm not having that.'

'Oh, Jake's not the hero,' said Juliet. 'You are. Only I didn't notice cos you weren't posh. So I get what I deserve. Ron Fox.'

'Christ,' said Struan, 'he's not that bad.'

'No,' said Juliet, 'he really isn't. He's always pleased to see me, you know?'

'Aye,' said Struan, 'there's a lot to be said for that.'

The murky, brownish sky above them cleared briefly, showing a smoky moon. The light revealed a bench, on which they sat down. Struan pulled Juliet into the shelter of his arm.

'You'll have to look after your dad for me, when I'm gone,' he said.

'Thought Jake was doing that,' said Juliet.

'You know what I mean,' said Struan.

'Yeah,' said Juliet, 'and I will. I'll even have the time. I just lost my job, you know. Major shoplifting on my watch.'

'Och, you didnae?' said Struan. 'I'm sorry.'

Then Juliet said: 'Struan, don't feel bad about my dad, OK? The thing is, my dad is not that

272

nice. You haven't met him.'

'Aye,' said Struan, 'I have. I've been washing his arse since July.'

'No,' said Juliet, 'my real dad I mean, not the old guy in the wheelchair. I mean, *I* like the wheelchair guy too. My real dad, though, I've been thinking about him a lot, and I think he was a bully, you know? Not just to me or Mum, but Jake as well?'

'Nobody's perfect,' said Struan.

'No,' said Juliet, 'but he wanted to be. He wanted to be the perfect writer. And then we all had to be sort of his scenery; like the perfect family to the famous writer. You know, like Talking Heads? *You may tell yourself: this is not my beautiful wife?*'

'*When the days go by, and there's no automobile?*' said Struan.

'Yeah,' said Juliet. 'That's the best song. So Mum was his beautiful wife, and he had the MG and Giles and all that, but when she got fat and old, she didn't fit, any more, and so he just dumped her. And Jake, Jake was his beautiful son, all right, but actually, if you think about it, that can't be much good really, even for Jake, because he knows he's only loved if he stays the beautiful son. So then Jake has to control everything too. I mean, I'm not saying Jake's not a total shit, cos he is, but I think Dad made him that way.'

'How come, then,' said Struan, accepting this analysis, 'that you're nice?'

'Because I never made the picture at all,' said Juliet. 'Because I'm too plain and thick.'

273

'Maybe your mum was nice to you when you were wee?' suggested Struan.

'Possibly,' said Juliet, 'or my Grandma Davies. But I can't remember it, and there's the truth.' Then the cloud re-closed, and they walked home again in the perfect blackness, holding each other's hand.

★　★　★

Of course, it was all very well Struan spouting that stuff. Happy to be going, Jake's responsibility, all that all that and all that. It didn't mean he believed it at three o'clock in the morning. Oh, he didn't disbelieve Juliet. He thought the evidence was fairly clear, from Phillip's books and his ex-wife and his son, and from all those wee bits Giles let slip, that Phillip had been a steel-clad ocean-going shit, at least for some of his life. But that wasn't the Phillip he had met. Or not the Phillip he had invented, from bits of his own dad, most like.

But even that wasn't the point. The point was, Phillip was stuck in his body, the way prisoners had been stuck in the bottle-dungeon in the castle at St Andrews, target of successive trips from Cuik High School. The *Oubliette*. And the point was, Struan had sworn, on each of those school trips, that no one could deserve that, whatever they might have done, and that should he, Struan Robertson, ever come across someone in a bottle-dungeon, he would not *oublie* them, but get busy with the sandwiches and the string. And now here he was, on the lip of the dungeon,

274

fully equipped with string and sandwiches and unique knowledge of *The Pit and Its Men*, and he was about to walk away. Struan rolled out of bed and crouched on the floorboards of the attic, looking at his fists.

Bill, he thought, might take on the job, for a bit. He seemed distinctly underemployed. And maybe Mr Fox could come over for the typing. It was him that was so damn keen on the play in the first place. And Jake, for Christ's sake, could do a hand's turn for his dad.

But each of those thoughts foundered on the fact of Shirin, Shirin going away soon after him. Then the house would go to Myfanwy, because who else? Giles wouldn't stop her, because he couldn't, and because he wouldn't, because he'd throw up his hairy hands and say, 'But what can I do, old chap, really?' Because Giles hated Phillip, too, at least a bit. He was nice to him because Bill was into it, Struan reckoned, because it was part of how Giles and Bill got on. But that wouldn't keep Phillip out of a Home. So Myfanwy would put Phillip in a Home and sell the house, if not to this rich American, then to the next one. And there would be no Struan, no Bill, no Mr Fox, no *Pit and Its Men*, no Scrabble board, no Amstrad in Phillip's bottle-dungeon then, just the mossy, granite walls, and Juliet visiting, when she remembered.

From below, Struan heard the click of Shirin, entering the collection rooms, the sigh of a filing cabinet opening. He wondered why he thought Shirin should do her painting and take Phillip's money and yet thought Jake Prys was a thief,

275

and an arse for the way he talked about his acting, and couldn't come up with an answer. He thought of Shirin as he first saw her, drawing Phillip in the study, direct in a shaft of sun. He remembered the strange, still quality of her profile in thought, and the sun shining from his wee picture, and he pushed his body into the boards and let it want what it wanted.

From below came another, furtive, rustling sound and he thought of Shirin taking her grandmother's jewels from the vault under a bed in a house in Tehran, when she was younger than Juliet was now. He remembered her saying, of her grandmother, 'We were four who were young and she was one who was old.' Then leaving, as he was to leave now.

But he was to leave first. Struan sat up on the floor. That's what Shirin had told him: leave first. Not that she despised him, not that he was too young, but that he was to go. She, not he, would be the one to abandon Phillip. She was going to carry that one for him.

Struan knelt on the floor of the attic, dazzled by the harsh bright gift Shirin had given him for his birthday, by the possibilities of his life. And after a while he crawled into bed, thinking she was right, she was kind, she was clever, and still he could not sleep, that first night of his majority, of his nineteenth year.

★　★　★

Myfanwy Prys wanted her house back, that was all. It was not too much to ask. Each night, as she listened to Underground trains shunt to their bays in the underused wasteland of Cricklewood Station; as she shuddered to the random cries — cats? Youths? — from the Cricklewood street: she longed for the peace of Yewtree Row, the faint hum of traffic interrupted only by cinema-goers returning from the Everyman, broadcasting their clever talk.

She missed the solid walls of Yewtree, leaning sympathetically over the winding street. She missed the sash windows, lovingly maintained by Mr Riley, squaring the southern light. She missed the fine stair of Yewtree, hung like a rib-cage in the wide high hall. She missed the cupboards of Yewtree, set in the bays of the sitting room, in the curved walls of the collection rooms, in the depths of the kitchen. The cupboards: the ancient wallpaper and stippling at the back of them, their broad, hand-smoothed, hardwood shelves. There were no cupboards here in Cricklewood, any more than there were linings to the walls or full-sized furniture: she had set it all up that way, to make the rooms look larger, and now clothes bulged out of the horrid canvas arrangements she had set under the eaves, now the sitting room was disfigured by stacks of CDs, and the wicker settee already sagged.

Tonight, into Myfanwy's undersized iron-framed bed, came the sounds of her son Jake joyously poking his girlfriend against the too-thin party wall. Celia's parents would be on the warpath tomorrow. Myfanwy hoped they didn't have the Cricklewood number, or that Juliet would have the sense not to hand it over. She rolled over in bed, pulled the pillow over her ears, and tried to think herself to sleep, as she often did, with a plan for reordering and repainting Yewtree, from the primrose distemper in the new kitchen to the restoration of the drawing room, to the modern brick finish in the attic flat she was planning for Jake.

Tomorrow, she thought, she would go back there. The return of Celia to Jake marked surely the end of the episode of the pond, of the exaggerated worship of Struan Robertson who still, in her mind, needed to answer questions about the missing cash from Phillip's desk. She would go in at a quiet time, using her key, and just walk around a little, checking, for example, whether her plan for a bathroom/bedroom for Juliet in the cellar really was practical, in terms of plumbing; see if perhaps the collection rooms, where she planned a new master suite, had been left unlocked.

And so, drifting in her mind down Yewtree's staircase, turning the china handles of the heavy doors, dandling the lead weights of its darling sash windows, Myfanwy Prys sought sleep, and met it, finally, in the larder, that small shelved room where her daughter Juliet was even then finishing Struan Robertson's birthday cake, and deciding to lose her virginity the very next day to a mostly amiable man named Fox.

27

But Juliet went to work the next day, after all, Miriam having found the Von Estorhof scarf stuffed behind the lingerie. She was on a warning for untidiness, mind, and grumbled a good deal as she strapped herself into her shop-wear jump-suit.

'Will you be here when I get back, Struan?' she asked anxiously at the door.

'Oh,' said Struan, 'aye. I'm going up to see my gran first, you see. Night bus. I've got my return ticket.'

So Juliet hugged him, and left. Struan went in to Phillip, and took his hand. 'Pond?' he said, sighing, and felt the jerk for yes, then another, for no.

'Amstrad?' he said. 'Writing?' and they gave themselves over.

On the first 'P' of Pip, Struan flicked to the last act. Pip and Angharad, about to split for ever.

'I love you, Angharad, but there is a passion greater?' he asked Phillip, and the old man signalled, 'Yes.' Phillip looked well this morning, thought Struan, he had more colour than he'd seen for days. He turned his attention back to Armprys, to the part in the play where Angharad tries to keep Pip in the village with a terrifying description of domestic bliss.

'But I also have a passion,' he ad-libbed for

279

Angharad, and Phillip gave his moth's consent. 'I have,' he went on, borrowing Pip's lines now, from earlier in the play, 'a passion for the body . . . ' And he fair went off on one then: a mixture of the Song of Solomon, the *Supplementary Material*, and *Portnoy's Complaint*, with which Phillip was thoroughly familiar, judging by his rapid twitches.

Phillip was having a terrific time, the best morning for simply years. The writing thing, the writing thing, see its magic: the village of Armprys rising around him, its narrow streets, its over-hanging slag, the narrow portals of the school house. Would Pip stay there? Never. Would he leave Angharad there, flower of the valleys, thrusting stem of white Welsh bluebell, to become downtrodden and bosomy and start whitewashing larders for no good reason; or to slump on her knees on a doorstep, righteous and smug, no care but for her child?

No! Not Angharad, not this girl, making her speech now to Pip, to the world! What a claiming of female energy, lovely among the lilies, queen of the apple down, pounding on her pony, yes she will, she will yes! The eyes on her, the thighs, the nice firm arse, the curious Scottish accent! Off to hit London in her own right! What a creation: nothing like her had yet hit the stage, Giles, eh?

That was the problem with Osborne, Giles, when you thought about it, his girls had nothing to say, just all that ironing, but listen to Angharad, listen to her now, touch of the *Milk Woods*, touch of Dylan, touch of Joyce, touch of

280

Phillip Prys, eh, eh, this hymn to lust, to the body, to the deep harmony of man and woman. Who but Phillip Prys could pull that one out, eh, out of the Welsh pits straight to the West End stage?

Angharad and Pip would leave Armprys behind. They would come to London, together; they would take the West End by storm; they would live in a rattling house with a wooden staircase and make love in the drawing room; and for them there would be no disappointments, no retractions, no compromise, no Melissa, no Linda, no children standing slack-limbed in reproach, no fat Juliet, no angry Jake, no gin, no binges, no Brighton, no contracts disappearing, no day when there was no more story to tell, no Giles in a restaurant saying *Angela sells, old chap, she sells*.

'Yes,' said Struan, 'yes, I will, yes?' But Phillip's eyes were closed now, and his hand was still.

'Are you going to print it?' asked Shirin. 'He likes that.'

She was just standing there, beside Phillip's chair. She was wearing jeans and a white shirt, hair pushed off her forehead, tired around the eyes. She looked so young. She looked just his age.

'Yes,' said Struan, and he began the ponderous process, as it was in 1989, of the saving onto floppy disk, filing and formatting. On his knees, he plugged in the printer, checked its supply of paper, aligned its carbon paper, pulled its ribbon straight.

Then he looked up. Shirin was gone.

So Struan set the little hammer running, and pulled the wheelchair round to where Phillip could see it working. Phillip opened one eye, and shut it again.

'That's OK,' said Struan, 'it was a pleasure.' And he pulled the blanket up over Phillip's knees, and adjusted the pillow under his head.

'Struan,' called Shirin, in a voice clear as the chime of a clock. He looked up, over the dome of Phillip's head. She was standing in the doorway of the study, and she was unbuttoning the white shirt, and taking it off, and reaching behind and unhooking her white bra, matter-of-fact as getting ready for swimming. 'Struan,' she said. 'I thought, you could come with me, to Iran.'

Then Struan left Phillip Prys lying there, and crossed the room in two strides and picked Shirin up in his arms, easily, with his young man's strength, and carried her up the stairs to her high-windowed bedroom. For there were one or two activities — driving, the butterfly, life-saving — at which Struan Robertson was a natural, a pure talent, and now, in Phillip Prys's wide bed, he found another.

28

When Phillip woke, his son Jake was beside him, smoking a cigarette.

'Hello, Dad,' he said, 'the nurse let me in. She thought I was Stru-anne. And she was pleased to see us, because she needed to bugger off to another job. House was empty, you know. Looks like your wife's fucked off somewhere, Dad. And that Stru-anne.'

Phillip did not react.

Jake regarded him a while, then stood up, and toured the study, lounging and handsome in his ragged jeans. He flipped the handle on the lift-up bed, peeped at the photos of himself on the mantel, lifted books from the shelves tenderly as a dealer, blowing the dust from the gathered pages.

'Mum's here too, by the way,' he said, to the shape of his father. 'She went upstairs. Just in case she, you know, startles you.' He checked the back of the Lowry above the fireplace. 'These,' he said, 'are starting to be worth a mint. Clever buy, old man, clever buy.'

Jake stubbed out his cigarette on the marble ashtray on the mantelpiece, then picked it up, and strolled back to his father, and sat beside him in the best chair, the one Struan had lined up in the circle of Phillip's vision.

'Dad,' he said, smiling his long smile, narrowing his long-lashed eyes, 'Dad, how about you have a cig? This ashtray is horribly clean.'

Phillip shut one eye. Jake winked back.

'Oi, oi,' he said. 'Dirty winks all around.'

And Jake lit, with a flare and snort of saltpetre, a Marlboro Light, and when it was burning, blew a little blue cloud of cigarette smoke up his father's nose.

'How's that?' he asked, his handsome head cocked to one side, a gesture of his since he was on the telly, England's prettiest boy. And slowly Phillip winked again, and then Jake knelt by his chair, and they smoked together, the smoke clouds blue and sculptural in the angled November light.

★ ★ ★

Out in the hall, Myfanwy considered her house. It smelled different: less untipped fag, more Dettol and gesso and Impulse Body Spray. The hall was silent, abandoned — a Jane Fonda tape by the door, a pile of unopened mail on the bottom step. Quietly, Myfanwy looked it over, tucked a statement or two from the bank in the deep Scandinavian pocket of her Narda Artwear frock. Upstairs, the panelled door of Shirin's bedroom was slung open, sending a dusty shaft of winter sun onto the polished landing. Carefully, standing on the least creaky portion of each tread, Myfanwy walked up.

'Is this your Amstrad?' said Jake to his dad, approaching the computer. 'Stru-anne sent me your latest productions. Is this where it switches on?'

The Amstrad grunted and spat into life. Jake

284

touched a key and the message 'system error' appeared in green all down the screen. Jake snorted.

'I haven't the foggiest,' he said, 'do you know, about these machines.' There was a manuscript by the wheel-chair table, though. 'This yours, Dad?' he said. 'Your latest thing? *The Posthumous Version?* Let's have a read.' And he picked up the crackling pages, settled back in the armchair.

★   ★   ★

Myfanwy crept through Shirin's room, where Shirin's bed lay flagrant and open, and slid into the en suite, noting the paint marks on the shelves, the splashes on the grass-green bath. Shirin's work was all around her: sketches, and black gesso outlines, the strange, hyper-bright, super-finished miniatures with their towers and stylized flowers and tiny, averted faces. They reminded Myfanwy of her mother's porcelain collection, the shepherdesses and bunny rabbits, and she wondered why this stuff, too, was not, as Cecil would have said, *irredeemably lower middle.*

A series of tiny paintings were pinned by their wide edges to the window frame. Shirin seemed to have given up painting allegorical corpuscles, and turned her attention to women wearing elaborate housecoats, kneeling in bowers. One old lady held a jewel box, opened, with lush *Arabian Nights* strings of pearls spilling out. A younger woman, her hair in a vertiginous pile, held a miniature tower block, each lit fly's-wing window gilded. Myfanwy thought again she

285

could make nothing of it: it was all impossible, like Shirin's clothes, so smart and finished and almost tarty; so much in another code; on their way to a different party.

There was a white board arrangement propped over the basin, with a paper pinned to it and the elaborate tools of gold-leafing laid out next to it. Myfanwy peered at it: the painting was gesso'd and partially painted: an elaborate bower blacked in against a stiff, fanciful green and yellow garden, with one central thumbnail shining in enamelled pink. A face: but the body was part of the bower, part of the building. Myfanwy crouched down; put her glasses on her nose: and when her own face, circa 1962, peeped back, she staggered back and swiftly out of the room, as if discovered.

★ ★ ★

Jake put down the bunched pages of *The Posthumous Version*.

'Dad,' he said, to the slumped form on the wheelchair, 'it's terrific, you know. Just terrific. I'll put it on at the Burton Taylor. I'll do Pip myself. What do you say?'

But Phillip didn't say anything. On the Amstrad, the green cursor winked on a black screen. 'Dad,' said Jake, after a while, 'I think I need a reply. How does Stru-anne do it? You don't actually type, do you?' Laboriously, he wheeled the chair to the Amstrad, put his father's fingers on the keys. They slid off.

'No,' said Jake, 'clearly not.'

* ★ ★

Myfanwy crept on, upstairs. The front room was unlocked, open, in fact, the door ajar. Myfanwy had not been over that threshold for more than two years. Now, she stepped in, breathed the dusty air.

No bloodied heads. It was emptier than she had thought, and tidier. The outlines of her pictures were still visible on the grey dimity wallpaper; the sprigged Laura curtains hung faded at the windows. Two filing cabinets were shoved against the walls where her bed had been, and there was a neat stack of sealed cardboard boxes by the fireplace, labelled by year in a hand she did not recognize. The old chesterfield was still in the window, still very much in need of an expensive restuffing. She had left it here on purpose, given it up as a bad job.

Now she sat on its sagging springs, hugged the patchwork cushion she had made from Laura Ashley scraps when you could still buy them in bags, and remembered the last, bad years of her marriage: Phillip and she roaring and cursing as the good parts, the good crits, their good selves, fell away from them; as they sank into fat and age and drink; Jake out of the house, with boys then with girls; Juliet, mulish on the stairs in a stupid school hat, refusing all of it.

Myfanwy wiped her eyes and turned her head, and a little collage of photos stuck to the filing cabinet caught her eye: herself, in the late fifties, the sixties, in a string of tight dresses, dark eyeliners, pale lips, smiles. Look: the cutting from the *Daily Mirror*, her in her knickers, getting the milk. Myfanwy fell forwards on her knees to look more closely. There was the famous picture of her and Phillip backstage at the first production of *The Pit*, grinning over mugs of tea. The studio shot in the cashmere jumper. Only Phillip could have put these up.

★ ★ ★

Jake's eye fell on the Scrabble board.

'What about this thing?' he said. 'How about, I twirl, you wink at the letter?' Slowly, Phillip winked.

So Jake pulled up Struan's favourite upright chair and sat in it backwards, dropping its cushion to the floor. He draped his arms and the Scrabble board over its back.

'Okey-dokey, Dad,' he said, and twirled. And several goes later, Phillip winked on a 'B'. Jake looked round for a pen, couldn't find one, typed into the Amstrad.

'There,' he said, 'cracked it now, Dad. Next letter.'

There was an 'L' and an 'E' and an 'S'.

'Another 's'?' enquired Jake. 'Shall I put one in?' He looked at the green word, flashing on the screen. 'Bless,' he said, 'well, that's rather lovely.'

He did think so. It was quite a moment, in his life. Tears came to Jake Prys' eyes, and he stood and called up the stair of his father's large house in Hampstead: 'Mum, come down. Dad can talk!'

And also in a friendly, softened spirit,

288

Myfanwy Prys came down the stairs, eyes also full of tears, still holding, for comfort, the cushion made from Laura Ashley scraps. She approached her former husband, with a heart full of tenderness and her hands full of patchwork, but the sight of her, pillow in hand, caused in the body of Phillip Prys a surge of adrenalin, which briefly opened his arteries a little wider, and released, in the complex branches of his arterial tree, the ripe black fruit of an embolus, which travelled swiftly to his brain, and lodged deep in his cerebral cortex.

★   ★   ★

In Archway, Juliet Prys walked gingerly on the grey street with her lover, Ron Fox. In Highgate, Giles Van der Piet was walking to the Heath with his lover Bill, discussing the range of self-help books they were planning in time for the nineteen nineties. Juliet said: 'Bloody hell, I feel like I just got off a horse.' And Bill, who had in fact a practical bent and was going to make a great deal of money with his books, correctly said that the nineties was going to be a beautiful new decade for him and Giles. And on Hampstead Heath, in the fragile autumn sun, Struan Robertson reached out to his lover Shirin, knowing that she would yield, that he was permitted to kiss her. All of him swooned, it seemed the very air bent and swooned, it was the happiest moment of his life.

Then in the house in Yewtree Row Phillip Prys died, silently, and fell forward onto the computer keyboard. The shift/break key, responding to the pressure of his nose and the archaic command system of those times, reproduced the word BLESS all down the screen. When his son Jake realized what had happened, he lifted his father's head, already so heavy, back against the pillow, then fell to his knees by the desk, and watched the screen fill again and again with BLESS in twitching acid green. Cautiously, he started to weep. Myfanwy put down the cushion and called the ambulance, then sat and stared for a long time unbelieving out of the window, and noticed that Shirin had sold the car.

And Struan kissed Shirin on her bruised lips; and Ron Fox slung his arm round his small cross Juliet; and Giles said, 'I am terrifically happy, you know,' to Bill. And if there was a grander moment of loss at Phillip's death; some parting and healing of the blue meniscus of the sky, these six did not notice it; they all walked on, full of their separate hopes: for this was 1989; the year the world changed; and the walls came down; and all the old tyrants were suddenly dead.

We do hope that you have enjoyed reading this large print book.

Did you know that all of our titles are available for purchase?

We publish a wide range of high quality large print books including:
Romances, Mysteries, Classics
General Fiction
Non Fiction and Westerns

Special interest titles available in large print are:
The Little Oxford Dictionary
Music Book
Song Book
Hymn Book
Service Book

Also available from us courtesy of Oxford University Press:
Young Readers' Dictionary
(large print edition)
Young Readers' Thesaurus
(large print edition)

For further information or a free brochure, please contact us at:
Ulverscroft Large Print Books Ltd.,
The Green, Bradgate Road, Anstey,
Leicester, LE7 7FU, England.
Tel: (00 44) 0116 236 4325
Fax: (00 44) 0116 234 0205

Other titles published by
The House of Ulverscroft:

THE WOMAN WHO DIVED INTO THE HEART OF THE WORLD

Sabina Berman and Lisa Dillman

Following the tragedy of her sister's death, Isabelle moves from her home in California to her birthplace in Mexico to take over the running of the family business. There, in her sister's dilapidated house, she is woken in the night by a wild child — a thing with no name, who could just be the niece she never knew she had. So she sets herself the task of turning it into a human being, named Karen. To start, she must teach Karen her first word: Me. And then begins the greatest journey of all, as Karen learns how to become 'Me'. It will take Isabelle to the bottom of the ocean, to the farthest reaches of the planet . . . and into the heart of the world.

THE FOLLOWING GIRLS

Louise Levene

When Amanda Baker was fourteen, she found a letter written by her runaway mother to her unborn child: 'Dear Jeremy (or Amanda)', it began. Now, in the 1970s, she is in the hands of disaffected parents seeking to find a new school for their disappointing daughter. The happiest days of your life? Not for Baker, sixteen and sick of it as she moves miserably between lessons packed with palm fibre and the use of the dative. Baker's only solace is her fifth-form gang, The Four Mandies, and a low-calorie diet of king-sized cigarettes — until she teams up with Julia Smith, games captain and consummate game-player. So begins a passionate friendship that will threaten Baker's future, menace her sanity, and risk the betrayal of everything and every-one she holds dear . . .

HOMECOMING

Susie Steiner

Up on the North Yorkshire moors, the Hartle family is about to have a life-changing year. Ann and Joe, with more than thirty years of marriage between them, are torn between giving up and pressing on with their struggling farm. Max, their elder son, is set to inherit the farm, and his wife Primrose has news to share, but is he ready for these new responsibilities? The younger son, Bartholomew, escaped to the south as soon as he could, building a new life for himself with his girlfriend Ruby. But when tragedy strikes, he is forced to return home — and come to terms with his past, in order to create a future. *Homecoming* is a big-hearted drama about how a family falls apart and comes back together again.